EOIN COLFER
ARTEMIS FOWL

ARTEMIS FOWL is a child prodigy from Ireland who has dedicated his brilliant mind to criminal activities. When Artemis discovers that there is a fairy civilization below ground, he sees it as a golden opportunity. Now there is a whole new species to exploit with his ingenious schemes. But Artemis doesn't know as much as he thinks about the fairy People. And what he doesn't know could hurt him . . .

EOIN COLFER

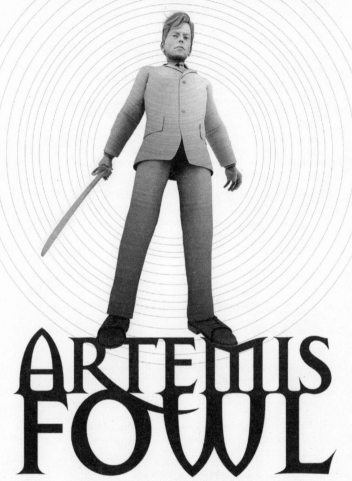

ARTEMIS FOWL

AND THE
LAST GUARDIAN

PUFFIN

PUFFIN BOOKS

Published by the Penguin Group
Penguin Books Ltd, 80 Strand, London WC2R 0RL, England
Penguin Group (USA) Inc., 375 Hudson Street, New York, New York 10014, USA
Penguin Group (Canada), 90 Eglinton Avenue East, Suite 700, Toronto, Ontario, Canada M4P 2Y3
(a division of Pearson Penguin Canada Inc.)
Penguin Ireland, 25 St Stephen's Green, Dublin 2, Ireland (a division of Penguin Books Ltd)
Penguin Group (Australia), 250 Camberwell Road, Camberwell, Victoria 3124, Australia
(a division of Pearson Australia Group Pty Ltd)
Penguin Books India Pvt Ltd, 11 Community Centre, Panchsheel Park, New Delhi – 110 017, India
Penguin Group (NZ), 67 Apollo Drive, Rosedale, Auckland 0632, New Zealand
(a division of Pearson New Zealand Ltd)
Penguin Books (South Africa) (Pty) Ltd, Block D, Rosebank Office Park, 181 Jan Smuts Avenue,
Parktown North, Gauteng 2193, South Africa

Penguin Books Ltd, Registered Offices: 80 Strand, London WC2R 0RL, England

puffinbooks.com

First published 2012
001 – 10 9 8 7 6 5 4 3 2 1

Set in Perpetua by Palimpsest Book Production Ltd, Falkirk, Stirlingshire
Printed in Great Britain by Clays Ltd, St Ives plc

British Library Cataloguing in Publication Data
A CIP catalogue record for this book is available from the British Library

HARDBACK
ISBN: 978–0–141–34081–4

TRADE PAPERBACK
ISBN: 978–0–141–34433–1

www.greenpenguin.co.uk

ALWAYS LEARNING   PEARSON

*For all the Fowl fans who journeyed to
the Lower Elements with me. Thank you.*

Contents

Contents

PROLOGUE

Ériú, Present Day

THE Berserkers lay arranged in a spiral under the rune stone, looping down, down into the earth – boots out, heads in as the spell demanded. Of course, after ten thousand years underground, there were no physical boots or heads. There was just the plasma of black magic holding their consciousness intact and even that was dissipating, tainting the land, causing strange strains of plants to appear and infecting the animals with uncommon aggression. In perhaps a dozen full moons the Berserkers would be gone utterly and their last spark of power would flow into the earth.

We are not all disappeared yet, thought Oro of the Danu, captain of the Berserkers. *We are ready to seize our glorious moment when it comes and to sow chaos among the humans.*

He sent the thought into the spiral and was proud to feel his remaining fairy warriors echo the sentiment.

Their will is as keen as their blades once were, he thought.

Though we are dead and buried, the spark of bloody purpose burns bright in our souls.

It was the hatred of humankind that kept the spark alive – that and the black magic of the warlock Bruin Fadda. More than half of their company of warriors had already expired and been drawn to the afterlife, but still five score remained to complete their duties should they be called upon.

Remember your orders, the elfin warlock had told them all those centuries ago even as the clay was falling on their flesh. *Remember those who have died and the humans who murdered them.*

Oro did remember and always would. Just as he could never forget the sensation of stones and earth rattling across his dying skin.

We will remember, he sent into the spiral. *Remember and return.*

The thought drifted down, then echoed up from the dead warriors, who were eager to be released from their tomb and see the sun once more.

CHAPTER I: A COMPLEX SITUATION

FROM THE CASE NOTES OF DOCTOR JERBAL ARGON, PSYCH BROTHERHOOD

1. **ARTEMIS** Fowl, once self-proclaimed *teenage criminal mastermind*, now prefers the term *juvenile genius*. Apparently he has changed. (Note to self: *harrumph*.)

2. For the past six months Artemis has been undergoing weekly therapy sessions at my clinic in Haven City in an attempt to overcome a severe case of Atlantis Complex, a psychological condition that he developed as a result of meddling in fairy magic. (Serves him right, silly Mud Boy.)

3. Remember to submit outrageous bill to Lower Elements Police.

4. Artemis appears to be cured, and in record time too. Is this likely? Or even possible?

5. Discuss my theory of relativity with Artemis. Could

make for a very interesting chapter in my v-book: *Foiling Fowl: Outsmarting the Smarty-pants*. (Publishers love the title: *cha-ching!*)

6.   Order more painkillers for my blasted hip.
7.   Issue clean bill of mental health for Artemis. Final session today.

Doctor Argon's Office, Haven City, the Lower Elements

Artemis Fowl grew impatient. Doctor Argon was late. This final session was just as unnecessary as the past half dozen had been. He was completely cured, for heaven's sake, and had been since week eighteen. His prodigious intellect had accelerated the process and he should not have to twiddle his thumbs at the behest of a gnome psychiatrist.

At first Artemis paced the office, refusing to be calmed by the waterwall with its gently pulsing mood lights, then he sat for a minute in the oxygen booth, which he found calmed him a little too much.

Oxygen booth indeed, he thought, quickly ducking out of the glass-walled chamber.

Finally the door hissed and slid aside on runners, admitting Doctor Jerbal Argon to his own office. The squat gnome limped directly to his chair. He dropped into the embrace of its many pads, slapping the armrest controls until the gel sac under his right hip glowed gently.

'Aaaah,' he sighed. 'My hip is killing me. Nothing helps, honestly. People think they know pain, but they have no idea.'

'You're late,' noted Artemis in fluent Gnommish, his voice devoid of sympathy.

Argon sighed blissfully again as the heated chair pad went to work on his hip. 'Always in a hurry, eh, Mud Boy? Why didn't you have a puff of oxygen or meditate by the water-wall? Hey-Hey Monks swear by those waterwalls.'

'I am not a pixie priest, Doctor. What Hey-Hey Monks do after first gong is of little interest to me. Can we proceed with my rehabilitation? Or would you prefer to waste more of my time?'

Argon huffed a little, then swung his bulk forward, opening a sim-paper file on his desk. 'Why is it that the saner you get the nastier you are?'

Artemis crossed his legs, his body language relaxed for the first time. 'Such repressed anger, Doctor. Where does it all stem from?'

'Let's stick to your disposition, shall we, Artemis?' Argon snagged a stack of cards from his file. 'I am going to show you some ink blots and you tell me what the shapes suggest to you.'

Artemis's moan was extended and theatrical. 'Ink blots. Oh, please. My lifespan is considerably shorter than yours, Doctor. I prefer not to waste valuable time on worthless pseudo tests. We may as well read tea leaves or divine the future in turkey entrails.'

'Ink blots are a reliable indication of mental health,' Argon objected. 'Tried and tested.'

'Tested by psychiatrists for psychiatrists,' snorted Artemis.

Argon slapped a card down on the table. 'What do you see in this ink blot?'

'I see an ink blot,' said Artemis.

'Yes, but what does the blot suggest to you?'

Artemis smirked in a supremely annoying fashion. 'I see card five hundred and thirty-four.'

'Pardon me?'

'Card five hundred and thirty-four,' repeated Artemis. 'Of a series of six hundred standard ink-blot cards. I memorized them during our sessions. You don't even shuffle.'

Argon checked the number on the back of the card: 534. Of course.

'Knowing the number does not answer the question. What do you see?'

Artemis allowed his lip to wobble. 'I see an axe dripping with blood. Also a scared child and an elf clothed in the skin of a troll.'

'Really?' Argon was interested now.

'No. Not really. I see a secure building, perhaps a family home, with four windows. A trustworthy pet and a pathway leading from the door into the distance. I think, if you check your manual, you will find that these answers fall inside *healthy* parameters.'

Argon did not need to check. The Mud Boy was right, as usual. Perhaps he could blindside Artemis with his new theory. It was not part of the programme but might earn him a little respect.

'Have you heard of the theory of relativity?'

Artemis blinked. 'Is this a joke? I have travelled through time, Doctor. I think I know a little something about relativity.'

'No. Not that theory; my theory of relativity proposes that all things magical are related and influenced by ancient spells or magical hotspots.'

Artemis rubbed his chin. 'Interesting. But I think you'll find that your postulation should be called the theory of *relatedness.*'

'Whatever,' said Argon, waving the quibble away. 'I did a little research and it turns out that the Fowls have been a bother to fairy folk off and on for thousands of years. Dozens of your ancestors have tried for the crock of gold, though you are the only one to have succeeded.'

Artemis sat up straight; this *was* interesting. 'And I never knew about this because you mind-wiped my forefathers.'

'Exactly,' said Argon, thrilled to have Artemis's full attention. 'When he was a lad, your own father actually managed to hog-tie a dwarf who was drawn to the estate. I imagine he still dreams of that moment.'

'Good for him.' A thought struck Artemis. 'Why was the dwarf attracted to our estate?'

'Because the residual magic there is off the scale. Something happened on the Fowl Estate once. Something huge, magically speaking.'

'And this lingering power plants ideas in our heads and nudges the Fowls towards a belief in magic,' Artemis murmured almost to himself.

8

'Exactly. It's a goblin-and-egg situation. Did you think about magic and then find magic? Or did the magic make you think about looking for magic?'

Artemis took a few notes on his smartphone. 'And this huge magical event, can you be more specific?'

Argon shrugged. 'Our records don't go back that far. I'd say we're talking about back when fairies lived on the surface, more than ten thousand years ago.'

Artemis rose and loomed over the squat gnome. He felt he owed the doctor something for the theory of *relatedness*, which would certainly bear some investigation.

'Doctor Argon, did you have turned-in feet as a child?'

Argon was so surprised that he blurted an honest answer to a personal question, very unusual for a psychiatrist. 'Yes. Yes, I did.'

'And were you forced to wear remedial shoes with stacked soles?'

Argon was intrigued. He hadn't thought about those horrible shoes in centuries; he had actually forgotten them until this moment.

'Just one, on my right foot.'

Artemis nodded wisely, and Argon felt as though their roles had been reversed and he was the patient.

'I would guess that your foot was pulled into its correct alignment, but your femur was twisted slightly in the process. A simple brace should solve your hip problem.' Artemis pulled a folded napkin from his pocket. 'I sketched a design while you kept me waiting these past few sessions. Foaly should be able to build the brace for you. I may have been a few millimetres off with my estimate of your dimensions, so best to get measured.' He placed ten fingers flat on the desk. 'May I leave now? Have I fulfilled my obligation?'

The doctor nodded glumly, thinking that he would possibly omit this session from his book. He watched Artemis stride across the office floor and duck through the doorway.

Argon studied the napkin drawing and knew instinctively that Artemis was right about his hip.

Either that boy is the sanest creature on Earth, he thought. *Or he is so disturbed that our tests cannot even begin to scratch the surface.*

Argon pulled a rubber stamp from his desk and on the cover of Artemis's file stamped the word FUNCTIONAL in big red letters.

I hope so, he thought. *I really hope so.*

Artemis's bodyguard, Butler, waited for his principal outside Doctor Argon's office in the large chair that had been a gift from the centaur Foaly, technical consultant to the Lower Elements Police.

'I can't stand to look at you perched on a fairy stool,' Foaly had told him. 'It offends my eyes. You look like a monkey passing a coconut.'

'Very well,' Butler had said in his gravelly bass. 'I accept the gift, if only to preserve your eyes.'

In truth he had been mightily glad to have a comfortable

chair, being more than six and a half feet tall in a city built for three-footers.

The bodyguard stood and stretched, flattening his palms against the ceiling, which was double-height by fairy standards. Thank God Argon had a taste for the grandiose or Butler wouldn't even have been able to stand up straight in the clinic. To his mind the building, with its vaulted ceilings, gold-flecked tapestries and retro sim-wood sliding doors, looked more like a monastery where the monks had taken a vow of wealth, rather than a medical facility. Only the wall-mounted laser hand-sanitizers and the occasional elfin nurse bustling past gave any hint that this place was actually a clinic.

I am so glad this detail is coming to an end, Butler had been thinking at least once every five minutes for the past fortnight. He had been in tight spots many times, but there was something about being confined in a city clamped to the underside of the Earth's crust that made him feel claustrophobic for the first time in his life.

Artemis emerged from Argon's office, his self-satisfied smirk even more pronounced than usual. When Butler saw this expression, he knew that his boss was back in control of his faculties and his Atlantis Complex was certified as cured.

No more counting words. No more irrational fear of the number four. No more paranoia and delusions. Thank goodness for that.

He asked anyway, just to be certain. 'Well, Artemis, how are we?'

Artemis buttoned the jacket of his navy woollen suit.

'We are fine, Butler. That is to say that I, Artemis Fowl the Second, am one hundred per cent functional, which is about five times the functionality of an average person. Or to put it another way: one point five Mozarts. Or three quarters of a da Vinci.'

'Only three quarters? You're being modest.'

'Correct,' said Artemis, smiling. 'I am.'

Butler's shoulders sagged a little with relief. Inflated ego, supreme self-confidence. Artemis was most definitely his old self.

'Very good. Let's pick up our escort and be on our way then, shall we? I want to feel the sun on my face. The real sun, not the UV lamps they have down here.'

Artemis felt a pang of sympathy for his bodyguard, an emotion he had been experiencing more and more in recent months. It was difficult enough for Butler to be inconspicuous among humans; down here he could hardly attract more attention if he were wearing a clown suit and juggling fireballs.

'Very well,' agreed Artemis. 'We will pick up our escort and depart. Where is Holly?'

Butler jerked a thumb down the hallway. 'Where she generally is. With the clone.'

Captain Holly Short of the Lower Elements Police Recon division stared at the face of her arch-enemy and felt only pity. Of course, had she been gazing at the real Opal Koboi and not a cloned version, then pity might not have been the last emotion on her list, but it would certainly have ranked far below *rage* and *intense dislike bordering on hatred*. But this was a clone, grown in advance to provide the megalomaniacal pixie with a body double so that she could be spirited from protective custody in the J. Argon Clinic if the LEP ever managed to incarcerate her, which they had.

Holly pitied the clone because she was a pathetic, dumb creature who had never asked to be created. Cloning was a banned science for both religious reasons and the more obvious fact that, without a life force or soul to power their systems, clones were doomed to a short life of negligent brain activity and organ failure.

This particular clone had lived out most of its days in an incubator, struggling for each breath since it had been removed from the chrysalis in which it had been grown.

'Not for much longer, little one,' Holly whispered, touching the ersatz pixie's forehead through the sterile gloves built into the incubator wall.

Holly could not have said for sure why she had begun to visit the clone. Perhaps it was because Argon had told her that no one else ever had.

She came from nowhere. She has no friends.

She had at least two friends now. Artemis had taken to joining Holly on her visits and would sit silently beside her, which was very unusual for him.

The clone's official designation was Unauthorized Experiment 14, but one of the clinic's wits had named her Nopal, which was a cruel play on the name Opal and the words *no pal*. Cruel or not, the name stuck and now even Holly used it, though with tenderness.

Argon assured her that Unauthorized Experiment 14 had no mental faculties, but Holly was sure that sometimes Nopal's milky eyes reacted when she visited. Could the clone actually recognize her?

Holly gazed at Nopal's delicate features and was inevitably reminded of her gene donor.

That pixie is poison, she thought bitterly. *Whatever she touches withers and dies.*

Artemis entered the room and stood beside Holly, resting a hand lightly on her shoulder.

'They're wrong about Nopal,' said Holly. 'She feels things. She understands.'

Artemis knelt down. 'I know. I taught her something last week. Watch.'

He placed his hand on the glass, tapping his fingers in sequence slowly, building up a rhythm. 'It is an exercise developed by Cuba's Doctor Parnassus. He uses it to generate a response from infants, even chimpanzees.'

Artemis continued to tap and slowly Nopal responded, raising her hand laboriously to Artemis's, slapping the glass clumsily in an attempt to copy his rhythm.

'There, you see,' said Artemis. 'Intelligence.'

Holly bumped him gently, shoulder to shoulder, which was her version of a hug. 'I knew your brains would eventually come in handy.'

The acorn cluster on the breast of Holly's LEP jumpsuit

vibrated and Holly touched her wi-tech earring, accepting the call. A quick glance at her wrist computer told her that the call was from LEP technical consultant Foaly, and that the centaur had labelled it *urgent*.

'Foaly. What is it? I'm at the clinic, babysitting Artemis.'

The centaur's voice was crystal clear over the Haven City wireless network.

'I need you back at Police Plaza, right now. Bring the Mud Boy.'

The centaur sounded theatrical, but then Foaly would play the drama queen if his carrot soufflé collapsed.

'That's not how it works, Foaly. Consultants don't give orders to captains.'

'We have a Koboi sighting coming through on a satellite. It's a live feed,' countered the technical consultant.

'We're on our way,' said Holly, severing the connection.

They picked up Butler in the corridor. Artemis, Holly and Butler, three allies who had weathered battlefields, rebellions and conspiracy together and had developed their own crisis shorthand.

Butler saw that Holly was wearing her business face.

'Situation?'

Holly strode past, forcing the others to follow. 'Opal,' she said in English.

Butler's face hardened. 'Eyes on?'

'Satellite link.'

'Origin?' asked the bodyguard.

'Unknown.'

They hurried down the retro corridor towards the clinic's courtyard. Butler outstripped the group and held open the old-fashioned hinged door with its stained-glass window depicting a thoughtful doctor comforting a weeping patient.

'Are we taking the Stick?' asked the bodyguard, his tone suggesting that he would rather not take *the Stick*.

Holly walked through the doorway. 'Sorry, big man. Stick time.'

Artemis had never been one for public transport, human or fairy, and so asked, 'What's the stick?'

The Stick was the street name for a series of conveyor belts that ran in parallel strips along Haven City's network of blocks. It was an ancient and reliable mode of transport from a less litigious time, which operated on a hop-on/hop-off basis similar to certain human airport-walkway systems. There were platforms throughout the city and all a person had to do was step on and grab hold of one of the carbon-fibre stalks that sprouted from the belt. Hence the name *Stick*.

Artemis and Butler had of course seen the Stick before, but Artemis had never planned to use such an undignified mode of transport and so had never even bothered to find out its name. Artemis knew that, with his famous lack of coordination, any attempt to hop casually on to the platform would result in a humiliating tumble. For Butler the problem was not one of coordination or lack of it. He knew that, with his bulk, it would be difficult just to keep his feet within the belt's width.

'Ah, yes,' said Artemis. '*The Stick*. Surely a green cab would be faster?'

'Nope,' said Holly, hustling Artemis up the ramp on to the platform, then poking him in the kidneys at just the right time so that he stepped unconsciously on to the belt, his hand landing on a stick's bulbous grip.

'Hey,' said Artemis, perhaps the third time in his life he had used a slang expletive. 'I did it.'

'Next stop, the Olympics,' said Holly, who had mounted the platform behind him. 'Come on, bodyguard,' she called over her shoulder to Butler. 'Your principal is heading towards a tunnel.'

Butler shot the elf a look that would cow a bull. Holly was a dear friend, but her teasing could be relentless. He tiptoed on to the belt, squeezing his enormous feet on to a single section and bending his knees to grasp the tiny stick. In silhouette he looked like the world's bulkiest ballerina attempting to pluck a flower.

Holly might have grinned had Opal Koboi not been on her mind.

The Stick belt trundled its passengers from the Argon Clinic along the border of an Italian-style piazza towards a low tunnel, which had been laser-cut from solid rock. Fairies lunching al fresco froze with forkfuls of salad halfway to their mouths as the unlikely trio passed by.

The sight of a jumpsuit-clad LEP officer was common enough on a Stick belt, but a gangly human boy dressed like an undertaker and a troll-sized, buzz-cut man-mountain were quite unusual.

The tunnel was barely a metre high so Butler was forced to prostrate himself over three sections, flattening several handgrips in the process. His nose was no more than a metre from the tunnel wall, which he noticed was engraved with beautiful luminous pictograms depicting episodes from the People's history.

So the young fairies can learn something about their own heritage each time they pass through. How wonderful, thought Butler, but he suppressed his admiration as he had long ago disciplined his brain to concentrate on bodyguard duties and not waste neurons being amazed while he was below ground.

Save it for retirement, he thought. *Then you can cast your mind back and appreciate art.*

Police Plaza was a cobbled crest into which the shape of the Lower Elements Police acorn insignia had been painstakingly paved by master craftsmen. It was a total waste of effort as far as the LEP officers were concerned, as they were not generally the type who were inclined to gaze out of the fourth-floor windows and marvel at how the sim-sunlight caught the rim of each gold-leafed cobble and set the whole arrangement a-twinkling.

On this particular day it seemed that everyone on the fourth floor had slid from their cubicles like pebbles on a tilted surface and gathered in a tight cluster by the situations room, which adjoined Foaly's office/laboratory.

Holly made directly for the narrowest section of the throng and used sharp elbows to inch through the strangely silent crowd. Butler simply cleared his throat once and the crowd peeled apart as though magnetically repelled from the giant human. Artemis took this clear path into the situations room to find Commander Trouble Kelp and Foaly standing before a wall-sized screen, raptly following unfolding events.

Foaly noticed the gasps that followed Butler wherever he went in Haven and glanced round.

'May the fours be with you,' the centaur whispered to Artemis. His standard greeting/joke for the past six months.

'I am cured as you well know,' said Artemis. 'What is going on here?'

Holly cleared a space beside Trouble Kelp, who seemed to be morphing into her former boss, Commander Julius Root, as the years went on. Commander Kelp was so brimful of gung-ho attitude that he had taken the name Trouble upon graduation and had once tried to arrest a troll for littering, which accounted for the sim-skin patch on the tip of his nose that glowed yellow from a certain angle.

'Haircut's new, Skipper,' Holly said. 'Beetroot had one just like it.'

Commander Kelp did not take his eyes from the screen. Holly was joshing because she was nervous and Trouble knew it. She was right to be nervous. In fact, outright fear would be more appropriate, given the situation that was being beamed in to them.

'Watch the show, Captain,' he said tightly. 'It's pretty self-explanatory.'

There were three figures on screen, a kneeling prisoner and two captors, but Holly did not place Opal Koboi straight away because she was searching for the pixie among the standing pair. She realized with a jolt that Opal was the prisoner.

'This is a trick,' she said. 'It must be.'

Commander Kelp shrugged. *Watch it and see.*

Artemis stepped closer to the screen, scanning the picture for information. 'You are sure this is live?'

'It's a live feed,' said Foaly. 'I suppose they could be sending us a pre-record.'

'Where is it coming from?'

Foaly checked the tracer map on his own screen. The call line ran from a fairy satellite down to South Africa and from there to Miami and then on to a hundred other places like the scribble of an angry child.

'They jacked a satellite and ran the line through a series of shells. Could be anywhere.'

'The sun is high,' Artemis mused aloud. 'I would guess by the shadows that it is early noon. If it is actually a live feed.'

'That narrows it down to a quarter of the planet,' said Foaly caustically.

The hubbub in the room rose as, on screen, one of the two bulky gnomes standing behind Opal drew a human automatic handgun, the chrome weapon looking like a cannon in his fairy fingers.

It seemed as though the temperature had suddenly dropped in the situations room.

'I need quiet,' said Artemis. 'Get these people out of here.'

On most days Trouble Kelp would argue that Artemis had no authority to clear a room and would possibly invite more people into the cramped office just to prove his point, but this was not most days.

'Everybody out,' he barked at the assembled officers. 'Holly, Foaly and the Mud Boy, stay where you are.'

'I think perhaps I'll stay too,' said Butler, shielding the top of his head from lamp burn with one hand.

Nobody objected.

Usually the LEP officers would shuffle with macho reluctance when ordered to move, but in this instance they rushed to the nearest monitor, eager not to miss a single frame of unfolding events.

Foaly shut the door behind them with a swing of his hoof, then darkened the window glass so there would be no distraction from outside. The remaining four stood in a ragged semicircle before the wall screen, watching what would appear to be the last minutes of Opal Koboi's life. One of the Opal Kobois at any rate.

There were two gnomes on screen, both wearing full-face anti-UV party masks that could be programmed to resemble anyone. These had been modelled on Pip and Kip, two popular kitty-cat cartoon characters on PPTV, but the figures were still recognizable as gnomes because of their stocky barrel torsos and bloated forearms. They stood before a nondescript grey wall, looming over the tiny pixie who knelt in the mud tracks of some wheeled vehicle, waterline creeping along the legs of her designer tracksuit. Opal's wrists were bound and her mouth taped, and she seemed genuinely terrified.

The gnome with the pistol spoke through a vox-box in the mask, disguising his voice as Pip the kitty-cat.

'I can't make it any plainer,' he squeaked and somehow the cartoon voice made him seem more dangerous. 'We got one Opal, you got the other. You let your Opal go and we don't kill this one. You had twenty minutes, now you have fifteen.'

Pip the kitty-cat cocked his weapon.

Butler tapped Holly's shoulder.

'Did he just say –?'

'Yeah. Fifteen minutes or Opal's dead.'

Butler popped a translator bud into his ear. This was too important to trust to his dubious grasp of Gnommish.

Trouble Kelp was incredulous. 'What kind of deal is that? Give us a terrorist or we kill a terrorist?'

'We can't just let someone be murdered before our eyes,' said Holly.

'Absolutely not,' agreed Foaly. 'We are not humans.'

Artemis cleared his throat.

'Sorry, Artemis,' said the centaur. 'But you humans are a bloodthirsty bunch. Sure, we may produce the occasional power-crazed pixie, but by and large the People are peace-loving folk. Which is probably why we live down here in the first place.'

ᛒ⚹◊⚶•¶○ᛇᛇ○ᚻᛒ•⚶ᚻᛇᛇᚱ◊ᛩ•○ᛒ•⚹⚶ᚱ◊

Trouble Kelp actually snarled, one of his leadership devices, which not many people could carry off, especially when they stood barely more than three feet high in what Artemis was sure were stacked boots, but Trouble's snarl was convincing enough to stifle the bickering.

'Focus, people,' he said. 'I need solutions here. Under no circumstances can we release Opal Koboi, but we can't just stand by and allow her to be murdered either.'

The computer had picked up the references to Koboi on screen and had elected to run her file on a side screen, in case anyone needed their memory refreshed.

OPAL KOBOI. Certified genius pixie industrialist and inventor. Orchestrated the goblin coup and insurrection. Cloned herself to escape prison and attempted to lead the humans to Haven. Responsible for the murder of Commander Julius Root. Had human pituitary gland implanted to manufacture growth hormone (subsequently removed). Younger version of Opal followed Captain Short from the past and is currently at large in present timeline. It is assumed she will attempt to free her incarcerated self and return to her own time-stream. Opal is in the unprecedented position of occupying places one and two on the LEP Most Dangerous list. Categorized as highly intelligent, motivated and psychotic.

This is a bold move, Opal, thought Artemis. *And with potentially catastrophic repercussions.*

He felt rather than saw Holly at his elbow.

'What do you think, Artemis?'

Artemis frowned. 'My first impression is to call it a bluff. But Opal's plans always take account of first impressions.'

'It could be a ruse. Perhaps those goblins would simply shoot her with a blank?'

Artemis shook his head. 'No. That would deliver no pay-off other than momentary horror on our part. Opal has planned this so that she wins whatever the eventuality. If you free her, then she's free. If the younger Opal dies, then . . . Then what?'

Butler weighed in. 'You can do all sorts of things with special effects these days. What if they computer graphic her head to explode?'

Artemis was disappointed in this theory, which he felt he had already discounted. 'No, Butler. Think. Again, there's nothing to gain.'

Foaly snorted. 'At any rate, if they do kill her, we will know very soon whether this whole thing is real or not.'

Artemis half laughed. 'True. We will certainly know.'

Butler groaned. This was one of those times when Artemis and Foaly were aware of something *sciencey* and assumed that everyone else in the room also had all the facts. Moments like this were guaranteed to drive Holly crazy.

'What are you talking about?' shouted Holly. 'What will we know? How will we know whatever it is?'

Artemis stared down at her as though waking from a dream. 'Really, Holly? You have two versions of the same individual occupying a time-stream and you are unaware of the ramifications?'

On screen the gnomes stood like statues behind the shivering pixie.
The armed one, Pip, occasionally checked a wristwatch by tugging
his sleeve with his gun barrel, but otherwise they waited patiently.
Opal pleaded with her eyes, staring at the camera lens, fat tears
streaming down her cheeks, sparkling in the sunlight. Her hair seemed
thinner than usual and unwashed. Her Juicy Couture tracksuit,
purchased no doubt from the children's section of some exclusive
store, was torn in several places, the rips caked in blood. The picture
was super-high-def and so clear that it was like looking through
a window. If this was a spurious threat, then young Opal did not
know it.

Trouble pounded the desk, an affectation of Julius Root's
that he had adopted.

'What are the ramifications? Tell me!'

'Just to be clear,' said Artemis. 'Do you wish to be told
what the word *ramifications* means? Or to know what the
ramifications are?'

Holly elbowed Artemis in the hip, speeding him along.
'Artemis, we're on a clock here.'

'Very well, Holly. Here is the problem . . . '

'Come on,' pleaded Foaly. 'Let me explain. This is my
kingdom and I will be simple and to the point, I promise.'

'Go on then,' said Trouble, who was known for his love
of *simple and to the point.*

Holly laughed. A single harsh bark. She could not believe
everyone continued to act like their everyday selves even
though a life was at stake.

We have become desensitized like the humans.

Whatever Opal had done, she was still a person. There had been dark days when Holly had dreamed of hunting the pixie down and issuing a little Mud-Man justice, but those days were gone.

Foaly tugged at his outrageously coiffed forelock.

'All beings are made of energy,' he began in the typical pompous *imparting important info* voice that he used at times like this. 'When these beings die, their energy slowly dissipates and returns to the earth.' He paused dramatically. 'But what if a being's entire existence is suddenly negated by a quantum anomaly?'

Trouble raised his arms. 'Whoa! Simple and to the point, remember?'

Foaly rephrased. 'OK. If young Opal dies, then old Opal cannot continue to exist.'

It took Trouble a second, but he got it. 'So, will it be like the movies? She will fizzle out of existence and we will all look a bit puzzled for a moment then forget about her?'

Foaly snickered. 'That's one theory.'

'What's the other theory?'

The centaur paled suddenly and uncharacteristically yielded the floor to Artemis.

'Why don't you explain this bit?' Foaly said. 'I just flashed on what could actually happen and I need to start making calls.'

Artemis nodded curtly. 'The *other* theory was first postulated by your own Professor Bahjee over five centuries ago.

Bahjee believes that if the time-stream is polluted by the arrival of the younger version of a being and that younger version subsequently dies, then the present-tense version of the being will release all its energy spontaneously and violently. Not only that but anything that exists because of the younger Opal will also combust.'

Violently and *combust* were words that Commander Kelp understood well.

'Release its energy? How violently?'

Artemis shrugged. 'That depends on the object or being. Matter is changed instantaneously into energy. A huge explosive force will be released. We could even be talking about nuclear fission.'

Holly felt her heart speed up. 'Fission? Nuclear fission?'

'Basically,' said Artemis. 'For living beings. The objects should cause less damage.'

'Anything Opal made or contributed to will explode?'

'No. Just the things she influenced in the past five years of our timeline, between her two ages, though there will probably be some temporal ripples on either side.'

'Are you talking about all her company's weapons that are still in commission?' asked Holly.

'And the satellites,' added Trouble. 'Every second vehicle in the city.'

'It is just a theory,' said Artemis. 'There is yet another theory that suggests nothing at all will happen other than one person dying. Physics trumps quantum physics and things go on as normal.'

Holly found herself red-faced with sudden fury. 'You're talking as though Opal is already dead.'

Artemis was not sure what to say. 'We are staring into the abyss, Holly. In a short time many of us could be dead. I need to stay detached.'

Foaly looked up from his computer panel. 'What do you think about the percentages, Mud Boy?'

'Percentages?'

'Theory-wise.'

'Oh, I see. How likely are the explosions?'

'Exactly.'

Artemis thought about it. 'All things considered, I would say about ninety per cent. If I were a betting man and there were someone to take this kind of bet, I would put my last gold coin on it.'

Trouble paced the small office. 'We need to release Opal. Let her go immediately.'

Now Holly was uncertain. 'Let's think about this, Trubs.'

The commander turned on her. 'Didn't you hear what the human said? Fission! We can't have fission underground.'

'I agree but it could still be a trick.'

'The alternative is too terrible. We turn her loose and hunt her down. Get Atlantis on the line now. I need to speak to the warden at the Deeps. Is it still Vinyáya?'

Artemis spoke quietly but with the commanding tone that had made him a natural leader since the age of ten.

'It's too late to free Opal. All we can do is save her life. That's what she planned for all along.'

•🙊◖⊗□→•⚙)⊗⦶◊•§⊖⑂⑂•☏⑂ꕤ§•□⚗

'Save her life?' objected Trouble. 'But we still have . . .' Commander Kelp checked the countdown clock. 'Ten minutes.'

Artemis patted Holly's shoulder, then stepped away from her. 'If fairy bureaucracy is anything like the human kind, you won't be able to get Opal into a shuttle in that time. What you might be able to do is get her down to the reactor core.'

Kelp had not yet learned the hard way to shut up and let Artemis explain and so kept asking questions, slowing down the process, wasting valuable seconds.

'Reactor core? What reactor core?'

Artemis raised a finger. 'One more question, Commander, and I will be forced to have Butler restrain you.'

Kelp was a breath away from ejecting Artemis or charging him with something, but the situation was critical and if there was a chance that this human could in some way help . . .

He clenched his fists till his fingers creaked. 'OK. Talk.'

'The Deeps is powered by a natural fission reactor in a uranium ore layer set on a bed of granite similar to the one in Oklo, Gabon,' said Artemis, tugging the facts from his memory. 'The People Power Company harvest the energy in small pods set into the uranium. These pods are constructed with science and magic to withstand a moderate nuclear blast. This is taught in schools here. Every fairy in the room knows this, correct?'

Everyone nodded. Technically it was correct, as they did know it now.

'If we can place Opal inside the pod before the deadline,

then the blast will at least be contained and theoretically, if we pump in enough anti-rad foam, Opal might even retain her physical integrity. Though *that* is something I would not bet my last gold coin on. Opal, apparently, is prepared to take the risk.'

Trouble was tempted to poke Artemis in the chest but wisely resisted. 'You're saying that all of this is an elaborate escape plan?'

'Of course,' said Artemis. 'And not all that elaborate. Opal is forcing you to release her from her cell. The alternative is the utter destruction of Atlantis and every soul in it, which is unthinkable to anyone except Opal herself.'

Foaly had already brought up the prison plans. 'The reactor core is less than a hundred metres below Opal's cell. I'm contacting the warden now.'

Holly knew that Artemis was a genius and there was no one more qualified to second-guess kidnappers, but they still had options.

She gazed at the figures on screen and was chilled by how casual the gnomes seemed in the light of what they were about to do. They slouched like adolescents, barely glancing at their captive, cocky in their abilities and not even a jot self-conscious about their cartoon-character smart-masks, which read their faces and displayed the appropriate emotions in exaggerated cartoon style. Smart-masks were very popular with the karaoke crowd who could look like their idols as well as trying to sound like them.

Perhaps they don't know exactly what's at stake here, Holly thought suddenly. *Perhaps they are as clueless as I was ten seconds ago.*

'Can they hear us?' she asked Foaly.

'They can, but we haven't responded yet. Just press the button.'

This was just an old figure of speech; there was of course no actual button, just a sensor on the touch screen.

'Hold it, Captain!' ordered Trouble.

'I am a trained negotiator, sir,' said Holly, hoping the respect in her tone would get her what she wanted. 'And I was once . . .' She glanced guiltily at Artemis, sorry that she had to play this card. 'I was once a hostage myself, so I know how these things go. Let me talk to them.'

Artemis nodded encouragingly and Holly knew that he understood her tactics.

'Captain Short is correct, Commander,' he said. 'Holly is a natural communicator. She even managed to get through to me.'

'Do it,' barked Trouble. 'Foaly, you keep trying to reach Atlantis. And assemble the Council; we need to begin evacuating both cities now.'

Though you could not see their real faces, the gnomes' cartoon expressions were bored now. It was in the slant of their heads and the bend of their knees. Perhaps this whole thing was not as exciting as they hoped it would be. After all, they could not see their audience and no one had responded to their threats. What had started out as a revolutionary action was now beginning to look like two big gnomes picking on a pixie.

Pip waggled his gun at Kip and the meaning was clear. Why don't we just shoot her now?

Holly activated the microphone with a wave of her hand.

'Hello, you there. This is Captain Holly Short of the LEP. Can you hear me?'

The gnomes perked up immediately and Pip even attempted a whistle, which came through the vox-box as a raspberry.

'Hey, Captain Short. We heard of you. I've seen pictures. Not too shabby, Captain.'

Holly bit back a caustic retort. Never force a kidnapper to demonstrate his resolve.

'Thank you, Pip. Should I call you Pip?'

'You, Holly Short, can call me anything and *any time* you like,' squeaked Pip and extended his free hand towards his partner for a knuckle bump.

Holly was incredulous. These two were about to totally incapacitate the entire fairy world and they were goofing about like two goblins at a fireball party.

'OK, Pip,' she continued evenly. 'What can we do for you today?'

Pip shook his head sorrowfully at Kip. 'Why are the pretty ones always stupid?' He turned to the camera. 'You know what you can do for us. We told you already. Release Opal Koboi or the younger model is gonna take a long sleep. And by that I mean get shot in the head.'

'You need to give us some time to show good faith. Come on, Pip. One more hour? For me?'

Pip scratched his head with the gun barrel, pretending to consider it. 'You are cute, Holly. But not that cute. If I give you another hour, you'll track me down somehow and drop a time-stop on my head. No thanks, Cap. You have ten minutes. If I was you, I would get that cell open or call the undertaker.'

'This kind of thing takes time, Pip,' persisted Holly, repeating the name, forging a bond. 'It takes three days to pay a parking fine.'

Pip shrugged. 'Not my problem, babe. And you can call me Pip all day and it won't make us BFFs. It ain't my real name.'

Artemis deactivated the microphone. 'This one is smart, Holly. Don't play with him, just tell the truth.'

Holly nodded and switched on the mike. 'OK, whatever your name is. Let me give it to you straight. There's a good chance that if you shoot young Opal, then we're going to have a series of very big explosions down here. A lot of innocent people will die.'

Pip waved his gun carelessly. 'Oh yeah, the quantum laws. We know about that, don't we, Kip?'

'Quantum laws,' said Kip. 'Of course we know about that.'

'And you don't care that good fairies, gnomes that could be related to you, will die?'

Pip raised his eyebrows so that they jutted over the top of the mask. 'You like any of your family, Kip?'

'Ain't got no family. I'm an orphan.'

'Really? Me too.'

And, while they bantered, Opal shivered in the dirt, trying to speak through the tape. Foaly would get voice analysis on the muffled mumbles later, if there were a later, but it didn't take a genius to figure out she was pleading for her life.

'There must be something you need?' said Holly.

'There is one thing,' replied Pip. 'Could I get your comcode? I sure would love to hook up for a sim-latte when this is all over. Might be a while, of course, what with Haven City being in ruins.'

Foaly put a text box on the screen. It read: *They're moving Opal now.*

Holly flickered her eyelids to show she understood, then continued with the negotiation. 'Here's the situation, Pip. We have nine minutes left. You can't get someone out of Atlantis in nine minutes. It's not possible. They need to suit up, pressurize maybe, go through the conduits to open sea. Nine minutes is not long enough.'

Pip's theatrical responses were getting a little hard to take. 'Well then, I guess a lot of people are going swimming. Fission can put a hell of a hole in the shield.'

Holly broke. 'Don't you care about anyone? What's the going rate for genocide?'

Pip and Kip actually laughed.

'It's a horrible feeling, impotency, ain't it?' said Pip. 'But there are worse feelings. Drowning, for example.'

'And getting crushed by falling buildings,' added Kip.

Holly banged her tiny fists on the console.

These two are so infuriating.

34

Pip stepped close to the camera so his mask filled the screen. 'If I don't get a call from Opal Koboi in the next few minutes, telling me she is in a shuttle on her way to the surface, then I will shoot this pixie. Believe it.'

Foaly rested his head in his hands. 'I used to love Pip and Kip,' he said.

CHAPTER 2: KILLING THE PAST

THE DEEPS, ATLANTIS

 OPAL Koboi was making a futile attempt to levitate when the guards came for her. It was something she had been able to do as a child before her chosen life of crime had stripped the magic from her synapses, the tiny junctions between nerve cells where most experts agreed magic originated. Her power might have regenerated if it hadn't been for the human pituitary gland she'd had briefly grafted to her hypothalamus. Levitation was a complicated art, especially for pixies with their limited powers, and usually only a state achieved by Hey-Hey Monks of the Third Balcony, but Opal had managed it while still in nappies, which was her parents' first sign that their daughter was a little bit special.

Imagine it, she thought. *I wished to be human. That was a mistake for which I will eventually find someone to blame. The centaur Foaly — he drove me to it. I do hope he is killed in the explosion.*

Opal smirked in self-satisfaction. There had been a time when she'd whiled away the prison monotony by concocting ever more elaborate death traps for her centaur nemesis, but now she was content to let Foaly die with the rest in the imminent explosions. Granted she had cooked up a little surprise for his wife, but this was merely a side project and not something she had spent too much time on.

It is a measure of how far I have come, Opal thought. *I have matured somewhat. The veil has lifted and I see my true purpose.*

There had been a time when Opal had simply been a ruthless business fairy with daddy issues, but somewhere during the years of banned experimentation she had allowed black magic to fester in her soul and let it warp her heart's desire until it was not enough to be lauded in her own city. She needed the world to bow down, and she was prepared to risk everything and sacrifice anyone to see her wish fulfilled.

This time it will be different for I will have fearsome warriors bound to my will. Ancient soldiers who will die for me.

Opal cleared her mind and sent out a probe searching for her other self. All that came back was the white noise of terror.

She knows, Opal realized. *Poor thing.*

This moment of sympathy for her younger self did not last long, as the imprisoned Opal had learned not to live in the past.

I am merely killing a memory, she thought. *That is all.*

Which was a convenient way of looking at it.

*

Her cell door phase-changed from solid to gas and Opal was unsurprised to see Warden Tarpon Vinyáya, a malleable pen-pusher who had never spent a night under the moon, fidgeting in her doorway, flanked by two jumbo pixie guards.

'Warden,' she said, abandoning her levitation attempt. 'Has my pardon arrived?'

Tarpon had no time for pleasantries. 'We're moving you, Koboi. No discussion, just come along.'

He gestured to his guards. 'Wrap her up, boys.'

The jumbo pixies strode rapidly into the room, wordlessly pinning Opal's arms to her sides. Jumbo pixies were a breed peculiar to Atlantis where the particular blend of pressurized environment and algae-based filtration had caused them to pop up with increased regularity over the years. What the jumbo pixies gained in brawn they generally sacrificed in brain and so they made the ideal prison guards, having no respect for anyone smaller than them who did not sign their pay cheque.

Before Opal could open her mouth to voice an objection, the pixies had bundled her into a lined anti-radiation suit and clipped three bungee cords round her torso.

The warden sighed as if he had been expecting Opal to somehow disable his guards. Which he had.

'Good. Good,' he said, mopping his high brow with a hempen handkerchief. 'Take her to the basement. Don't touch any of the pipes and avoid breathing if possible.'

The pixies hefted their captive between them, like a rolled

〈symbols〉

rug, and double-timed it from Opal's cell, across the narrow bridge that linked her cell-pod to the main prison and into the service elevator.

Opal smiled behind the heavy lead gauze of her headpiece.

This certainly is the day for Opal Kobois to be manhandled by burly boys.

She beamed a thought to her younger self on the surface.

I feel for you, sister.

The elevator cube flashed downwards through a hundred metres of soft sandstone to a small chamber composed entirely of hyper-dense material harvested from the crust of a neutron star.

Opal guessed they had arrived at the chamber and giggled at the memory of a stupid gnome in her high school who had asked what neutron stars were made from.

'*Neutrons, boy,*' Professor Leguminous had snapped. '*Neutrons! The clue is in the name.*'

This chamber held the record for being the most expensive room per square centimetre to construct anywhere on the planet, though it looked a little like a concrete furnace room. At one end was the elevator door, at the other were what looked like four missile tubes and in the middle was an extremely grumpy dwarf.

'You are bleeping joking me?' he said, belly thrust out belligerently.

The jumbo pixies dumped Opal on the grey floor.

'Orders, pal,' said one. 'Put her in the tube.'

The dwarf shook his head stubbornly. 'I ain't putting no one in a tube. Them tubes is built for rods.'

'I do believe,' said the second pixie, very proud of himself for remembering the information he was about to deliver, 'that one of them reactor sites is depleted so the tube do be empty.'

'That sounded pretty good, Jumbo, except for the *do be* at the end,' said the dwarf whose name was Kolin Ozkopy. 'But, even so, I need to know how the consequences of *not* putting a person in a tube are worse than the consequences of putting them in one?'

A sentence of this length would take a jumbo pixie several minutes to digest; luckily they were spared the embarrassment of being pressed for an explanation when Kolin's phone rang.

'Just a sec,' he said, checking caller ID. 'It's the warden.'

Kolin answered the phone with a flourish. 'Y'ello. Engineer Ozkopy here.'

Ozkopy listened for a long moment, interjecting three *uh-huh*s and two *D'Arvit*s before pocketing the phone.

'Wow,' he said, prodding the radiation suit with his toe. 'I guess you'd better put her in the tube.'

POLICE PLAZA, HAVEN CITY, THE LOWER ELEMENTS

Pip waggled his phone at the camera.

'You hear anything? Because I don't. No one is calling this number and I've got five bars. One hundred per cent planetary coverage. Hell, I once took a call on a spaceship.'

Holly swiped the mike sensor. 'We're moving as fast as we can. Opal Koboi is in the shuttle bay right now. We just need ten more minutes.'

Pip adopted a sing-song voice.

> '*Never tell a lie, just to get you by.*
> *Never tell a tale, lest you go to jail.*'

Foaly found himself humming along. It was the Pip and Kip theme song. Holly glared at him.

'Sorry,' he muttered.

Artemis grew impatient with the fruitless wrangling. 'This is futile and frankly embarrassing. They have no intention of releasing Opal. We should evacuate now, at least to the shuttle bays. They are built to withstand magma flares.'

Foaly disagreed. 'We're secure here. The real danger is in Atlantis. That's where the other Opal is. You said, and I concur, that the serious explosions, theoretical explosions, only occur with living beings.'

'Theoretical explosions are only theoretical until the theory is proven,' countered Artemis. 'And with so many –' He stopped mid-sentence, which was very unlike him as Artemis detested both bad grammar and poor manners. His skin tone faded from pale to porcelain and he actually rapped his own forehead.

'Stupid. Stupid. Foaly, we are both imbeciles. I don't expect lateral thinking from the LEP, but you . . .'

Holly recognized this tone. She had heard it during

previous adventures, generally before things went catastroph-
ically wrong.

'What is it?' she asked, afraid of the answer which must
surely be terrible.

'Yeah,' agreed Foaly, who always had time to feel insulted.
'Why am I an imbecile?'

Artemis pointed an index finger diagonally down and
south-west in the approximate direction they had come from
the J. Argon Clinic.

'The oxygen booth has addled my senses,' he said. 'The
clone. Nopal. She's a living being. If she explodes, it could
go nuclear.'

Foaly accessed the clone's file on Argon's website, navigat-
ing with blurred speed to the patient details.

'No. I think we should be OK there. Opal harvested her
own DNA before the timeline split.'

Artemis was angry with himself all the same for momentarily forgetting the clone.

'We were minutes into this crisis before the clone's rele-
vance occurred to me,' he said. 'If Nopal had been created at
a later date, my slow thinking could have cost lives.'

'There are still plenty of lives at stake,' said Foaly. 'We
need to save as many as we can.'

The centaur popped a plexiglass cover on the wall and
pressed the red button underneath. Instantly a series of Evac
sirens began to wail throughout the city. The eerie sound
spread like the keening of mothers receiving the bad news
of their nightmares.

Foaly chewed a nail. 'There's no time to wait for Council approval,' he said to Trouble Kelp. 'Most should make it to the shuttle bays. But we need to ready the emergency resuscitation teams.'

Butler was less than happy with the idea of losing Artemis. 'Nobody's death is impending.'

His principal didn't seem overly concerned. 'Well, technically, *everybody's* death is impending.'

'Shut up, Artemis!' snapped Butler, which was a major breach of his own professional ethics. 'I promised your mother that I would look after you, and yet again you have put me in a position where my brawn and skills count for nothing.'

'That is hardly fair,' said Artemis. 'I hardly think that I can be blamed for Opal's latest stunt.'

Butler's face blazed a few shades redder than Artemis could remember having seen it. 'I do think you can be blamed and I do blame you. We're barely clear of the consequences of your last misadventure, and here we are neck-deep in another one.'

Artemis seemed more shocked by this outburst than the *impending death* situation.

'Butler, I had no idea you were harbouring such frustration.'

The bodyguard rubbed his cropped head.

'Neither had I,' he admitted. 'But for the past few years it's been one thing after another. Goblins, time travel, demons. Now this place where everything is so . . . so . . . small.' He took a deep shuddering breath. 'OK. I said it, it's out there. And I am fine now. So, let's move on, shall we? What's the plan?'

'Keep evacuating,' said Artemis. 'No more empowering those hostage-taking nitwits; they have their instructions. Drop the blast doors which should help to absorb some of the shock waves.'

'We have our strategies in place, human,' said Trouble Kelp. 'The entire population can be at their assembly points in five minutes.'

Artemis paced, thinking. 'Tell your people to dump their weapons into the magma chutes. Leave anything that might have Koboi technology behind. Phones, games, everything.'

'All Koboi weaponry has been retired,' said Holly. 'But some of the older Neutrinos might have a chip or two.'

Trouble Kelp had the grace to look guilty. '*Some* of the Koboi weaponry has been retired,' he said. 'Budget cuts, you know how it is.'

Pip interrupted their preparations by actually rapping on the camera lens.

'Hey, LEP people. I'm getting old here. Somebody say something, anything. Tell us more lies, we don't care.'

Artemis's eyebrows furrowed and joined. He did not appreciate such flippant posturing when many lives were at stake. He pointed at the microphone.

'May I?'

Trouble barely looked up from his emergency calls and made a vague gesture that was open to interpretation. Artemis chose to interpret it as an affirmative.

He approached the screen. 'Listen to me, you low life. This is Artemis Fowl. You may have heard of me.'

Pip grinned and his mask echoed the expression. 'Oooh, Artemis Fowl. Wonder boy. We've heard of you all right, haven't we, Kip?'

Kip nodded, dancing a little jig. 'Artemis Fowl, the Oirish boy who chased leprechauns. Sure and begorra everyone has heard of that smarty-pants.'

These two are stupid, thought Artemis. *They are stupid and talk too much and I should be able to exploit those weaknesses.*

He tried a ruse. 'I thought I told you to read your demands and say nothing more.'

Pip's face was literally a mask of confusion. 'You told us?'

Artemis hardened his voice. 'My instructions for you two idiots were to read the demands, wait until the time was up then shoot the pixie. I don't recall saying anything about trading insults.'

Pip's mask frowned. *How did Artemis Fowl know their instructions?*

'Your instructions? We don't take orders from you.'

'Really? Explain to me then how I know your instructions to the letter.'

Pip's mask software was not able to cope with his rapid expression change and froze momentarily.

'I . . . ah . . . I don't . . .'

'And tell me how I knew the exact frequency to tap into.'

'You're not in Police Plaza?'

'Of course not, you idiot. I'm at the rendezvous point waiting for Opal.'

Artemis felt his heart speed up, and waited a second for his conscious mind to catch up with his subconscious and tell him what he recognized on screen.

Something in the background.

Something familiar.

The wall behind Pip and Kip was nondescript grey. Rendered with roughly finished plaster. A common finish for farm walls worldwide. There were walls like this all over the Fowl Estate.

Ba-boom.

There went his heart again.

Artemis concentrated on the wall. Slate-grey except for a network of jagged cracks that sundered the plasterwork.

A memory presented itself of six-year-old Artemis and his father walking the estate. As they passed the barn wall on the upper pasture, young Artemis pointed to the wall and commented, 'See, Father? The cracks form a map of Croatia, once part of the Roman, Ottoman and Austrian Habsburg empires. Were you aware that Croatia declared its independence from Yugoslavia in 1991?'

There it was. On the wall behind Pip and Kip. A map of Croatia, though fifteen-year-old Artemis saw now that the Dalmatian coastline was truncated.

They are at the Fowl Estate, he realized.

Why?

Something Doctor Argon had said resurfaced.

Because the residual magic there is off the scale. Something happened on the Fowl Estate once. Something huge, magically speaking.

Artemis decided to act on his hunch. 'I'm at the Fowl Estate waiting for Opal,' he said.

'You're at Fowl Manor too?' blurted Kip, prompting Pip to turn rapidly and shoot his comrade in the heart. The gnome was punched backwards into the wall, knocking clouds of dust from the render. A narrow stream of blood oozed from the hole in his chest, pulsing gently down his breastplate, as undramatic as a paint drip running down a jar. His kitty-cat cartoon face seemed comically surprised and, when the heat from his face faded, the pixels powered down leaving a yellow question mark.

The sudden death shocked Artemis, but the preceding sentence had shocked him more.

He had been correct on both counts: not only was Opal behind this but the rendezvous point was Fowl Manor.

Why? What had happened there?

Pip shouted at the screen. 'You see what you did, human? If you *are* human. If you *are* Artemis Fowl. It doesn't matter what you know, it's too late.'

Pip pressed the still-smoking barrel to Opal's head and she jerked away as the metal burned her skin, pleading through the tape over her mouth. It was clear that Pip wished to pull the trigger but he could not.

He has his instructions, thought Artemis. *He must wait until the allotted time has run out. Otherwise he cannot be certain that Opal is secure in the nuclear reactor.*

␡•▢•⧉⦵⦵•⸎•⦚⬡⟩⟨•␡⬠⟩⌐▢•⬡⬠•⟿

Artemis deactivated the microphone and was moving towards the door when Holly caught his arm.

'There's no time,' she said, correctly guessing that he was headed for home.

'I must try to save my family from the next stage of Opal's plan,' said Artemis tersely. 'There are five minutes left. If I can make it to a magma vent, we might be able to outrun the explosions to the surface.'

Commander Kelp quickly weighed his options. He could order Artemis to remain underground, but it would certainly be strategically advantageous to have someone to track Opal Koboi if she somehow escaped from Atlantis.

'Go,' he said. 'Captain Short will pilot you and Butler to the surface. Stay in contact if . . .'

He did not finish the sentence but everyone in the room could guess what he had been about to say.

Stay in contact if . . . there is anything left to contact.

CHAPTER 3: FIRE AND BRIMSTONE

 OPAL did not enjoy being forced into the depths of the tube by a flat-topped ramrod, but once she was down inside the neutron crust she felt quite snuggly, cushioned by a fluffy layer of anti-rad foam.

One is like a caterpillar in a chrysalis, she thought, only a little irked by the rough material of her anti-rad suit. *I am about to transform into the godhead. I am about to arrive at my destiny. Bow down, creatures, or bear thine own blindness.*

Then she thought, *Bear thine own blindness? Is that too much?*

There was a niggly doubt in the back of Opal's head that she had actually made a horrific mistake by setting this plan in motion. It was her most radical manoeuvre ever and thousands of fairies and humans would die. Worse still, she herself might cease to exist or morph into some kind of time-mutant. But Opal dealt with these worries by simply refusing to engage with them. It was childish she knew, but Opal was ninety per cent convinced that she was cosmically ordained to be the first Quantum Being.

The alternative was too abhorrent to be entertained for long: she, Opal Koboi, would be forced to live out her days as a common prisoner in the Deeps, an object of ridicule and derision. The subject of morality tales and school projects. A chimp in a zoo for the Atlantis fairies to stare at with round eyes. To kill everyone or even die herself would be infinitely preferable. Not that she would die. The tube would contain her energy and with enough concentration she would become a nuclear version of herself.

One feels one's destiny at hand. Any minute now.

HAVEN CITY

Artemis, Butler and Holly took the express elevator to Police Plaza's own shuttle port, which was connected to a magma vent from the Earth's core that supplied much of the city's power through geothermal rods. Artemis did not speak to the others; he simply muttered to himself and rapped the steel wall of the elevator with his knuckles. Holly was relieved to find that there was no pattern in the rappings, unless of course the pattern was too complicated for her to perceive it. It wouldn't be the first time Artemis's thought process had been beyond her grasp.

The elevator was spacious by LEP standards and so allowed

Butler enough headroom to stand up straight, though he still knocked his crown against the capsule wall whenever they hit a bump.

Finally Artemis spoke: 'If we can get into the shuttle before the deadline, then we stand a real chance of making it to the magma chutes.'

Artemis used the word *deadline*, but his companions knew that he meant *assassination*. Pip would shoot Opal when the time was up; none of them doubted that now. Then the consequences of this murder would unfold, whatever they might be, and their best chance of survival lay on the inside of a titanium craft that was built to survive total immersion in a magma chimney.

The elevator hissed to a halt on pneumatic pistons and the doors opened to admit the assorted noises of utter bedlam. The shuttle port was jammed with frantic fairies fighting their way through the security checkpoints, ignoring the usual X-ray protocols and jumping over barriers and turnstiles. Sprites flew illegally low, their wings grazing the tube lighting. Gnomes huddled together in crunchball formations, attempting to barge their way through the line of LEP crowd-control officers in riot gear.

'People are forgetting their drills,' muttered Holly. 'This panic is not going to help anyone.'

Artemis stared crestfallen at the melee. He had seen something like it once in JFK airport when a TV reality star had turned up in Arrivals. 'We won't make it through. Not without hurting people.'

Butler picked up his comrades and slung one across each shoulder. 'The heck we won't,' he said, stepping determinedly into the multitude.

Pip's attitude had changed since shooting his partner. No more chit-chat and posturing, now he was following his instructions to the letter: wait until his phone alarm beeped, then shoot the pixie.

That Fowl guy. That was bluff, right? He can't do anything now. It probably wasn't even Fowl.

Pip decided that he would never divulge what had happened here today. Silence was safety. Words would only bind themselves into strands and hang him.

She need never know.

But Pip knew that she would take one look in his eyes and know everything. For a second Pip thought about running, just disentangling himself from this entire convoluted master plan and being a plain old gnome again.

I cannot do it. She would find me. She would find me and do terrible things to me. And, for some reason, I do not wish to be free of her.

There was nothing for it but to follow the orders that he had not already disobeyed.

Perhaps, if I kill her, she will forgive me.

Pip cocked the hammer on his handgun and pressed it to the back of Opal's head.

ATLANTIS

In the reactor, Opal's head was buzzing with excitement. It must be soon. Very soon. She had been counting the seconds, but the bumpy elevator ride had disorientated her.

I am ready, she thought. *Ready for the next step.*

Pull it! she broadcast, knowing her younger self would hear the thought and panic. *Pull the trigger.*

POLICE PLAZA

Foaly felt his quiff droop under the weight of perspiration and tried to remember what his parting comment to Caballine had been that morning.

I think I told her that I loved her. I always do. But did I say it this morning? Did I?

It seemed very important to him.

Caballine is in the suburbs. She will be out of harm's way. Fine.

The centaur did not believe his own thoughts. If Opal was behind this, there would be serpentine twists to this plan yet to be revealed.

Opal Koboi does not make plans; she writes operas.

For the first time in his life Foaly was horrified to catch himself thinking that someone else might just be a little smarter than he was.

POLICE PLAZA SHUTTLE PORT

Butler waded through the crowd, dropping his feet with care. His appearance in the shuttle port only served to heighten the level of panic, but that could not be helped now. Some temporary discomforts would have to be borne by certain fairies if it meant reaching their shuttle in time. Elves shoaled around his knees like cleaner fish, several poking him with buzz batons and a couple spraying him with pheromone repellent spray, which Butler found to his great annoyance instantly shrank his sinuses.

When they reached the security turnstile, the huge body-guard simply stepped over it, leaving the majority of the frightened populace milling around on the other side. Butler had the presence of mind to dunk Holly in front of the retinal scanner so they could be beeped through without activating the terminal's security measures.

Holly called to a sprite she recognized on the security desk.

'Chix. Is our chute open?'

Chix Verbil had once been Holly's pod-mate on a stakeout and was only alive because she had dragged his wounded frame out of harm's way.

'Uh . . . yeah. Commander Kelp told us to make a hole. Are you OK, Captain?'

Holly dismounted from Butler's shelf-like shoulder, landing with sparks from her boot heels.

'Fine.'

'Unusual mode of transport,' commented Chix, nervously hovering half a metre from the floor, his reflection shimmering in the polished steel below like a sprite trapped in another dimension.

'Don't worry, Chix,' said Holly, patting Butler's thigh. 'He's tame. Unless he smells fear.'

Butler sniffed the air as though there were a faint scent of terror.

Chix rose a few centimetres, his wings a hummingbird blur. He tapped the v-board on his wrist computer with sweating digits. 'OK. You are set to go. The ground crew checked all your life support. And we popped in a fresh plasma cube while we were in there so you're good for a few decades. The blast doors are dropping in less than two minutes so I would get moving if I were you and take those two Mud Men . . . ah, humans . . . with you.'

Butler decided that it would be quicker to keep Artemis pinioned on his shoulder until they were in the shuttle, as he would probably trip over a dwarf in his haste. He set off at a quick lope down the metal tube linking the check-in desk to their berth.

Foaly had managed to get a remodelling order approved for the bay so that Butler could walk under the lintel with his chin tucked low. The shuttle itself was actually an off-road vehicle confiscated by the Criminal Assets Bureau from a tuna smuggler. The middle row of seats had been removed so that the bodyguard could stretch out in the back. Riding the off-roader was Butler's favourite part of his underworld visits.

'*Off-roader!*' Foaly had snorted. '*As if there is anywhere to go in Haven that doesn't have roads. Plasma-guzzling status symbols, that's all these clunkers are.*'

Which hadn't stopped him from gleefully ordering a refit so that the vehicle resembled an American Humvee and could accommodate two humans in the back. And, because Artemis was one of the humans, Foaly could not help but show off a little, stuffing more extras into the confined space than would be found in the average Mars probe: gel seats, thirty-two speakers, 3D HDTV; and, for Holly, oxy-boost and a single laser cutter in the hood ornament which was an imp blowing a long-stemmed horn. This was why the shuttle was referred to as the *Silver Cupid*. It was a little romantic-sounding for Artemis's taste and so Holly referred to it by name as often as possible.

The off-roader detected Holly's proximity and sent a message to her wrist computer enquiring whether it should pop the doors and start itself up. Holly confirmed without missing a step and the batwing doors swung smoothly upwards just in time for Butler to unload Artemis like a sack of kittens from his shoulder into the back seat. Holly slid into the single front seat in the nose of the blocky craft and locked on to the supply rail before the doors had sealed.

Artemis and Butler leaned back and allowed the safety cinches to drop over their shoulders, pulling comfortably close on tension-sensitive rollers.

Artemis's fingers scrunched the material of his trousers

at the knees. Their progress down the feeder rail seemed maddeningly slow down the feeder rail. At the end of the metal-panel-clad rock tunnel they could see the vent itself, a glowing crescent yawning like the gate to hell.

'Holly,' he said without parting his teeth. 'Please, a little acceleration.'

Holly lifted her gloved hands from the wheel. 'We're still on the feeder rail, Artemis. It's all automatic.'

Foaly's face appeared in a heads-up display on the windscreen. 'I'm sorry, Artemis,' he said. 'I really am. We've run out of time.'

'No!' said Artemis, straining against his belt. 'There are fifteen seconds left. Twelve at least.'

Foaly's eyes dropped to the controls before him. 'We have to close the doors to ensure everyone inside the blast tunnels survives. I really am sorry, Artemis.'

The off-roader jerked then halted as the power was cut to the rail.

'We can make it,' Artemis said, his voice close to a panic wheeze.

Up ahead the mouth to hell began to close as the giant dwarf-forged gears rolled the metre-thick slatted shutters down over the vent.

Artemis grasped Holly's shoulder. 'Holly? Please.'

Holly rolled her eyes and flicked the controls to manual. 'D'Arvit,' she said and pressed the accelerator to the floor.

The off-roader leaped forward, jerking free from its guide rail, setting off revolving lights and warning klaxons.

On screen, Foaly rubbed his eyelids with index fingers. 'Yeah, yeah. Here we go. Captain Short goes rogue once more. Hands up who's surprised. Anyone?'

Holly tried to ignore the centaur and concentrate on squeezing the shuttle through the shrinking gap.

Usually I pull this sort of stunt towards the end of an adventure, she thought. *Third act climax. We're starting early this time.*

The shuttle grated along the tunnel floor, the friction sending up twin arcs of sparks that bounced off the walls. Holly slipped control goggles over her eyes and automatically adjusted her vision to the curious double-focus necessary to send blink commands to the sensors in her lenses and actually look at what was in front of her.

'Close,' she said. 'It's going to be close.' And then, before they lost the link: 'Good luck, Foaly. Stay safe.'

The centaur tapped his screen with two fingers. 'Good luck to us all.'

Holly bought them an extra few centimetres by deflating the *Cupid*'s suspension pads and the off-roader ducked under the descending blast doors with half a second to spare, swooping into the natural chimney. Below, the Earth's core spewed up magma columns ten kilometres wide, creating fiery updraughts that blasted the small shuttle's scorched underside and set it spiralling towards the surface.

Holly set the stabilizers and allowed the headrest to cradle her neck and skull.

'Hold on,' she said. 'There's a rough ride ahead.'

*

Pip jumped when the alarm sounded on his phone as though he had not been expecting it, as though he had not been counting the seconds. Nevertheless he seemed surprised now that the moment had finally arrived. Shooting Kip had drained the cockiness from him, and his body language was clearly that of a reluctant assassin.

He tried to regain some of that old cavalier spirit by waving his gun a little and leering at the camera, but it is difficult to represent the murder of a childlike pixie as anything but that.

'I warned you,' he said to the camera. 'This is on you people, not me.'

In Police Plaza, Commander Kelp activated the mike.

'I will find you,' he growled. 'If it takes me a thousand years, I will find you and deliver you to a lifetime's imprisonment.'

This actually seemed to cheer Pip a little. 'You? Find me? Sorry if that doesn't worry me, cop, but I know someone who scares me a lot more than you.'

And without further discussion he shot Opal, once, in the head.

The pixie toppled forward as though struck from behind with a shovel. The bullet's impact drove her into the ground with some force, but there was very little blood except a small trickle from her ear almost as if young Opal had fallen from her bicycle in the schoolyard.

In Police Plaza the usually riotous operations centre grew quiet as the entire force waited for the repercussions of the murder they had just witnessed. Which quantum theory would prove correct? Perhaps nothing at all would happen apart from the death of a pixie.

'OK,' said Trouble Kelp after a long pregnant moment. 'We're still operational. How long before we're out of the troll's den?'

Foaly was about to run a few calculations on the computer when the wall screen spontaneously shattered, leaking green gas into the room.

'Hold on to something,' he advised. 'Chaos is coming.'

ATLANTIS

Opal Koboi felt herself die and it was a curious sensation, like an anxious gnawing at her insides.

So this is what trauma feels like, she thought. *I'm sure I'll get over it.*

The sour sickness was soon replaced by a fizzing excitement as she relished the notion of what she was to become.

Finally I am transforming. Emerging from my chrysalis as the most powerful creature on the planet. Nothing will stand in my way.

This was all very melodramatic, but Opal decided that under the circumstances her eventual biographer would understand.

It never occurred to the pixie that her theory of temporal paradox could simply be dead wrong and she could be left down a hole in a nuclear reactor having killed her only real ally.

I feel a tingle, she thought. *It's beginning.*

The tingle became an uncomfortable burning sensation in the base of her skull that quickly spread to clamp her entire head in a fiery vice. Opal could no longer nurture thoughts of future conquests as her entire being suddenly became fear and pain.

I have made a mistake, she thought desperately. *No prize is worth another second of this.*

Opal thrashed inside her anti-rad suit, fighting the soft constraints of the foam, which blunted her movements. The pain spread through her nervous system, increasing in intensity from merely unbearable to unimaginable. Whatever slender threads of sanity Opal had left snapped like a brig's moorings in a hurricane.

Opal felt her magic return to conquer the pain in what remained of her nerve endings. The mad and vengeful pixie fought to contain her own energy and not be destroyed utterly by her own power, even now being released as electrons shifted orbits and nuclei spontaneously split. Her body phase-shifted to pure golden energy, vaporizing the radiation suit and burning wormhole trails through the dissolving foam, ricocheting against the walls of the neutron chamber and back into Opal's ragged consciousness.

Now, she thought. *Now the rapture begins as I remake myself in my own image. I am my own god.*

And, with only the power of her mind, Opal reassembled herself. Her appearance remained unchanged for she was vain and believed herself to be perfect. But she opened and expanded her mind, allowing new powers to coat the bridges between her nerve cells. Focusing on the ancient mantras of the dark arts so that her new magic could be used to bring her soldiers up from their resting place. Power like this was too much for one body and she must excise it as soon as her escape was made, or her atoms would be shredded and swept away like windborne fireflies.

Nails are hard to reassemble, she thought. *I might have to sacrifice my fingernails and toenails.*

The ripple effects of young Opal's murder in the corner of a field were more widespread than even Artemis could have imagined, though in truth *imagine* is the wrong verb, as Artemis Fowl was not in the habit of imagining anything. Even as a small boy he had never nurtured daydreams of himself on horseback fighting dragons. What Artemis preferred to do was visualize an achievable objective and then work towards that goal.

His mother, Angeline, had once peered over eight-year-old Artemis's shoulder as he sketched in his journal.

'*Oh, darling, that's wonderful!*' she'd exclaimed, delighted that her boy had finally shown some interest in artistic creativity, even if the picture did seem a little violent. '*It's a giant robot destroying a city.*'

'*No, Mother,*' Artemis had sighed, ever the theatrical misunderstood genius. '*It's a builder drone constructing a lunar habitat.*'

Angeline had ruffled her son's hair in revenge for the sigh and wondered if little Arty might need to talk to someone professional.

*

Artemis had considered the widespread devastation that would be caused by the spontaneous energy exploding from all Opal-related material, but even he did not know the saturation levels Koboi products had achieved in the few years before her incarceration. Koboi Industries had many legitimate businesses that manufactured everything from weapons components to medical equipment, but she had also several shadow companies that illegally extended her influence to the human world and even into space, and the effects of these tens of thousands of components exploding ranged from inconvenient to downright catastrophic.

In the LEP lock-up two hundred assorted weapons, which were scheduled for recycling the following week, collapsed like melting chocolate bars, then radiated a fierce golden light that fried all local closed-circuit systems before exploding with the power of a hundred bars of Semtex. Fission was not achieved but the damage was substantial nonetheless. The warehouse was essentially vaporized and several of the underground city's load-bearing support pillars were toppled like children's building blocks.

Haven City Centre collapsed inwards, allowing a million tonnes of the Earth's crust to cave in on top of the fairy capital, breaking the pressure seal and increasing the atmosphere readings by almost a thousand per cent. Anything under the falling rock was squashed instantly. There were eighty-seven fatalities and property damage was absolute.

Police Plaza's basement collapsed, causing the bottom three floors to sink into the depression. Fortunately the upper floors were bolted to the cavern roof, which held firm and saved the lives of many officers who had elected to remain at their posts.

Sixty-three per cent of fairy automobiles had Koboi pistons in their engines, which blew simultaneously, causing an incredible synchronized flipping of vehicles, part of which was captured on a parking garage camera that had somehow survived compression and would in future years become the most viewed clip on the Underworld Web.

Koboi shadow labs had for years been selling obsolete fairy technology to human companies as it would seem cutting-edge to their shareholders. These little wonder chips or their descendants had wended their way into almost every computer-controlled device built within the past few years. These chips inside laptops, mobile phones, televisions and toasters popped and pinged like kinetically charged ball bearings in tin cans. Eighty per cent of electronic communication on planet Earth immediately ceased. Humanity was heaved back to the paper age in half a second.

Life-support systems spat out bolts of energy and died. Precious manuscripts were lost. Banks collapsed as all financial records for the past fifty years were completely wiped out. Planes fell from the sky, the Graum II space station drifted off into space and defence satellites that were not supposed to exist stopped existing.

People took to the streets, shouting into their dead mobile phones as if volume could reactivate them. Looting spread across countries like a computer virus while actual computer viruses died with their hosts, and credit cards became mere rectangles of plastic. Parliaments were stormed worldwide as citizens blamed their governments for this series of inexplicable catastrophes.

Gouts of fire and foul blurts of actual brimstone emerged from cracks in the earth. These were mostly from ruptured pipes, but people took up a cry of Armageddon. Chaos reigned and the survivalists eagerly unwrapped the kidskin from their crossbows.

Phase one of Opal's plan was complete.

CHAPTER 4: ENGINEER OZKOPY HAS THE LAST WORD

 LUCKILY for Captain Holly Short and the passengers in the *Silver Cupid*, Foaly was so paranoid where Opal was concerned and so vain about his own inventions that he insisted nothing but branded Foaly-tech parts be used in the shuttle's refit, going so far as to strip out any Koboi or generic components that he could not trace back to a parent company. But, even with all of Foaly's paranoia, he still missed a patch of filler on the rear bumper that contained an adhesive Killer Filler developed by Koboi Labs. Fortunately, when the adhesive fizzled and blew, it took the path of least resistance and spun away from the ship like a fiery swarm of bees. No operating systems were affected though there was an unsightly patch of primer left visible on the spoiler, which everyone in the shuttle would surely have agreed was preferable to them being dead.

66

The shuttle soared on the thermals, borne aloft like a dandelion seed in the Grand Canyon – if you accept that there are dandelions in the Grand Canyon in spite of the arid conditions. Holly nudged them into the centre of the vast chimney, though there was little chance of them striking a wall in the absence of a fully fledged magma flare. Artemis called to her from the rear, but she could not hear with the roar of core wind.

Cans, she mouthed, tapping the phones in her own helmet. 'Put on your headphones.'

He pulled a pair of bulky cans from their clip on the ceiling and adjusted them over his ears. 'Do you have any kind of preliminary damage report from Foaly?' he asked.

Holly checked her coms. 'Nothing. Everything is down. I'm not even getting static.'

'Very well, here is the situation as I see it. As our communications are down, I assume that young Opal's murder has thrown the entire planet into disarray. There will be mayhem on a scale not seen since the last world war. Our Opal doubtless plans to emerge from the ashes of this global pyre as some form of pixie phoenix. How she intends to do this, I do not know, but there is some connection to my home, the Fowl Estate, so that is where we must go. How long will the journey take, Holly?'

Holly considered what was under the hood. 'I can shave fifteen minutes off the usual, but it's still going to be a couple of hours.'

Two hours, thought Artemis. *One hundred and twenty minutes to concoct a workable strategy wherein we three tackle whatever Opal has planned.*

Butler adjusted the headphone's microphone. 'Artemis. I know this has occurred to you, because it occurred to me.'

'I predict, old friend,' said Artemis, 'that you are about to point out that we are rushing headlong to the exact place where Opal is strongest.'

'Exactly, Artemis,' confirmed the bodyguard. 'Or as we used to say in Delta: we are running blindfolded into the kill box.'

Artemis's face fell. *Kill box?*

Holly shot Butler a withering glance. *Nicely put, big guy. Artemis's family live in that kill box.*

She flexed her fingers then wrapped them tightly round the controls. 'Maybe I can shave twenty minutes off the usual time,' she said, and set the shuttle's sensors searching for the strongest thermals to bear them aloft towards whatever madness Opal Koboi had orchestrated for the world.

ATLANTIS

Opal took a few moments to congratulate herself on once again being absolutely correct in her theorizing and then lay absolutely still to see if she could feel the panic seeping through from above.

One does feel something, Opal concluded. *Definitely a general wave of fear, with a dash of desolation.*

It would have been nice to simply lie a while and generate

power, but, with so much to do, that would have been an indulgence.

Work, work, work, she thought, turning her face to the tunnel mouth. *I must away.*

With barely a flicker of her mind, Opal emitted a corona of intense light and heat, searing through the solidified anti-rad foam that encased her, and levitated to the tube hatch, which hindered her barely more than the foam. After all, she had the power now to change the molecular structure of whatever she concentrated on.

Already the power is fading, she realized. *I am leaking magic and my body will soon begin to disintegrate.*

A dwarf stood in the chamber beyond the fizzled hatch seeming most unperturbed by the wonders before him.

'This is Frondsday,' proclaimed Kolin Ozkopy, chin jutting. 'I could be doing without all this bleeping nonsense on a Frondsday. First I lose reception on my phone so I have no idea who is winning the crunchball match, and now a golden pixie is floating in my chamber. So pray tell me, pixie lady, what is going on? And where are your nails?'

Opal was amazed to find that she felt compelled to answer. 'Nails are difficult, dwarf. I was prepared to forgo nails to save time.'

'Yep, that makes a lot of sense,' said Ozkopy, displaying far too much lack of awe for Opal's taste. 'You want to know what's difficult? Standing here getting blasted by your aura, that's what. I should be covered in SPF one thousand.'

In fairness to Ozkopy, he was not being psychotically blasé

about this whole affair. He was actually in shock and had a pretty good idea who Opal was and that he was probably about to die, and so was trying to brazen it out.

Opal's golden brow creased with a frown like rippling lava. 'You, dwarf, should be honoured that the final image seared into your worthless retinas is one of my glorious . . . glory.'

Opal was not entirely happy with how that sentence had ended, but the dwarf would be dead momentarily and the poor sentence construction forgotten. Ozkopy was not entirely happy with Opal insulting his retinas.

'Worthless retinas!' he spluttered. 'My dad gave me these retinas . . . not that he directly plucked 'em out of his own head, you understand, but he passed 'em down.' To his eternal cosmic credit, Ozkopy decided to go out with some flair. 'And, seeing as we're insulting each other, I always thought you'd be taller. Plus your hips are wobbly.'

Opal bristled angrily, which resulted in her radioactive corona expanding by a radius of three metres, totally atomizing anything in the sphere, including Kolin Ozkopy. But, even though the dwarf was gone, the sting of his parting comments would live on in Opal's mind-drawer of unfinished business for the rest of her life. If Opal had one flaw that she would admit to, it was a tendency to rashly dispose of those who had offended her, letting them off the hook as it were.

I mustn't let that dwarf get me down, she told herself, ascending with blinding speed towards the surface. *My hips are most definitely not wobbly.*

*

Opal's ascent was blinding and divine in appearance, like a supernova that shot towards the ocean's surface, the fierce heat of her black magic repelling the walls of Atlantis and the crushing ocean with equal offhandedness, reorganizing the atomic structure of anything that stood in her way.

She rode her corona of black magic onwards and upwards towards the Fowl Estate. She did not need to think about her destination as the lock called to her. The lock called and she was the key.

CHAPTER 5: HARMA-GEDDON

Ériú, aka the Fowl Estate

BURIED in a descending spiral around the lock, the Berserkers grew agitated as magic was let loose in the world above.

Something is coming, Oro, Captain of the Berserkers, realized. Soon we will be free and our swords will taste human blood once more. We will bake their hearts in clay jars and call forth the ancient dark forces. We will infiltrate what forms we must to hold the humans back. They cannot kill us for we are already dead, held together by a skein of magic.

Our time will be short. No more than a single night after all this time, but we will cover ourselves in glory and blood before we join Danu in the afterlife.

Can you feel the shift? Oro called down to the spirits of his warriors. Be prepared to push forward when the gate is opened.

72

We are ready, *replied his warriors.* When the light falls upon us, we will seize the bodies of dogs, badgers and humans and subvert them to our wills.

Oro could not help thinking: I would rather inhabit a human than a badger.

For he was proud and this pride had cost him his life ten thousand years ago.

Gobdaw, who lay to his left, sent out a shuddering thought that could almost be a chuckle. Yes, he said. But better a badger than a rat.

If Oro's heart had been flesh and blood, it would have burst with a new pride, but this time for his warriors.

My soldiers are ready for war. They will fight until their stolen bodies drop then finally be free to embrace the light.

Our time is at hand.

Juliet Butler was holding the fort, and not just in the sense of looking after things while Artemis's parents were away at an eco-conference in London; she was actually holding a fort.

The fort in question was an old Martello tower that stood sentry on a hillock overlooking Dublin Bay. The fort had been worn down to a nub by the elements, and strange black ivy had thrown tendrils along the walls as though trying to reclaim the stone for the Earth. The would-be conquerors were Artemis Fowl's brothers: four-year-old Myles and his twin Beckett. The boys had rushed the tower several times with wooden swords, but were rebuffed by Juliet and sent gently tumbling into the long grass. Beckett squealed with laughter, but Juliet could see that Myles grew more and more frustrated by the failure of his assaults.

Just like Artemis that one, Juliet thought. *Another little criminal mastermind.*

For the past ten minutes the boys had been rustling behind a bush, plotting their next attack. Juliet could hear muffled giggles and terse commands as Myles no doubt issued a complicated series of tactical instructions to Beckett.

Juliet smiled. She could just imagine the scenario. Myles would say something like: *You go one way, Beck, and I go the other. 'S called flanking.*

To which Beckett would respond with something like: *I like caterpillars.*

It was true to say that the brothers loved each other more than they loved themselves, but Myles lived in a state of constant frustration that Beckett could not, or would not, follow the simplest instruction.

Any second now Beckett will grow bored with this tactical meeting, thought Butler's younger sister, *and come wandering from the bush brandishing his toy sword.*

Moments later, Beckett did indeed stumble from the bush, but it was not a sword which he brandished.

Juliet swung her leg over the low parapet and called suspiciously, 'Beck, what have you got there?'

Beckett waved the item. 'Underpants,' he said frankly.

Juliet looked again to confirm that the grubby triangle was indeed a pair of underpants. Because of the knee-length Wimpy Kid T-shirt he had worn for the past forty-eight days, it was impossible to ascertain whether or not the underpants were Beckett's own, though it seemed likely given that the boy's legs were bare.

Beckett was something of an unruly character and in her few months as nanny/bodyguard Juliet had seen a lot worse things than underpants — for example, the worm farm that Beckett had constructed in the downstairs loo and fertilized *personally*.

'OK, Beck,' she called down from the tower. 'Just put the underpants down, kiddo. I'll get you a clean pair.'

Beckett advanced steadily. 'Nope. Beckett is sick of stupid underpants. These're for you. A present.'

The boy's face glowed with innocent enthusiasm, convinced that his Y-fronts were about the best present a girl could get — besides a pair of his Y-fronts with a handful of beetles cradled inside.

Juliet countered with: 'But it's not my birthday.'

Beckett was at the foot of the worn tower now, waving the pants like a flag. 'I love you, Jules — take the present.'

He loves me, thought Juliet. *Kids always know the weak spot.*

She tried one last desperate ploy. 'But won't your bottom be chilly?'

Beckett had an answer for that. 'Nope. I don't ever feel cold.'

Juliet smiled fondly. It was easy to believe. Bony Beckett gave off enough heat to boil a lake. Hugging him was like hugging a restless radiator.

At this point, Juliet's only way to avoid touching the

underpants was a harmless lie. 'Rabbits love old underpants, Beck. Why don't you bury them as a gift for Papa
Rabbit?'

'Rabbits don't need underpants,' said a sinister little voice
behind her. 'They are warm-blooded mammals and their fur
is sufficient clothing in our climate.'

Juliet felt the tip of Myles's wooden sword in her thigh
and realized that the boy had used Beckett as a distraction
then circled round to the back steps.

I didn't hear a thing, she mused. *Myles is learning to creep.*

'Very good, Myles,' she said. 'How did you get Beckett to
follow your instructions?'

Myles grinned smugly and the resemblance to Artemis
was uncanny. 'I didn't give him soldier's orders. I 'gested to
Beck that his bum might be itchy.'

This boy is not yet five, thought Juliet. *Wait till the world gets
a load of Myles Fowl.*

From the corner of her eye she saw something triangular
sail through the air towards her and instinctively snatched it.
No sooner had her fingers closed on the material than it
dawned on her what she was holding.

Great, she thought. *Hoodwinked by two four-year-olds.*

'Righto, boys,' she said. 'Time to go back to the house for
lunch. What's on the menu today?'

Myles sheathed his sword. 'I would like a croque-madame,
with chilled grape juice.'

'Bugs,' said Beckett, hopping on one foot. 'Bugs in
ketchup.'

Juliet hiked Myles on to her shoulder and hopped down from the tower's low wall. 'Same as yesterday then, boys.'

Memo to self, she thought. *Wash your hands.*

The boys were waist-high in the pasture when the faraway chaos began. Beckett paid the sudden distant cacophony little attention as his internal soundtrack generally featured explosions and screaming, but Myles knew something was wrong.

He headed back to the Martello tower and clambered up the stone steps, displaying a lack of motor skills reminiscent of Artemis, which amused Beckett greatly as he was sure-footed to the same extent his brothers were not.

'Armageddon,' Myles announced when he reached the top step. 'The end of the world.'

Beckett was dismayed. 'Not Disneyland too!'

Juliet ruffled his sun-bleached hair. 'No, of course not Disneyland.' In her stomach she felt a growling of disquiet. Where were these noises coming from? It sounded as though there was a war zone nearby.

Juliet followed Myles to the compacted mud floor on top of the tower. From there they had a clear view down into the distant city. Usually the only sounds to ride the breeze this far north were the occasional beeps of traffic-jammed horns from cars stuck on the ring road. But today the highway to Dublin seemed more like the road to hell. Even from this distance it was clear that the six lanes of traffic had come to a complete stop. Several engines exploded as they watched, and a pick-up truck threw an unexpected forward flip.

Further into the city bigger explosions rumbled from behind buildings and smoke belches drifted into the afternoon sky – a sky that had troubles of its own as a small aircraft landed in the centre of a football stadium – and an honest-to-God communications satellite dropped from space like a dead robot on to the roof of the U2 hotel.

Beckett climbed the steps and took Juliet's hand. 'It is Harma-geddon,' he said quietly. 'The world is going boom.'

Juliet pulled the boys close. Whatever was developing seemed too big to be directed specifically at the Fowl family, but there was a growing list of people who would happily destroy the entire county of Dublin just to get at Artemis.

'Don't worry, boys,' she said. 'I will protect you.'

She reached into her pocket. In situations like this, where things were violently weird, the first course of action was always the same: call Artemis.

She scrolled through the list of networks on her phone and was not overly surprised to see that the only available one was the FOX system that Artemis had set up for emergency secure calls.

I imagine that Artemis is the only teenager in the world to have built and launched his own satellite.

She was about to select Artemis's name from her contacts when a bulky forearm appeared in space three metres in front of her. There was a hand at the end of the arm and it clutched a fairy Neutrino blaster.

'Nighty night, Mud Wench,' said a voice from nowhere,

and a blue bolt of crackling power erupted from the tip of the weapon.

Juliet was familiar enough with fairy weapons to know that she would survive a blue bolt, but that she would probably suffer a contact burn and wake up inside a cocoon of pain.

Sorry, my boys, she thought. *I have failed you.*

Then the bolt from Pip's weapon hit her in the chest, scorched her jacket and knocked her from the tower.

Oro of the Berserkers felt a moment of doubt.

Perhaps this anticipation of freedom is merely a yearning, he thought.

No. This was more than his own longing. The key was coming. He could feel the rush of power as it approached their tomb.

Gather yourselves, he sent down to his warriors. *When the gate is open, take whatever shape you must. Anything that lives or has lived can be ours.*

Oro felt the earth shake with the roar of his warriors.

Or perhaps that was mere yearning.

CHAPTER 6: RÍSE, MY BEAUTÍES

TARA SHUTTLE PORT, ÍRELAND

 WHEN Captain Holly Short attempted to dock in her assigned shuttle bay, she found Tara's electromagnetic clamps to be inoperable and so was forced to improvise a landing in the gate's access tunnel. This was more or less what the Tara shuttle port supervisor would write in his Extraordinary Incident report when he got out of rehab, but the sentence did not convey the sheer trauma of the situation.

For their entire approach, Holly's instruments had assured her that everything was hunky-dory, and then, just as she swung the *Silver Cupid*'s tail round to dock with the clamps, Tara's flight-control computer had made a noise like raw meat hitting a wall at speed, then shut itself down, leaving Holly with no choice but to reverse into the shuttle port's access tunnel and pray that there were no unauthorized personnel in there.

Metal crumpled, Perspex shattered and fibre-optic cables stretched like warm toffee and snapped. The *Silver Cupid*'s reinforced hide took the punishment, but the hood ornament flew off like its namesake and would be found three months later in the belly of a soft drinks machine, corroded to a barely recognizable stick figure.

Holly hauled on the brake as sparks and shards rained down, pockmarking the windscreen. Her pilot's gyro harness had absorbed most of the shock meant for her body, but Artemis and Butler had been tossed around like beads in a rattle.

'Everybody alive?' she called over her shoulder and the assortment of groans that wafted back confirmed her passengers' survival if not their *intact* survival.

Artemis crawled out from under Butler's protective huddle and checked the shuttle's readings. Blood dripped from a slit on the youth's brow, but he appeared not to notice.

'You need to find a way out, Holly.'

Holly almost giggled. Driving the *Cupid* out of here would mean wilfully destroying an entire LEP installation. She would not just be tearing up the rulebook, she would be shredding the pages then mixing them with troll dung, baking the concoction and tossing the biscuits on a campfire.

'Dung biscuits,' she muttered, which made no sense if you didn't know her train of thought.

'You may be making *dung biscuits* of the rulebook,' said Artemis, who could apparently track trains of thought, 'but Opal must be stopped for all our sakes.'

●✥◻◊●●✷❖◊⊛✇●✉✕◊✇●✕♭✦●✕●♧⊖

Holly hesitated.

Artemis capitalized on her hesitation. 'Holly. These are *extraordinary circumstances*,' he said urgently. 'Do you remember Butler's phrase? *Kill box*. That's where my brothers are at this moment. In the kill box. And you know how much Juliet will sacrifice to save them.'

Butler leaned forward, grasping a hanging hand-grip loop and pulling it from its housing in the process.

'Think tactically,' he said, instinctively knowing how to galvanize the fairy captain. 'We need to proceed under the assumption that we are the only small force standing between Opal and whatever form of world domination her twisted mind has cooked up in solitary. And remember: she was prepared to sacrifice herself. She *planned* for it. We need to go. *Now, soldier!*'

Butler was right and Holly knew it.

'OK,' she said, punching parameters into the *Cupid*'s route finder. 'You asked for it.'

A sprite in a hi-vis jacket was flying down the access tunnel, wings tapping the curved walls in his haste. Sprite wing tips were sensitive bio-sonar sensors that took decades to heal, so the sprite must have been in some considerable distress for such reckless flight.

Holly moaned. 'It's Nander Thall. Mister By-the-Book.'

Thall was paranoid that the humans would somehow contaminate Haven on the way in or steal something on the way out so he insisted on full scans every time the *Cupid* docked.

'Just go,' Butler urged. 'We don't have time for Thall's regulations.'

Nander Thall hollered at them through a megaphone. 'Power down, Captain Short. What in Frond's name do you think you are doing? I knew you were a wild card, Short. I knew it. Unstable.'

'No time,' said Artemis. 'No time.'

Thall hovered a metre from the windscreen. 'I'm a-looking in your eyeball, Short, and I see chaos. We're in lockdown here. The shield has failed, do you understand that? All it would take is some Mud Man with a shovel to unearth the entire shuttle port. It's all hands to the fortifications, Short. Power down. I'm giving you a direct order.'

Nander Thall's eyes bulged in their sockets like goose eggs and his wings beat erratically. This was a sprite on the edge.

'Do you think if we ask for permission he will let us go in time?' said Artemis.

Holly doubted it. The access tunnel stretched out behind Thall, passengers huddled nervously in the pools of light cast by emergency beacons. The situation would be difficult enough to contain without her driving up the panic levels.

The on-board computer beeped, displaying the optimum escape route on the screen and it was this beep that spurred Holly.

Sorry, she mouthed at Nander Thall. 'Gotta go.'

Thall's wings beat with nervous rapidity. 'Don't you mouth *sorry* at me! And you do not *gotta go* anywhere.'

But Holly *was* sorry and she did gotta go. So she went.

Straight up towards the luggage conveyor, which generally trundled overhead, luggage floating along on a transparent smart-water canal that displayed the identity of the owner through the Perspex. Now the conveyor canal was stagnant and the suitcases bumped each other like abandoned skiffs.

Holly nudged the joystick with one thumb, settling the *Cupid* into the canal, which the computer assured her was wide enough to accommodate the vehicle. It was, with barely two centimetres to spare on each side of the wheel arches.

Incredibly Nander Thall was in pursuit. He bobbed alongside the canal, his comb-over blown back like a windsock, shouting into his little megaphone.

Holly shrugged theatrically. *Can't hear you*, she mouthed. *Sorry.*

And she left the sprite swearing at the baggage tunnel, which flowed in gentle sloped circles towards the Arrivals hall.

Holly piloted the *Cupid* along the tunnel's curves, guided by twin headlights that revealed Perspex walls embedded with kilometres of dead circuitry. Dim shapes could be seen beavering at circuit boxes, stripping out smoking capacitors and fuses.

'Dwarfs,' said Holly. 'They make the best electricians. No lighting required and small dark spaces a bonus. Plus they eat the dead components.'

'Seriously?' wondered Butler.

'Absolutely. Mulch assures me that copper is very cleansing.'

Artemis did not involve himself in the conversation. It was trivial and he was deep in visualization mode, picturing every conceivable scenario that would face them when they reached Fowl Manor and plotting how to emerge from these scenarios as the victor.

In this respect Artemis's methodology was similar to that of American chess master Bobby Fischer, who was capable of computing every possible move an opponent could make so that he could counteract it. The only problem with this technique was that there were some scenarios that Artemis simply could not face and these had to be shuffled to the end of his process, rendering it flawed.

And so he plotted, realizing that it was probably futile as he did not know most of the constants in this equation, not to mention the variables.

A dark promise drifted below the surface of his logic.

If my loved ones are harmed, then Opal Koboi shall pay.

Artemis tried to banish the thought as it served no useful purpose, but the notion of revenge refused to go away.

Holly had only a few hundred pilot hours logged in the *Cupid*, far too little for what she was attempting, but then again there weren't enough pilot hours in a lifetime for this kind of driving.

The *Cupid* sped along the canal, its chunky tyres finding purchase in the Perspex trough, the tiny rocket disguised as an exhaust pipe boiling a short-lived trough in the smart-water. Suitcases were crushed under its treads or popped like mortars along the belt's scoop, showering those below with fluttering garments, cosmetics and smuggled human memorabilia. The security guards on duty had had the presence of mind to confiscate most of these artefacts, but nobody ever figured out who had managed to stuff a life-size Gandalf cardboard cut-out into a suitcase.

Holly drove on, concentrating through squinted eyes and gritted teeth. The luggage canal took them out of the terminal into bedrock. Upwards they spiralled, through archaeological strata, past dinosaur bones and Celtic tombs, through Viking settlements and Norman walls until the *Cupid* emerged in a large baggage hall with a transparent roof that opened directly to the elements – a real James Bond super-villain lair kind of place complete with spidery metallic building struts and a shuttle-rail system.

Generally the Sky Window would be camouflaged using projectors and shields, but these security measures were out of commission until all Koboi parts could be replaced with technology that hadn't exploded. On this afternoon, bruised Irish rainclouds drifted across the bevelled panes and the baggage hall would be completely visible from above if anyone cared to photograph the fairy baggage handlers or forklift trucks that stood with smoking holes in their bodywork as though the victims of a sniper.

Holly asked the computer whether there was another way out besides the one it was suggesting. The on-board avatar informed her dispassionately that indeed there was, but it was three hundred kilometres away.

'D'Arvit,' muttered Holly, deciding that she wasn't going to worry about rules any more, or property damage. There was a bigger picture to consider here and nobody likes a whiner.

Nobody likes a whiner. Her father had always said that.

She could see him now, spending every free minute in his precious garden, feeding algae to his tubers under the sim-sunlight.

You have to do your share of the housework, Poppy. Your mother and I work long hours to keep this family going. He would stop then and stroke her chin. *The Berserkers made the ultimate sacrifice for the People long ago. Nobody's asking you to go that far, but you could do your chores with a smile on your pretty face.* He would stiffen then, playing at sergeant major. *So hop to it, Soldier Poppy. Nobody likes a whiner.*

Holly caught sight of her reflection in the windscreen. Her eyes brimmed with melancholy. Daughters had always carried the nickname Poppy in her family. No one could remember why.

'Holly,' barked Artemis. 'Security is closing in.'

Holly jerked guiltily and checked the perimeter. Several security guards were edging towards the *Cupid*, trying to bluff her with useless Neutrino handguns, using the smoking hulk of a flipped shuttle for cover.

One of the guards snapped off a couple of shots, dinging the front fender.

A custom weapon, Holly realized. *He must have built it himself.*

The shots had little effect on the *Cupid*'s plates, but if the guard had gone to the trouble of cobbling together his own back-up pistol, perhaps he had thought to bolt on an armour-piercing barrel.

As if reading her mind, the guard fumbled at his belt for a clip of ammunition.

That's the difference between me and you, thought Holly. *I don't fumble.*

She switched all power to the jets and sent the *Cupid* rocketing towards the Sky Window, leaving the security guards pretending to fire useless weapons at her, a couple even going so far as to make *bang bang* noises, though fairy weapons hadn't gone *bang bang* in centuries.

The Sky Window is reinforced Perspex, thought Holly. *Either it breaks or the Cupid does. Probably a bit of both.*

Though she would never know it, Holly's gamble would not have paid off. The Sky Window was built to withstand direct impact from anything short of a low-yield nuclear warhead, a fact that was proudly announced over the terminal's speakers a hundred times a day, which Holly had somehow managed to avoid hearing.

Luckily for Captain Short and her passengers, and indeed the fate of much of the wider world, her potentially fatal ignorance would never come to light as Foaly had anticipated a situation where a fairy craft would be heading at speed for the Sky Window and it would refuse to open. The centaur also guessed that because of the universal law of maximum doo-doo displacement – which states that, when the afore-mentioned doo-doo hits the fan, the fan will be in your hand

and pointed at someone important who can have you fired – the Sky Window would probably refuse to open at a crucial time. And so he had come up with a little proximity organism that ran on its own bio-battery/heart, which he had grown from the stem cells of *appropriated* sprite wings.

The whole process was dubious at best and illegal at worst and so Foaly hadn't bothered to log a blueprint and simply had the sensors installed on his say-so. The result was that a cluster of these proximity beetles scuttled along the Sky Window pane edges and if their little antennae sensed a vehicle drawing too close to a certain pane, then they excreted a spray of acid on the window and quickly ate the pane. The energy required to complete their task in time was massive and so when the beetles were finished they curled up and died. It was impressive, but, pretty much like the man with the exploding head, it was a one-time trick.

When the beetles sensed the *Cupid*'s ascent, they rushed to action like a minute company of cavalry and devoured the pane in less than four seconds. When their job was done, they winked out and dropped like ball bearings on to the vehicle's hood.

'That was easy,' Holly said into her microphone, as the *Cupid* passed through a *Cupid*-shaped hole. 'So much for Foaly's great Sky Window.'

Ignorance, as they say, is usually fatal but sometimes it can be bliss.

Holly powered up the *Cupid*'s shield, though with every single human satellite out of commission she really needn't have bothered, and set a course for Fowl Manor.

Which gives us about five minutes before Opal has us exactly where she wants us.

A less-than-comforting thought that she did not voice, but all it took was a glance in the rear-view mirror at Butler's expression to see that the bodyguard was thinking more or less the same thing.

'I know,' he said, catching her eye. 'But what choice do we have?'

İRİSH AİRSPACE

Opal could not have turned her face from the lock now if she had put all her enhanced pixie might to the task. She was the key and the two were paired. Their collision was as inevitable as the passage of time. Opal felt the skin on her face stretch towards the lock and her arms were pulled until the sockets creaked.

The elfin warlock was indeed powerful, she thought. *Even after all this time his magic holds.*

Her trajectory took her in a regular arc to the Atlantic's surface and across the afternoon sky to Ireland. She descended like a fireball in a slingshot towards the Fowl Estate, with no time to wonder or worry about, or for that matter revel in, the imminent proof of her theories.

I will raise the dead, she had often thought in her cell. *Even Foaly cannot make that boast.*

Opal hit the Fowl Estate like a comet come to Earth,

directly on the worn nub of Martello tower with its alien creeping vine. Like a dog snuffling after a bone, her corona of magic destroyed the tower and cleared a path for itself, spiralling six metres down, past centuries of deposit, revealing another more ancient tower below. The magic sniffed out the roof lock, settling over it like a shimmering man-o'-war.

Opal lay face down, floating, dreamily watching events unfold. She saw her fingers splay and twitch, spark streams shooting from the tips. She saw the cloaking spell stripped from what had seemed to be a simple metamorphosed boulder, revealing it to be a rough stone tower with complicated intertwined runes etched into its surface. The magical ectoplasm sank into the engraved runes, electrifying them, sending burning rivulets coursing through the grooves.

Open yourself to me, thought Opal, though this is an interpretation of her brain patterns. Another interpretation would be *Aaaaaaargghhhhhh*.

The lock's runes teemed with magic, becoming animated, slithering like snakes on hot sands, nipping at each other, fat ones swallowing the lines of lesser magic until all that remained was a simple couplet in Gnommish:

Here be the lock first of two
See it open and live to rue

Opal had enough consciousness left to smirk inside her cocoon. *Fairy medieval poetry. Typically blunt. Bad grammar, obvious rhyme and melodrama coming out of its metaphorical ears.*

I shall see it open, she thought. *And Artemis Fowl will live to rue. But not for long.*

Opal gathered herself and placed her right hand flat on the stone, fingers splayed, magic clouding the tips. The hand sank in like sunlight through the darkness, cracks radiating from the contact.

Rise, she thought. *Rise, my beautiful warriors.*

ÉRIÚ, AKA THE FOWL ESTATE

The Berserkers were expelled from holy ground and into the air as though shot from cannon. The afterlife's tug lessened and the warriors felt free to complete their mission. The next death, they knew, would be their last, and finally the gates to Nimh would be open to them. This had been promised; they longed for it. For it is ever true that, though the dead long for life, souls are made for heaven and will not rest until they reach it. This was something unknown to the elfin warlock when he forged the lock and key. He did not know that he had doomed his warriors to ten thousand years with their faces turned from the light. And to turn from the light for too long could cost a person his soul.

But, now, all the promises that had been whispered into their dying ears as the priests lugged their limp heavy bodies to the trench were on the verge of fulfilment. All they need do was defend the gate in their stolen bodies and their next death would open the gates of paradise. The Berserkers could go home.

But not before human blood was spilled.

The soil fizzled and danced as the ectoplasm of a hundred fairy warriors burst through it. Upwards they surged, impatient for the light. They were drawn inexorably towards the key who lay over the stone lock, and they passed through the conduit of her magic one by one.

Oro was first.

It is a pixie, *he realized with no little surprise, as pixies were known for their lack of magical ability.* And a female! But, for all that, this one's magic is powerful.

As each successive warrior flashed through Opal's being, she felt their pain and despair and absorbed their experiences before expelling them into the world with one command.

Obey me. You are my soldier now.

And so were Oro and his band of Berserkers placed under *geasa* or fairy bond to follow Opal wherever she would command. They tumbled into the sky, searching for a body to inhabit inside the magic circle.

As leader, Oro had first choice of available ciphers and he had, like many of his warriors, spent many thousands of hours considering what creature would make the ideal host for his talents. Ideally he would choose an elf with a bit of muscle to him and a long arm for swordplay, but it was unlikely that such a fine specimen would be readily available, and, even if it were, it would be such a shame to take one elf and replace him with another. Recently Oro had settled on a troll as his vehicle of choice if there should happen to be one lumbering around.

Imagine it. A troll with an elf's mind. What a formidable warrior that would make!

But there were no trolls, and the only available fairy was a feeble gnome with protection runes criss-crossing his chest. No possessing that one.

There were humans, three of the hated creatures. Two males and a female. He would leave the female for Bellico, one of only two she-fairies in their ranks. So that left the boys.

Oro's soul circled above the males. Two curious little man-eens who were not displaying the awe that this situation would seem to call for. Their world had dissolved to a maelstrom of magic, for Danu's sake. Should they not be quaking in their boots, bubbling from the nose and begging for a mercy that would not be forthcoming?

But, no, their reactions were surprising. The dark-haired boy had moved swiftly to the fallen girl and was expertly checking her pulse. The second, a blond one, had uprooted a clump of reeds, with surprising strength for one his size, and he was even now accosting the doltish gnome, forcing him backwards towards a ditch.

That one interests me, thought Oro. *He is young and small, but his body fizzes with power. I will have him.*

And it was as simple as that. Oro thought it and so it became deed. One second he was hovering above Beckett

Fowl and the next he had become him and was beating the gnome with a fistful of whippety reeds.

Oro laughed aloud at the senses assaulting his nerve endings. He felt the sweat in the wrinkles of his fingers, the glistening smoothness of the reeds. He smelled the boy, the youth and energy of him like hay and summer. He felt a youthful heartbeat like a drum in his chest.

'Ha!' he said exultantly and continued to thrash the gnome, for the sheer fun of it, thinking: *The sun is warm, praise be Belenos. I live once more, but I will die gladly this day to see humans in the ground beside me.*

For it is ever true that resurrected fairy warriors are super noble in their thought patterns and don't have much in the way of a sense of humour.

'Enough of this playfulness,' he said in Gnommish and his human tongue mangled the words so that he sounded like an animal grunting speech. 'We must assemble.'

Oro looked to the skies where his plasmic warriors sloshed about him like a host of translucent deep-sea creatures. 'This is what we have waited for,' he called. 'Find a body inside the circle.'

And they dispersed in a flash of ozone, scouring the Fowl Estate for vessels that would become their hosts.

The first bodies to be taken were the nearby humans.

It was a poor day to hunt for ciphers on the Fowl Estate. On an average weekday the manor would be a virtual throng of humanity. And presiding over everything would be Artemis

Senior and Angeline Fowl, master and mistress of the manor. But on this fateful day the manor was virtually shut down for the approaching Christmas holidays. Artemis's parents were in London attending an eco-conference with one personal assistant and two maids in tow. The rest of the staff was on early leave with only the occasional holiday visit to keep the manor ticking over. The Fowl parents had planned to scoop up their offspring on the tarmac in Dublin Airport once Artemis had concluded his therapy and then point the Green Jet's composite nose cone towards Cap Ferrat for Christmas on the Côte d'Azure.

Today, nobody was home except for Juliet and her charges. Not a nugget of humanity to be preyed on, much to the frustration of the circling souls who had been dreaming of this moment for a very long time. So choices were limited to various wildlife, including eight crows, two deer, a badger, a couple of English pointer hunting dogs that Artemis Senior kept in the stables, and corpses with a bit of spark in them, which were more plentiful than you might think. Corpses were far from ideal hosts as decay and desiccation made quick thinking and fine motor movements tricky. Also bits were liable to fall off when you needed them most.

The first corpses to go were fairly well preserved for their ages. Artemis Senior had, in his gangster days, stolen a collection of Chinese warrior mummies, which he had yet to find a safe way to repatriate and so stored them in a dry-lined secret basement. The warriors were more than surprised to find their brain matter reanimated and rehydrated and their consciousness being ridden shotgun by warriors even older than they were. They clanged into action in rusty armour and smashed through the glass in mounted display cases to reclaim their swords and polearm spears, steel tips polished to a deadly glitter by a loving curator. The basement door splintered quickly under their assault and the mummies crashed through the manor's great hall into the sunlight, pausing for a moment to feel its warm touch on their upturned brows, before lumbering towards the pasture and their leader, forcing themselves to hurry in spite of their awakening senses, which longed to stop and smell any plant life. Even the compost heap.

The next corpses to be reanimated were those of a bunch of rowdy lads interred by a cave-in, in a cave, back in the eighteenth century while burying a plundered galleon's worth of treasure, which they had transferred from the breached hull of HMS *Octagon* to their own brigantine *The Cutlass*. The feared pirate Captain Eusebius Fowl and ten of his only slightly less feared crew were not crushed by the falling rock but sealed in an airtight bubble that would admit not so much as a sparrow's whistle for them to suck into their lungs.

The pirates' bodies jittered as though electrocuted, shrugged off their blankets of kelp and squeezed through a recently eroded hole in their tomb wall, heedless of the popped joints and sprung ribs that the journey cost.

Apart from these groups there were sundry corpses who found themselves dragged from their resting places to become accomplices in Opal Koboi's latest bid for power. The spirit had already moved on from some, but, for those who had died violently or with unfinished business, a ghost of their very essence remained which could do nothing but lament the rough treatment heaped upon their bodies by the Berserkers.

Opal Koboi slumped on the ancient rock, and the runes that had slithered like fiery snakes settled once more, congregating around Opal's handprint in the centre of the magical key.

The first lock has been opened, she thought, her senses returning in nauseating waves. *Only I can close it now.*

The gnome heretofore referred to as Pip, but whose actual name was the considerably more unwieldy Gotter Dammerung, hobbled into the crater, climbed the tower steps and wrapped a glittering shawl round Opal's shoulders.

'Star cloak, Miss Opal,' he said. 'As requested.'

Opal stroked the material and was pleased. She found that there was still enough magic in her fingertips to calculate the thread count.

'Well done, Gunter.'

'That's Gotter, Miss Koboi,' corrected the gnome, forgetting himself.

Opal's stroking fingers froze, then gripped a handful of the silken cloak so tightly that it smoked. 'Yes, Gotter. You shot my younger self?'

Gotter straightened. 'Yes, miss, as ordered. Gave her a nice burial, like you said in the code.'

It occurred to Opal that this fairy would be a constant reminder that she had sacrificed her younger self for power.

'It is true that I ordered you to kill Opal the younger, but she was terrified, *Gotter*. I felt it.'

Gotter was perplexed. This day was not turning out at all as the gnome had imagined. He'd nurtured images of painted elfin warriors, their bone-spiked braids streaming behind them, but instead he was surrounded by human children and agitated wildlife.

'I don't like those rabbits,' he blurted, possibly the most monumentally misjudged non sequitur of his life. 'They look weird. Look at their vibrating ears.'

Opal did not feel a person of her importance should have to deal with comments like these and so she vaporized poor Gotter with a bolt of plasmic power, leaving nothing of the loyal gnome but a smear of blackish burn paste on the step. A poorly judged use of plasma as it turned out because Opal certainly could have used a moment to fully charge up a second bolt to deal with the armoured shuttle that suddenly appeared over the boundary wall. It was shielded, true, but Opal had enough dark magic in her to see to the heart of the shimmer before her. She reacted a little hastily and sent a weak bolt careering to the left, managing only to clip the engine housing and not engulf the entire craft. The errant magic flew wild, knocking a turret from the estate wall before collapsing into squibs that whizzed skywards.

Though the *Cupid* was merely clipped, the contact was sufficient to melt its rocket engine, disable its weapons and send it into an earthbound nosedive, which even the most skilful pilot would not be able to soften.

More avatars for my soldiers, thought Opal, pulling the star cloak tight around her and skipping nimbly down the tower steps. She climbed the crater wall and followed the furrow ploughed through the meadow by the mortally wounded shuttle. Her warriors were close behind, still half-drunk on new sensations, tottering in their new bodies, trying to form words in unfamiliar throats.

Opal glanced overhead and saw three souls streaking towards the smoking craft, which had come to an awkward rest crammed into the lee of a boundary wall.

'Take them,' she called to the Berserkers. 'My gift to you.'

Almost all of the Berserkers had been accommodated by this point and were stretching tendons with great relish, or scratching the earth beneath their paws or sniffing at the autumn musk. All were catered for except three laggardly souls who had resigned themselves to a resurrection spent cramped and embarrassed inside the bodies of ducklings, when these new hosts arrived inside the circle.

Two humans and a fairy. The Berserkers' spirits lifted. Literally.

Inside the *Cupid* it was Holly who'd fared best from the crash though she had been closest to the impact. *Faring best*, however, is a relative term and probably not the one Holly would have chosen to describe her condition.

I fared best, she would probably fail to say at the earliest opportunity. *I only had a punctured lung and a snapped collarbone. You should have seen the other guys.*

Luckily for Holly, absent friends once again contributed to her not being dead. Just as Foaly's Sky Window bio-sensors had prevented a calamitous collision in the shuttle port, her close friend the warlock N°1 had saved her with his own special brand of demon magic.

And how had he done this? It had happened two days previously over their weekly sim-coffee in Stirbox, a trendy java joint in the Jazz Quarter. N°1 had been even more hyper than usual due to the double-shot espresso coursing through his squat grey body. The runes that embossed his frame's armour plating glowed with excess energy.

'I'm not supposed to have sim-coffee,' he confessed. 'Qwan says it disturbs my chi.' The little demon winked, momentarily concealing one orange eye. 'I could have told him that demons don't have chi, we have *qwa*, but I don't think he's ready for that yet.'

Qwan was N°1's magical master, and so fond was the little demon of his teacher that he pretended not to have surpassed him years ago.

'And coffee is great for *qwa*. Makes it zing right along. I could probably turn a giraffe into a toad now if I felt like it. Though there would be a lot of excess skin left over. Mostly neck skin.'

'That is a disturbing idea,' said Holly. 'If you want to perform some useful amphibian-related magic, why don't you do something about the swear toads?'

Swear toads were the result of a college prank during which a group of postgrads had managed to imbue a strain of toads with the power of speech. Bad language only. This had been hilarious for about five minutes until the toads began multiplying at a ferocious rate and spouting foul epithets at anything that moved, including kindergarten fairies and people's grandmothers.

Nº1 laughed softly. 'I like swear toads,' he said. 'I have two at home called Bleep and D'Arvit. They are very rude to me, but I know they don't mean it.' The little demon took another slurp of coffee. 'So, let's talk about your magic problem, Holly.'

'What magic problem?' asked Holly, genuinely puzzled.

'I see magic like another colour in the spectrum and you are leaking magic like swamp cheese leaks stink.'

Holly looked at her own hands as though the evidence would be visible. 'I am?'

'Your skeleton is the battery that stores your magic, but yours has been abused one time too many. How many healings have you undergone? How many traumas?'

'One or two,' admitted Holly, meaning *nine or ten*.

'One or two *this cycle*,' scoffed Nº1. 'Don't lie to me, Holly Short. Your electrodermal activity has increased significantly. That means your fingertips are sweating. I can see that too.' The little grey demon shuddered. 'Actually sometimes I see stuff that I have no desire to see. A sprite came into my office the other day and he had a bunch of microscopic hoop-worm larvae wriggling around his armpit. What is wrong with people?'

Holly didn't answer. It was best to let N°1 rant stuff out of his system.

'And I see you've been donating a spark or two of your magic every week to the Opal clone in Argon's clinic, trying to make it a little more comfortable. You're wasting your time, Holly. That creature doesn't have a spirit; magic is no use.'

'You're wrong, N°1,' said Holly quietly. 'Nopal is a person.'

N°1 held out his rough palms. 'Give me your hands,' he said.

Holly placed her fingers in his. 'Are we going to sing a sea shanty?'

'No,' replied N°1. 'But this might hurt a little.'

This might hurt a little is universal code for *this will definitely hurt a lot*, but, before Holly's brain could translate this, N°1's forehead rune spiralled – something it only did when he was building up to some major power displacement. She managed to blurt, 'Wait a –' before what felt like two electric eels wrapped themselves round her arms, slithering upwards, sinking into her chest. It was not a pleasant experience.

Holly lost control of her limbs, spasming like a marionette on the end of a giggling puppet master's strings. The entire episode lasted no more than five seconds, but five seconds of acute discomfort can seem like a long time.

Holly coughed smoke and spoke once her jaw stopped clicking. 'You had to do that in a coffee shop, I suppose?'

'I thought we wouldn't see each other for a while and I worry about you. You're so reckless, Holly. So eager to help anyone but yourself.'

Holly flexed her fingers and it was as though her joints

had been oiled. 'Wow, I feel great now that the blinding pain has faded.' Suddenly the rest of Nº1's words registered. 'And why wouldn't we see each other for a while?'

Nº1 looked suddenly serious. 'I've accepted an invitation to the Moon Station. They want me to have a look at some micro-organisms and see if I can extract some race memory from their cells.'

'Uh-huh,' said Holly, understanding all of the first sentence, but nothing of the second beyond the individual words. 'How long will you be gone?'

'Two of your Earth years.'

'Two years,' stammered Holly. 'Come on, Nº1. You're my last single fairy friend. Foaly got hitched. Trouble Kelp is hooked up with Lily Frond, though what he sees in that airhead is beyond me.'

'She's pretty and she cares about him, but besides that I have no idea,' said Nº1 archly.

'He'll find out what Frond is really like when she ditches him for someone more senior.'

Nº1 thought it politic not to mention Holly's three disastrous dates with Commander Kelp, the last of which ended with them both being thrown out of a crunchball match.

'There's always Artemis.'

Holly nodded. 'Yeah. Artemis is a good guy, I suppose, but whenever we meet it ends in shots fired, or time travel or brain cells dying. I want a quiet friend, Nº1. Like you.'

Nº1 took her hand again. 'Two years will fly by. Maybe you can get a lunar pass and come to visit me.'

'Maybe. Now, enough changing the subject. What did you just do to me?'

Nº1 cleared his throat. 'Well, I gave you a magical make-over. Your bones are less brittle, your joints are lubed. I bolstered your immune system and cleared out your synapses which were getting a little clogged with magical residue. I filled your tank with my own personal blend of power and made your hair a little more lustrous than it already is and bolstered your protection rune so you will never be possessed again. I want you to be safe and well until I come back.'

Holly squeezed her friend's fingers. 'Don't worry about me. Routine operations only.'

Routine operations only, thought Holly now, groggy from the impact and the magic coursing through her system, repairing her fractured collarbone and knitting the lattice of slices in her skin.

The magic would have liked to shut her down for repairs, but Holly could not allow that. She pawed the first-aid pack from its niche on her belt and slapped an adrenalin patch on to her wrist, the hundreds of tiny needles releasing the chemical into her bloodstream. An adrenalin shot would keep her alert while allowing the magic to do its work. The *Cupid*'s cab was smashed, and only the vehicle's toughened exoskeleton had prevented a total collapse that would have crushed the passengers. As it was, the shuttle had ridden its last magma flare. In the back of the vehicle, Butler was shrugging off the concussion that was threatening to drag him to oblivion and Artemis lay wedged into the floor space between the seats like a discarded action figure.

I like you, Artemis, Holly thought. *But I need Butler.*

And so Butler got the first shot of healing magic, a bolt that hit the bodyguard like a charged defibrillator, sending him spasming through the back window to the meadow beyond.

Wow, thought Holly. *Nice brew, N°1.*

She was more careful with Artemis, flicking a drop of magic from her fingertip on to the middle of his forehead. Still the contact was enough to set his skin rippling like pond water.

Something was coming. Holly could see the doubly distorted images through the shattered windows and her cracked visor. A lot of somethings. They looked small but moved surely.

I don't get it. I am not getting it yet.

N°1's magic completed its healing journey through her system and, as the blood cleared from her left eye, Holly got a good look at what was coming her way.

A menagerie, she thought. *Butler can handle it.*

But then N°1's magic allowed her a flickering glimpse of the souls floating like tattered translucent kites in the air and she remembered the stories her father had told her so many times.

The bravest of the brave. Left behind to protect the gate.

Berserkers, Holly realized. *The legend is true. If they take Butler, we are finished.*

She crawled over Artemis, through the back window and rolled into the trough carved out by the *Cupid*'s crash, freshly scythed earth crumbling over her head. For a moment Holly had the irrational fear that she was being buried alive, but then the tumbling earth rattled past her limbs and she was clear.

Holly felt the throbbing afterpain of a healed break in her shoulder, but otherwise she was physically fine.

My vision is still blurred, she realized. *Why?*

But it was not her vision; it was the helmet lenses that were cracked. Holly raised her visor and was greeted by the crystal-clear sight of an attacking force being led by Artemis's little brothers that seemed to include a phalanx of ancient armoured warriors and various woodland animals.

Butler was on all fours beside her, shaking off the magic fugue like a grizzly bear shaking off river water. Holly found another adrenalin patch in her pack and slapped it on to his exposed neck.

Sorry, old friend. I need you operational.

Butler jumped to his feet as though electrified but swayed, disorientated for a moment.

The assortment of possessed figures halted suddenly, arranged in a semicircle, obviously itching to attack, but held at bay for some reason.

Little Beckett Fowl was at the forefront of the motley group, but he seemed less a child now, carrying himself as he did with a warrior's swagger, a fistful of bloody reeds swinging in his grip. The vestiges of N°1's magic allowed Holly to glimpse the spirit of Oro lurking inside the boy.

'I am a fairy,' she called in Gnommish. 'These humans are my prisoners. You have no quarrel with us.'

Opal Koboi's voice drifted over the ranks. 'Prisoners? The big one doesn't appear to be a prisoner.'

'Koboi,' said Butler, coherent at last. Then the big bodyguard noticed his sister in the group. 'Juliet! You're alive.'

Juliet stepped forward, but awkwardly as though she were not familiar with her own workings. 'Braddur,' she said, her voice cracked and strangely accented. 'Embrash me.'

'No, old friend,' warned Holly, glimpsing the flickering warrior inside Butler's sister. 'Juliet is possessed.'

Butler understood immediately. They had previously encountered fairy possession when Artemis had been wrapped up in his Atlantis Complex.

The bodyguard's features sagged and in that moment his decades of soldiering were written on his face.

'Jules. Are you in there?'

The warrior queen, Bellico, used Juliet's memories to answer, but the vocal cords were not under her complete control. Her words were unclear as though heard through tinny speakers and the accent was a blend of thick Scandinavian and Deep South American, an unusual blend.

'Yesh, braddur. It ish I. Zooooliet.'

Butler saw the truth. The body might be his sister's, but the mind certainly wasn't.

Artemis joined them, laying a hand on Holly's shoulder,

a blotch of blood on his shirt where he had coughed. As usual, he found the most pertinent question to ask.

'Why do they not attack?'

Holly physically jerked.

Why not? Of course why not?

Butler reiterated. 'Why aren't they attacking? They've got numbers over us and emotionally we're a mess. That thing is my sister, for heaven's sake.'

Holly remembered why they remained unmolested.

We are hosts inside the circle. They need us.

The souls flapped overhead, rearing up to descend.

I can explain what I am about to do, thought Holly. *Or I can just do it.*

Easier to just do it and hope there was an opportunity to apologize later.

She expertly flicked the settings wheel on the barrel of her Neutrino and shot Butler on his exposed neck and Artemis on the hand in blurred succession.

Now we won't be possessed, she thought. *But on the downside these Berserkers will probably simply kill us.*

The souls dropped on to their intended hosts like sheets of wet polythene. Holly felt ectoplasm cram itself into her mouth, but the spirit would not be able to possess her because of the rune under her collar.

Hold on, she told herself. *Hold on.*

Holly tasted clay and bile. She heard echoes of screams from ten thousand years earlier and experienced the Battle of Taillte as though she herself had stood on that plain where blood ran through the stake pits, and waves of humanity rolled across the meadow, blackening the grass with their passage.

It all happened just the way my father told me, Holly realized.

The soul howled in frustration as it lost purchase and was repelled, flapping into the air.

Two Berserker souls fought for entry into Artemis and Butler, but were repulsed. Butler had keeled over like a felled redwood when Holly's shot hit him and Artemis clasped his hand, stunned that their friend Holly would burn their bare skin with her Neutrino beams. Artemis had quickly and mistakenly concluded that Holly had been possessed by one of the Danu. Something he now knew all about from the soul who had tried to occupy him.

He sank to his knees and watched through pain-slitted eyes as the Berserker warriors advanced towards them. Was Holly an enemy or friend now? He could not be sure. She seemed herself and had swung her weapon at the horde.

Opal's voice came from beyond the throng, shielded by its mass.

'They have protected themselves. Kill them now, my soldiers. Bring their heads to me.'

Artemis coughed. *Bring their heads to me? Opal used to be a little more subtle. It's true what they say: prison does not rehabilitate people. Not pixies at any rate.*

His own baby brothers advanced towards him with murder in their eyes. Two four-year-olds moving with increasing grace and speed.

Are they stronger now? Could Myles and Beckett actually succeed in killing us?

And, if they didn't, perhaps those pirates would with their rusting cutlasses.

'Butler,' Artemis rasped. 'Retreat and evaluate.' It was their only option.

There is no proactive move open to us.

This realization irritated Artemis, even though he was in mortal danger.

'Retreat and try not to injure anybody except those pirates. The Chinese warrior mummies and I will not be overly upset if a few animals are harmed. After all, it is us or them.'

But Butler was not listening to Artemis's uncharacteristically nervous diatribe because Holly's shot had pulsed his vagus nerve and knocked him out cold. A shot in a million.

It was up to Holly to defend the group. It should be fine. All Captain Short had to do was set her custom Neutrino on a wide burst to buy them some time. Then a pirate's cosh twirled from the fingers of a pirate's skeletal hand and cracked Holly's nose, sending her tumbling backwards on top of Butler's frame.

Artemis watched the possessed creatures advance the final steps towards him and was dismayed that at the end it all came down to the physical.

I always thought my intellect would keep me alive, but now I shall be killed by my own baby brother with a rock. The ultimate sibling rivalry.

Then the ground opened beneath his feet and swallowed the group whole.

Opal Koboi elbowed through her acolytes, to the edge of the chasm that had suddenly appeared to suck her nemeses from their fate.

'No!' she squealed, tiny fists pounding the air. 'I wanted their heads. On spikes. You people do that all the time, right?'

'We do,' admitted Oro, through the mouth of Beckett. 'Limbs too, betimes.'

Opal could have sworn that, underneath her stamping feet, the ground burped.

CHAPTER 7: LICKETY-SPIT

THE FOWL ESTATE, SEVERAL METRES BELOW GROUND

 ARTEMIS tumbled down and down, striking knees and elbows against the crooks of roots and sharp limestone corners that protruded like half-buried books. Clumps of wet earth crumbled around him and stones rattled down his shirt and up his trouser legs. His view was obstructed by the twirl of tumble and layers of earth, but there was a glowing above. And below too? Was that possible?

Artemis was confused by the thump of wood behind one ear and the luminous glow from below. It was below, wasn't it?

I feel like Alice falling to Wonderland.

A line came to him: *It would be so nice if something made sense for a change.*

No fall can last forever when gravity is involved, and Artemis's descent was mercifully gradual as the crater funnelled to a bottleneck, which Butler and Holly had the decency to block with their tangled frames and limbs before they plopped through the hole. Rough hands grabbed at Artemis, tugging him through to a tunnel beneath.

Artemis landed on the body heap and blinked the mud from his eyes. Someone or something stood naked before him, an ethereal figure glowing with divine light from head to foot. It reached out a shining hand and spoke in a deep movie promo voice.

'Pull my finger.'

Artemis relaxed neck muscles that he hadn't realized were tensed. 'Mulch.'

'The one and only. Saving your brainiac butt once more. Remind me, who's supposed to be the genius around here?'

'Mulch,' said Artemis again.

Mulch pointed his proffered finger like a gun. 'Aha. You're repeating yourself. You once told me that repeating yourself is an exercise in redundancy. Well, who's redundant now, Mud Boy? What good did your genius do you with those freaks up there?'

'None,' admitted Artemis. 'Can we argue later?'

'Cos you're losing the argument,' scoffed Mulch.

'No, because *those freaks* are on our tail. We need to retreat and regroup.'

'Don't worry about that,' said Mulch, reaching a forearm into a hole in the tunnel wall and yanking out a thick root. 'Nobody's following us anywhere once I collapse the tunnel mouth, but you might want to scoot forward a metre or two.'

The earth above them rumbled like thunderclouds cresting a low mountain and Artemis was gripped with a sudden certainty that they were all about to be crushed. He scurried forward and flattened himself against the cold dark mud wall as if that could possibly make any difference.

But Mulch's tunnel held its integrity and only the spot where Artemis had been was completely blocked.

Mulch wrapped his fingers round Butler's ankle and with some effort hauled the unconscious bodyguard along the tunnel floor.

'You carry Holly. Gently now. By the looks of your hand, she drove those spirits away and saved your life. Before I saved it. Probably just after Butler saved it. You seeing a pattern emerging, Artemis? You starting to realize who the liability is here?'

Artemis looked at his hand. He was branded with a spiral rune where Holly had blasted him. The last globs of Berserker ectoplasm slicking his hair caused him to shudder at the sight.

A protection rune. Holly had branded them to save them. And to think he had doubted her.

Artemis scooped up Holly and followed the glowing dwarf, tentatively feeling his way with tapping toes. 'Slow down,' he called. 'It's dark in here.'

Mulch's voice echoed along the tunnel. 'Follow the globes, Arty. I gave 'em an extra coating of dwarf spit, the magical solution that can do it all from glow in the dark to repel ghostly boarders. I should bottle this stuff. Follow the globes.'

Artemis squinted at the retreating glow and could indeed

distinguish two wobbling globes that shone a little brighter than the rest. Once he realized what the globes were, Artemis decided not to follow too closely. He had seen those globes in action and still had the occasional nightmare.

The tunnel undulated and curved until Artemis's internal compass surrendered what little sense of direction it had. He traipsed behind Mulch's glowing rear end, glancing down at his unconscious friend in his arms. She seemed so small and frail, though Artemis had seen her take on a horde of trolls in his defence.

'The odds are against us as they have been so often, my friend,' he whispered, as much to himself as to Holly. He ran a rough calculation, factoring in the desperate situations they had endured over the past few years, the relative IQ of Opal Koboi and the approximate number of opponents he had glimpsed above ground. 'I would estimate our chances of survival to be less than fifteen per cent. But, on the plus side, we have survived, indeed been victorious, against greater odds. Once.'

Obviously Artemis's whispers carried down the tunnel, for Mulch's voice drifted back to him.

'You need to stop thinking with your head, Mud Boy, and start thinking with your heart.'

Artemis sighed. The heart was an organ for pumping oxygen-rich blood to the cells. It could no more *think* than an apple could tap-dance. He was about to explain this to the dwarf when the tunnel opened to a large chamber and Artemis's breath was taken away.

The chamber was the size of a small barn with walls sloping to an apex. There were feeder tunnels dotted at various heights and blobs of glowing gunk suckered to exposed rock served as a lighting system. Artemis had seen this particular system before.

'Dwarf phlegm,' he said, nodding at a low cluster of tennis-ball-sized blobs. 'Hardens once excreted and glows with a luminescence unmatched in nature.'

'It's not all phlegm,' said the dwarf mysteriously, and for once Artemis did not feel like getting to the bottom of Mulch's mystery, as the bottom of Mulch's mysteries was generally in the vicinity of Mulch's mysterious bottom.

Artemis placed Holly gently on a bed of fake fur coats and recognized a designer label. 'These are my mother's coats.'

Mulch dropped Butler's leg. 'Yep. Well, possession is nine-tenths of the law, so why don't you take your tenth back up to the surface and talk larceny with the thing that used to be Opal Koboi?'

This was a good point. Artemis had no desire to be booted out of this sanctuary.

'Are we safe down here? Won't they follow us?'

'They can try,' said Mulch, then spat a glowing wad of spit on top of a fading spatter. 'But it would take a couple of days with industrial drills and sonar. And even then I could bring the whole thing down with a well-placed burst of dwarf gas.'

Artemis found this hard to believe. 'Seriously. One *blast* and this entire structure comes tumbling down?'

Mulch adopted a heroic pose, one foot on a rock, hands

on hips. 'In my line of work, you gotta be ready to move on. Just walk away.'

Artemis did not appreciate the heroic pose. 'Please, Mulch, I beg you. Put on some trousers.'

Mulch grudgingly agreed, tugging faded tunnelling breeches over his meaty thighs. This was as far as he was prepared to go, and his furry chest and prodigious gut remained glowing and bare.

'The trousers I will wear for Holly's sake, but this is my home, Artemis. In the cave, Diggums keeps it casual.'

Water dripped from a stalactite into a shimmering pool. Artemis dipped his hand in, then laid his palm on Holly's forehead. She was still unconscious following her second physical trauma in as many minutes, and a single spark of magic squatted on her head wound, buzzing like an industrious golden bee. The bee seemed to notice Artemis's hand and skipped on to the brand, calming his skin but leaving a raised scar. Once it had finished its work, the magic returned to Holly and spread itself like a salve across her forehead. Holly's breathing was deep and regular and she seemed more like a person asleep than unconscious.

'How long have you been here, Mulch?'

'Why? Are you looking for rent arrears?'

'No, I am simply collating information at the moment. The more I know, the more comprehensively I can plan.'

Mulch nudged the lid from a cooler, which Artemis recognized from an old picnic set of the family's, and pulled out a blood-red salami.

'You keep saying that 'bout comprehensive planning *et cetera*, and we keep ending up eyeball-deep in the troll hole without spring boots.'

Artemis had long ago stopped asking Mulch to explain his metaphors. He was desperate for any information that might give him an edge, something that would help him to wrest control of this desperate situation.

Focus, he told himself. *There is so much at stake here. More than ever before.*

Artemis felt ragged. His chest heaved from recent healings and exertions. Uncharacteristically, he did not know what to do, other than wait for his friends to wake up. He shuffled across to Butler, checking his pupils for signs of brain injury. Holly had shot him in the neck and they had taken quite a tumble. He was relieved to find both pupils to be of equal size.

Mulch squatted beside him, glowing like a dumpy demigod, which was a little disturbing if you knew what the dwarf was actually like. Mulch Diggums was about as far from godliness as a hedgehog was from smoothliness.

'What do you think of my place?' asked the dwarf.

'This is . . .' Artemis gestured to their surroundings. 'Amazing. You hollowed all of this out yourself. How long have you been here?'

The dwarf shrugged. 'Coupla years. Off and on, you know. I have a dozen of these little bolt-holes all over the place. I got tired of being a law-abiding citizen. So I siphon off a little juice from your geothermal rods and pirate your cable.'

'Why live down here at all?'

'I don't *live* live here. I crash here occasionally. When things get hot. I just pulled a pretty big job and needed to hide out for a while.'

Artemis looked around. 'A pretty big job, you say? So, where's all the loot?'

Mulch wagged a finger that glowed like a party stick. 'That, as my cousin Nord would say, is where my improvised lie falls apart.'

Artemis put two and two together and arrived at a very unpleasant four.

'You were here to rob me!'

'No, I wasn't. How dare you?'

'You are lurking down here to tunnel into Fowl Manor. Again.'

'*Lurking* is not a nice word. Makes me sound like a sea serpent. I like to think I was hiding in the shadows. Cool, like a cat burglar.'

'You eat cats, Mulch.'

Mulch joined his hands. 'OK. I admit it. I might have been planning to have a peek into the art vault. But look at the funny side. Stealing stuff from a criminal mastermind. That's gotta be ironic. You brainiacs like irony, right?'

Artemis was appalled. 'You can't keep art here. It's damp and muddy.'

'Didn't do the pharaohs any harm,' argued the dwarf.

Holly, who lay on the ground beside them, opened her eyes, coughed, then executed a move that was much more

120

difficult than it looked by actually springing vertically from where she lay and landing on her feet. Mulch was impressed until Holly attempted to strangle him with his own beard, at which point he stopped being impressed and got busy choking.

This was a problem with waking up after a magical healing; often the brain is totally unharmed but the mind is confused. It is a strange feeling to be smart and dopey at the same time. Add a time lapse into the mix, and a person will often find it difficult to transition from a dream state to the waking world, so it is advisable to place the patient in tranquil surroundings, perhaps with some childhood toys heaped round the pillow. Unfortunately for Holly she had lost consciousness in the middle of a life-or-death struggle and awoke to find a glowing monster looming over her. So, she understandably overreacted.

It took about five seconds before she realized who Mulch was.

'Oh,' she mumbled sheepishly. 'It's you.'

'Yes,' said Mulch, then coughed up something that squeaked and crawled away. 'If you could please relinquish the beard, I just had a salon conditioning treatment done.'

'Really?'

'Of course not really. I live in a cavern. I eat dirt. What do you think?'

Holly finger-combed Mulch's beard a little, then climbed down from the dwarf's shoulders.

'I was just sitting in spit, right?' she said, grimacing.

'It's not *all* spit,' said Artemis.

'Well, Artemis,' she said, rubbing the faint red mark on her forehead. 'What's the plan?'

'And hello to you too,' said Mulch. 'And don't thank me. Saving your life once more has been my pleasure. Just one of the many services offered by Diggums Airlines.'

Holly scowled at him. 'I have a warrant out for you.'

'So why don't you arrest me then?'

'The secure facilities aren't really operating at the moment.'

Mulch took a moment to process this and the trademark bravado drained from his craggy features, crease by crease. It almost seemed like his glow dimmed a few notches.

'Oh, holy lord Vortex,' he said, tracing the sacred sign of the bloated intestine over his stomach to ward off evil. 'What has Opal done now?'

Holly sat on a mound, tapping her wrist computer to see if anything worked.

'She's found and opened the Berserker Gate.'

'And that's not the worst thing,' said Artemis. 'She killed her younger self, which destroyed everything Opal has invented or influenced since then. Haven is shut down and humans are back in the Stone Age.'

Holly's face was grim in the glow of luminous spit. 'Actually, Artemis, finding the Berserker Gate *is* the worst thing, because there are two locks. The first releases the Berserkers . . .'

Mulch jumped into the pause. 'And the second? Come on, Holly, this is no time for theatrics.'

Holly hugged her knees like a lost child. 'The second releases Armageddon. If Opal succeeds in opening it, every single human on the surface of the Earth will be killed.'

Artemis felt his head spin as the bloody scale of Opal's plan became clear.

Butler chose this moment to regain his senses. 'Juliet is on the surface with Masters Beckett and Myles, so I guess we can't let that happen.'

They sat in a tight group round a campfire of glowing spit while Holly told what had been considered a legend, but was now being treated as pretty accurate historical fact.

'Most of this you will already know from the spirits who tried to invade you.'

Butler rubbed his branded neck. 'Not me. I was out cold. All I have is fractured images. Pretty gross stuff, even for me. Severed limbs, people being buried alive. Dwarfs riding trolls into battle? Could that have happened?'

'It all happened,' Holly confirmed. 'There was a dwarf corps that rode trolls.'

'Yep,' said Mulch. 'They called themselves the Troll Riders. Pretty cool name, right? There was a group that only went out at night who called themselves the Night Troll Riders.'

Artemis couldn't help himself. 'What were the daytime troll riders called?'

'Those gauchos were called the Daytime Troll Riders,' answered Mulch blithely. 'Head to toe in leather. They smelled like the inside of a stinkworm's bladder, but they got the job done.'

Holly could have wept with frustration, but she'd learned during her brief period as a private investigator when Mulch had served as her partner that the dwarf would shut up only when he was good and ready. Artemis, on the other hand, should know better.

'Artemis,' she said sharply. 'Don't encourage him. We are on a timetable.'

Artemis's expression seemed almost helpless in the luminescence. 'Of course. No more comments. I am feeling a little overwhelmed, truth be told. Continue, Holly, please.'

And so Holly told her story, her features sharply lit from below by the unconventional glow. Butler could not help but be reminded of horror stories told to him and his fellow scouts by Master Prunes on weekend trips to the Dan-yr-Ogof cave in Wales. Holly's delivery was bare bones, but the circumstances sent a shiver along his spine.

And I do not shiver easily, thought the big man, shifting uncomfortably on the muddied root that served as a seat.

'When I was a child, my father told me the story of Taillte almost every night so that I would never forget the sacrifice our ancestors made. Some laid down their lives, but a few went beyond even that and deferred their afterlives.' Holly closed her eyes and tried to tell it as she had heard it. 'Ten thousand years ago, humans fought to eradicate the fairy families from the face of the Earth. There was no reason for them to do this. Fairies are in the main peace-loving people and their healing abilities and special connection to the land were of benefit to all, but always among the humans there are those individuals who would control all they see and are threatened by that which they do not understand.'

Artemis refrained from making the obvious point that it was one of the fairy folk who was more or less attempting to destroy the world presently, but he filed it away to trot out at a later date.

'And so the People took refuge on the misty isle of Ériú, the home of magic, where they were most powerful. And they dug their healing pits and massed their army at the Plains of Taillte for a last stand.'

The others were silent now as Holly spoke for they could see the scene in their own memories.

'It was a brief battle,' said Holly bitterly. 'The humans showed no mercy and it was clear by the first night that the People were doomed to extermination. And so the Council decided that they would retreat to the catacombs below the earth from whence they had come before the dawn of the age of man. All except the demons, who used magic to lift their island out of time.'

'OK,' said Mulch. 'I was sticking with it, but then you said "whence", so now I have to go to the fridge.'

Holly scowled briefly then continued. By now everyone knew that eating was how Mulch handled bad news, and good news, and banal news. All news really.

'But the Council reasoned that even their underground refuge would be in danger from the humans and so they built a gate with an enchanted lock. If this lock were ever opened, then the souls of the Berserker warriors buried round the gate would rise up and possess what bodies they could to prevent the humans from gaining access.'

Artemis could still remember the sickly stench he'd experienced when the fairy Berserker had attempted to occupy his mind.

'And if the Berserker Gate were opened by fairy hand, then the warriors would be in thrall to that fairy to fight at his or her command. In this case, Opal Koboi. This spell was conjured to last for a century at least until the People were safely away and the location of the gate forgotten.'

Holly's lip curled as she said this and Artemis made a deduction.

'But there was a betrayal?'

Holly's eyes flickered in surprise. 'How . . . Yes, of course you would guess, Artemis. We were betrayed by the infamous gnome warlock Shayden Fruid, once known as Shayden the Bold but since called Shayden the Shame of Taillte. There's an inverted statue of Shayden in the chapel of Hey-Hey, which is not meant as a compliment, believe me.'

'What happened, Holly?' said Artemis, urging her on.

'Shayden Fruid hid in a conjured mist until the dying Berserkers were buried around the gate and the People had descended into the underworld, then he attempted to tamper with the lock. Not only did he intend to open the lock for the humans but also to lead the enthralled Berserkers against their own people.'

'This guy was a real sweetheart,' Mulch called, his face bathed in fridge glow. 'Legend has it he once sold his own mother down the river. And I'm not talking metaphorically here. He actually put his mother in a boat and traded her in the next village downstream. That should have been a red flag right there.'

'But Shayden's plan failed, didn't it?' said Artemis.

'Yes, because the secret stage of the plan called for someone to stay behind and collapse the valley on top of the gate. A great warlock who could maintain the mist until the gate was buried and then use it to cover his getaway. As the demons had already left, only the elfin warlock Bruin Fadda, whose hatred of the humans was legendary, could complete the mission, climbing to the lip of the valley to conjure the collapse that had been prepared by a team of dwarf engineers.'

Somehow it seemed to Artemis, Butler and Holly that they had all experienced what had happened. Perhaps it was the last remnant of Berserker plasma on their brows, but suddenly they could hear the breath in Bruin Fadda's throat as he raced down the hillside, screaming at Shayden to step away from the lock.

'They struggled fiercely, each mighty warrior mortally wounding the other. And, at the end, Bruin, dying and driven mad with pain, hate and despair, conjured a second lock using his own blood and forbidden black magic. If that lock were to be opened, then Danu, the Earth mother, would surrender her magic to the air in a blast of power that would annihilate every human on the surface and the People would be safe forever.'

'Just humans?'

Holly woke from her reverie. 'Just humans. The hated oppressor. Bruin had lost every member of his family in a raid. He was beyond reason.'

Butler rubbed his chin. 'Every weapon has a sell-by date, Holly. It's been ten thousand years. Couldn't this spell have a half-life or something?'

'It's possible. But the Berserkers are loose and the first lock worked just fine.'

'Why would Opal want to open the second lock?'

Artemis knew the answer to that one. 'It's political. There is a huge lobby in Haven that has been advocating full-scale war for years. Opal would be a hero to them.'

Holly nodded. 'Exactly. Plus Opal is so far gone now that she seriously believes that her destiny is to be some kind of messiah. You saw what she was prepared to do just to escape.'

'Do tell,' said Mulch.

'She had her younger self kidnapped and she then set up a fake ransom demand for her present self so that we would put her inside a natural nuclear reactor thus helping her to generate enough black magic for her to open the first lock.'

Mulch slammed the fridge door. 'I am sincerely sorry I asked. This is typical of the kind of mess you get us into, Artemis.'

'Hey,' snapped Holly. 'This is not the time to blame Artemis.'

⊗•⬭⟩⌇⚚⮞•⟜⬡⟩•⊙ ⟔⬭⟅⬚⮜•⬤•⟔⟩⊗⟟⬤

'Thank you,' said Artemis. 'Finally.'

'There will be plenty of time to blame Artemis later when this is resolved.'

Artemis folded his arms with exaggerated movements. 'That is uncalled for, Holly. I am as much a victim here as everyone else. Even those Berserkers are being used to fight a war that ended ten thousand years ago. Couldn't we simply tell them the war is over? They are guarding a gate that I presume doesn't even lead anywhere any more.'

'That's true. We haven't used the old networks for millennia.'

'Can't you somehow communicate that?'

'No. They are under fairy bonds. Nothing we say will make an impact.'

'How much time do we have?' asked Artemis.

'I don't know,' admitted Holly. 'My father told me the legend as a bedtime story. It was passed down to him from his father. The whole thing came from the mind of an empath warlock who synched with Bruin Fadda in his final moments. All we know is that the second lock is complex magic. Opal is running on black magic now, but that has a high price and fades fast. She will want to get it open before dawn while the fairy moon is still high. Her Berserkers will be bare wisps of their former selves after all this time, and they can't last much longer than that. Some will give in to the afterlife's call before then.'

Artemis turned to Butler for a question about tactics. This was the bodyguard's area of expertise.

'How should Opal deploy her forces?'

'Opal will have most of those Berserkers gathered round her watching her back while she picks that magical lock. The rest will guard the walls and run roving patrols round the estate, armed to the teeth no doubt. Probably with my arms.'

'Do we have any weapons?' asked Artemis.

'I lost my Neutrino after the crash,' said Holly.

'I had to sign in my handgun at Haven immigration,' said Butler. 'Never had a chance to pick it up.'

Mulch returned to the campfire. 'You did say every human on the surface would be killed. I just want to point out that you are underground. So you could, you know, just stay here.'

Holly shot him a pretty raw poisonous look.

'Hey, no need for that. It's good to explore all the options.'

'If Opal does open the second lock, not only will it kill billions of humans but it will spark off an unprecedented civil war among the People. After which Opal Koboi would probably declare herself supreme empress.'

'So you're saying we should stop her?'

'I'm saying we *have* to stop her, but I don't know how.'

Artemis looked towards the heavens as if divine inspiration were forthcoming, but all he could see were the glowing walls of Mulch's subterranean refuge and the inky blackness of tunnel mouths dotted along their surfaces.

'Mulch,' he said, pointing. 'Where do those tunnels lead?'

CHAPTER 8: MOTLEY CREW

DALKEY ISLAND, SOUTH COUNTY DUBLIN

THERE is a common misconception that trolls are stupid. The fact is that trolls are only *relatively* stupid.

Compared to astrophysicists and Grand High Hey-Hey Monks, trolls could be considered a bit lacking in the IQ department, but even a below-average troll will solve a puzzle faster than any chimpanzee or dolphin on the planet. Trolls have been known to fashion crude tools, learn sign language and even grunt out a few intelligible syllables. In the early Middle Ages, when troll sideshows were legal, the famous performing troll Count Amos Moonbeam would be fed honey punch by his dwarf handler until he belched out a fair approximation of 'The Ballad of Tingly Smalls'.

So, trolls stupid?

Definitely not.

What trolls *are* is stubborn. Pathologically so. If a troll suspects that someone wishes it to exit through door A, then it will definitely choose door B possibly after relieving itself all over door A on the way out.

This made it difficult for trolls to integrate in the Lower Elements. The LEP even have a special troll division of trained handlers who log the most overtime hours per capita tracking down rogue trolls who refuse to be corralled in the tunnels of suburban Haven. At any given time there are a hundred-plus trolls who have chewed out their tracking chips and are crawling through cracks in the Earth's crust, moving inexorably towards magical hotspots on the surface.

Trolls are drawn to magical residue like dwarfs are drawn to stuff that doesn't belong to them. Trolls feed on residue. It nourishes them and increases their life spans. And, as they grow older, they grow craftier.

The oldest troll on record had been known by many names in his lifetime: his mother may have named him Gruff or she may have been trying to say *get off*. To LEPtroll he was simply Suspect Zero and to the humans he was the Abominable Snowman, Bigfoot or El Chupacabra, depending on which area he had been spotted in.

Gruff had stayed alive for several extra centuries by being prepared to hike across the globe in search of magical residue. There was not a continent he had not visited under cover of darkness and his greying hide was criss-crossed with the scars and scorch marks of a hundred tussles with the LEP and various human hunters. If Gruff could put a sentence together, he would probably say:

Maybe I look beat up, but you should see the other guys.

Gruff was currently residing in a cave on Dalkey Island off the coast of south Dublin, and he would swim ashore to a private slipway and help himself to livestock from surrounding farms. He had been spotted a few times by the owner of the slipway, an eccentric Irishman who now sang to him nightly from across the bay. Gruff knew that he would either have to move on or eat the human in the next couple of days, but for this particular evening he was content to lay his head on the carcass of a sheep, which would serve as a pillow for now and as breakfast later on.

His sleep was interrupted by the activation of a sixth sense that inhabited the space in his brain somewhere between taste and smell. There was magical activity nearby, which set the inside of his skull a-tingling as though fireflies had hatched in there. And, where there was magic, there would undoubtedly be residue. Enough to cure the ache in his back and seal up the running sore on his haunch where a walrus had gored him.

Gruff scooped sausages of offal from the sheep's innards and swallowed them whole to sustain him for the trip. And, as he lowered himself into the sea for the short swim to the mainland, he felt the magic's lure grow stronger and his spirits lifted.

Gruff longed for the sweet nectar of residue to cure what ailed him. And when a troll has its stout heart set on something there are not many things on this Earth capable of blocking its way.

CHAPTER 9: SPEWING THE BITTER POISON

THE FOWL ESTATE

 OPAL stood on the edge of the collapsed tunnel feeling mildly thwarted but not in the least downhearted. After all, she was a veritable dynamo of black magic for the time being and Artemis Fowl was buried beneath a tonne of rubble, if not dead then certainly dishevelled, which would vex the Mud Boy almost as much.

Dead or not, the plan remained the same.

Oro knelt and picked up Holly's weapon from the crumbled clay. 'What is this, mistress?'

Opal held the handgun cupped in her tiny hands and communicated with its energy until the energy agreed to transfer itself across to her person. It was undramatic to watch – the weapon simply exhaled and crumpled.

'I must open the second lock,' she said to Oro, refreshed by this morsel of power. 'I have until morning. Then my magic will evaporate with the dawn dew and I will be left defenceless.'

'The second lock?' said Oro, Beckett's vocal cords mangling the Gnommish. 'Are you certain, mistress?'

'*Queen*,' corrected Opal. 'You will refer to me as Queen Opal. By opening the first lock of the Berserker Gate I have bonded you to me. But I would prefer that you referred to me as little as possible as your silly human voice box irritates me. And stop scowling. The expression looks ridiculous on your little boy face. Mummy is tempted to spank you.'

'But the second lock?' persisted Oro. 'That will unleash the power of Danu.'

'Firstly, what did I just say about referring to me? Secondly, take a peek inside the brain of your human. A little Danu wave is the best thing for this planet.'

Oro seemed puzzled, but his bonds forbade him to argue and Opal knew that even if the Berserker could argue, his points would be presented in turgid Middle Ages prose with simplistic logic.

'Let me speak to the human boy,' she said, reasoning that a Fowl child, however young, would appreciate what she had accomplished here. Plus it would be fun to watch a human squirm.

Oro sighed, wishing that his old friend Bruin Fadda had built a little leeway into the fairy bonds, then shuddered as he allowed his own consciousness to be subsumed temporarily by Beckett Fowl's.

The centuries dropped from Oro's face and Beckett

emerged shiny and smiling. 'I was dreaming,' he said. 'In my dream I looked like me but with more fingers.'

Opal spread her arms wide, allowing the black magic to pulse in orange cables along her limbs. 'Are you not terrified, boy?'

Beckett hopped monkey-like into his version of a ninja pose. 'Nope. *You* should be terror-fied.'

'Me?' said Opal, laughing. 'You cannot harm me. The fairy bonds prevent it.'

Beckett punched Opal in the stomach, from the shoulder like Butler taught him. 'Oh yeah. I'm pretty fast. Faster than your stupid fairy bonds. Butler says I'm a natch-u-ral.'

Opal's breath left her in a huff and she stumbled backwards, cracking her elbow on the Berserker Gate's raised dais. Luckily for her, the fairy bonds kicked in and Oro reclaimed control of the body, otherwise four-year-old Beckett Fowl might have put an end to Opal's world domination plans right there.

Oro rushed to help Opal up. 'My queen, are you harmed?'

Opal waved her hand, unable to speak, and was forced to endure several seconds of Oro pumping her torso up and down like a bellows until her breath returned.

'Release me, you stupid elf. Are you trying to break my spine?'

Oro did as he was told. 'That boy is a quick one. He beat the bonds. Not many could do that.'

Opal rubbed her stomach with a magic hand, just in case there was bruising. 'Are you sure you didn't give the boy a little help?' she said suspiciously.

'Of course not, my queen,' said Oro. 'Berserkers do not help humans. Do you wish to speak with the boy again?'

'No!' Opal squeaked, then regained her composure. 'I mean . . . no. The boy has served his purpose. We must move ahead with the plan.'

Oro knelt, scooping a handful of loose earth. 'We should at least give chase to our attackers. The elf has battle skills; the big human is also a formidable warrior. They will most definitely attempt sabotage.'

Opal was prepared to concede this point. 'Very well, tiresome elf. Send your craftiest lieutenant with a few soldiers. Make sure to include the other boy in your party. Fowl may be reluctant to kill his own brother.' Opal blew through her lips, a small action that made it abundantly clear that she herself would not hesitate to kill any family member were she in Fowl's position. In fact, she would see any hesitation to hack down a sibling as a lack of commitment to the plan.

After all, she thought, *did I not have myself killed to escape prison?*

But fairies were weak and humans were weaker. Perhaps Fowl would hold back for the second it took for his little brother to plant a dagger in his side.

'Do not waste too much time or resources. I want a circle of Berserker steel behind me while I work on the second lock. There are complex enchantments to unravel.'

Oro stood, closing his eyes for a second to enjoy the breeze on his face. From beyond the walls he could hear the crackle of enormous flames and when he opened his eyes the smoulder of distant destruction licked the night clouds.

'We are eager but few, my queen. Shall there be more enemies on the way?'

Opal made a sound that was almost a cackle. 'Not until morning. My enemies are experiencing certain difficulties. Mummy saw to that.'

The part of Oro's mind that was still his own and not in thrall to a glowing orange pixie thought: *It is unseemly that she refers to herself as our mother. She is mocking us.*

But such is the strength of fairy *geasa*, or bonds, that even this rebellious thought caused the Berserker captain physical pain.

Opal noticed his wince. 'What are you thinking, Captain? Nothing seditious, I hope?'

'No, my queen,' said Oro. 'This puny body is unable to contain my bloodlust.' This lie cost him another twinge, but he was ready for it and bore it without reaction.

Opal frowned. That one had ideas of his own, but no matter. Oro's energy was already fading. The Berserkers would barely last the night and by then the second lock would be open and the Koboi era would truly begin.

'Go then,' she snapped. 'Choose a hunting party, but *your* duty is to protect the gate. I have arranged for the humans to be occupied for the moment, but once the sun rises they will come in a wave of destruction to destroy the last of our kind.' Opal decided to go all Gothic so Oro would get the point. 'Without mercy in their cold merciless hearts they shall come unto us.'

This kind of talk seemed to penetrate and Oro stamped away to pick his hunting party.

The entire situation was, Opal had to admit to herself, absolutely perfect. The Berserkers would guard the perimeter, pitiful in their mistaken belief that their big gloomy gate actually led somewhere. And then they would simply evaporate into the afterlife, unaware of the unnecessary genocide they had helped to commit.

Ghosts make such unreliable tribunal witnesses, Opal thought, smirking.

But, as enjoyable as self-congratulatory smirking might be, there was actual work to be done that required the entirety of her intellect. The lock remained locked, and she could only hold on to the black magic for so long before it consumed her physical body. Already she could feel blisters rising between her shoulder blades. The magic would leave her soon, but before then it would wreak havoc on her system. Her power healed the blisters as soon as they rose, but that cost her magic and the blisters came back anyway.

Why can't I solve this problem by killing someone? she thought petulantly, then comforted herself with the mantra that had kept her going in prison.

'Soon all the humans will be dead,' she said, droning in the time-honoured fashion of gurus everywhere. 'And then Opal will be loved.'

And even if I'm not loved, she thought, *at least all the humans will be dead.*

*

Oro stumped on little legs down the age-old steps that ran round the Berserker Gate and for a moment remembered clearly the day when he had helped construct this squat tower. There had been more magic involved than heavy lifting though. Old Bruin Fadda had his team pouring every spark of power they could get their hands on into the lock. A big circle of warlocks hurling lightning bolts into the stone.

Whoever opens this gate will get more than they bargained for, Bruin had promised later that week, even as Oro and his men lay dying. Bruin had been wrong. Queen Opal got exactly what she had been expecting.

How did she know? Oro wondered. *I was almost certain that the world had forgotten us.*

The Berserkers were bristling with repressed violence and anxious to inflict damage on humankind. They tried to stand still as Oro addressed them, but it was a struggle, especially for the pirates who were unable to stop their exposed bones rattling.

Oro stood on a tree stump so that the small body he occupied could be seen by all and held his fist aloft for silence.

'My warriors!' he shouted over the ranks. 'Our day has finally come!'

This was met with a chorus of yells, whoops, barks and whistles as the various creatures inhabited by the Berserkers voiced their approval. Oro could not hide a wince. These were not the warriors he remembered, who fought and suffered mortal wounds on the Plains of Taillte, but they were what they were and the will to fight was there if not the ability. There were foxes in their ranks, for Danu's sake. How was a fox supposed to heft a sword? Still, better to get his warriors' blood going with some rhetoric. Oro had always been proud of his speechifying.

'We will drink the bitter poison of our defeat and spew it at our enemies!' he shouted, his voice carrying across the meadow.

His warriors cheered, roared and howled their approval, except for one.

'Pardon?' said his lieutenant, Gobdaw.

'What?' said Oro.

The lieutenant who lurked inside the body of the second Mud Boy wore a puzzled expression on his pasty face. In truth puzzlement of any kind was new for Gobdaw. He was usually an *ask no questions* kind of fairy who did his talking with an axe. Generally Gobdaw loved a nice bit of rhetoric.

'Well, Oro,' said Gobdaw, seeming a little surprised by the words coming out of his mouth. 'What does that mean exactly? Spewing the bitter poison of our defeat at our enemies?'

This question took Oro by surprise. 'Well, it simply means . . .'

'Because, if you don't mind me saying, using the word *defeat* in a motivational speech sends a little bit of a mixed message.'

Now it was Oro's turn to be perplexed. 'Motivational? Mixed message? What do these terms even mean?'

Gobdaw looked as though he might cry. 'I don't know, Captain. It's my human host. He's a strong one.'

'Pull yourself together, Gobdaw. You have always appreciated my rhetoric.'

'I did. I do, Captain. The young one refuses to be silenced.'

Oro decided to distract Gobdaw with duty. 'You have the honour of leading the search for enemies. Take the hounds, Bellico and those mariners too. Everybody else, surround the gate. Queen Opal labours at the second lock. Understood?'

'Yes, Captain,' roared Gobdaw, shaking his fist. 'As you command.'

Oro nodded. That was more like it.

Gobdaw, Bellico and the Fowl hunting hounds circled the collapsed tunnel. Bellico was feeling pretty good about herself, encased as she was in the body of Juliet Butler. This was a better host than she could have hoped for: an excellent physical specimen equipped with the knowledge of several ancient fighting styles which, thanks to Juliet's memories, she knew how to put into practice very well indeed.

Bellico checked her reflection in the blade of a pirate's knife and was pleased with what she saw.

Not too ugly, for a human. It is almost a pity my life force will sustain me no more than a single night. Perhaps if we had been called upon within fifty years of being laid in the ground, then the magic could have sustained us for longer, but now our spirits are weakened by time. The spell was not constructed to keep us earthbound for this long.

•⚲⟊⧗⟡⧓⟠⟆⟅•⊗⬚⬡•⟅⟗⟊⟩⟆⬤⟐⊕⟊•⟦⟡⟊⟩

Bellico's memory contained images that painted an ugly picture of Opal Koboi, but she had been warned that human visions of the fairy folk were unreliable. Such was the Mud Men's hatred of the People that even their memories would be skewed.

The pirates were less pleased with their inherited corpses, which disintegrated even as they walked.

'It's costing me all my magic just holding this skin sack of maggots together,' complained the one-time warrior giant Salton Finnacre, who inhabited the body of Eusebius Fowl the lung-sucking pirate.

'At least you've got legs,' grumbled his battle partner J'Heez Nunyon, who hobbled along on a pair of wooden stumps. 'How am I supposed to do my signature dervish move on these things? I'm gonna look like a bleepin' drunk dwarf falling over.'

It was worse for the English pointer hounds, who could only form the most rudimentary sounds with their vocal cords.

'Fowl,' barked one, being very familiar with Artemis's scent. 'Fowl. Fowl.'

'Good boy,' said Gobdaw, reaching up to pat the hound's head with Myles's little hand, which the dog did not think was very funny at all and would have bitten the hand had it not belonged to a superior officer.

Gobdaw called to his soldiers. 'Warriors. Our noble brothers inside these beasts have picked up a trail. Our mission is to find the humans.'

No one asked, *What then?* Everybody knew what you did to humans when you found them. Because, if you didn't do it to them, they would do it to you and your entire species and probably anyone your species had ever shared a flagon of beer with.

'And the elf?' asked Bellico. 'What of her?'

'The elf made her choice,' said Gobdaw. 'If she steps aside, then we let her live. If she stands her ground, then she becomes as a Mud Person to us.' Sweat rolled down Gobdaw's brow though the night was growing cool and he spoke through clenched teeth, trying to hold back Myles Fowl's consciousness, which bubbled up inside him like mental indigestion.

This exchange was cut short when the English pointers streaked away from the collapsed tunnel mouth and across the meadow towards the large human dwelling that crested the hill.

'Ah,' said Bellico, taking off after the dogs. 'The humans are in the stone temple.'

Gobdaw tried to stop himself from talking, but failed. 'He says to tell you that it's called a manor. And that all girls are stupid.'

Artemis, Holly and Butler squirmed along a tunnel that Mulch had assured them would emerge in the wine cellar behind a rack of Château Margaux 1995.

Artemis was horrified with this revelation. 'Don't you know that your tunnel could affect the temperature of the cellar? Not to mention the humidity? That wine is an investment.'

'Don't worry about the wine, silly Mud Boy,' said Mulch in a very patronizing tone that he had developed and practised simply to annoy Artemis. 'I drank that months ago and replaced it. It was the only responsible thing to do – after all, the cellar's integrity had been compromised.'

'Yes, by you!' Artemis frowned. 'Replaced it with what?'

'Do you really want to know?' the dwarf asked, and Artemis shook his head, deciding that given the dwarf's history, in this particular case ignorance would be less disturbing than the truth.

'Wise decision,' said Mulch. 'So, to continue. The tunnel runs to the back of the cellar but the wall is plugged.'

'Plugged with what?' asked Artemis, who could be a bit slow in spite of his genius.

The dwarf finger-combed his beard. 'I refer you to my last question: do you really want to know?'

'Can we break through?' asked Butler, the pragmatist.

'Oh yes,' said Mulch. 'A big strong human like you. No problems. I'd do it for you, but apparently I have this other mission.'

Holly looked up from her wrist computer, which still wasn't picking up a signal. 'We need you to get the weapons in the shuttle, Mulch. Butler has some kit in the house, but Juliet could already be leading the Berserkers there. We need to move fast and on two fronts. A pincer movement.'

Mulch sighed. 'Pincer. I love crab. And lobster. Makes me a little gassy, but it's worth it.'

Holly slapped her knees. 'Time to go,' she said. Neither of the humans argued.

Mulch watched his friends climb into the manor tunnel and then turned back the way they had come, towards the shuttle.

I don't like retracing my steps, he thought. *Because there's usually someone chasing after me.*

So now here they were, wriggling along a claustrophobic tunnel with the heavy smell of earth in their noses and the ever-present threat of untold tonnage looming above them like a giant anvil.

Holly knew what everyone was thinking. 'This tunnel is sound. Mulch is the best digger in the business,' she said between grunts and breaths.

The tunnel meandered and their only light was from a mobile phone taped to Butler's forehead. Artemis had this sudden vision of the three of them stuck in there forever, like rodents in the belly of a snake, being slowly digested until not a trace remained.

No one will ever know what happened to us.

This was a redundant thought, Artemis knew, because if they didn't get out of this tunnel, then in all likelihood there would be no one left to wonder what had become of their small group. And he would never know if he had failed to save his parents or if they had already been killed somehow in London. Nevertheless Artemis could not shake the notion that they were about to die in this vast unmarked grave, and it grew stronger with every grasping reach of his hand that drew him further into the earth.

Artemis reached forward once more in the blackness and his scrabbling fingers met Butler's boot.

'I think we made it,' said the bodyguard. 'We've reached the blockage.'

'Is the blockage solid?' called Holly from the rear.

There followed a series of noises that would not sound out of place in a jelly factory and a smell that would be totally consistent with a burst sewage pipe.

Butler coughed several times, swore at length, then said a line heavy with dreadful implication. 'Only the crust is solid.'

They tumbled through the hole on to a fallen rack of broken wine bottles which had been knocked over by Butler's hurried entry. Usually he would have inched his way through the entrance, moving the rack bit by bit, but in this case speed was more important than stealth and so he simply crashed through Mulch's tunnel plug and into the cellar beyond. The other two quickly followed, happy to escape the confines of the tunnel.

Artemis sniffed the liquid pooling in concave curves of broken bottle fragments. 'That is most definitely not Château Margaux 1995,' he commented.

'It's not even snake wine,' said Butler, brushing himself off. 'Although I know a few mercenaries who would prob-ably drink it.'

Holly hiked up the tall seventeenth-century stone cellar steps, then pressed her ear to the door. 'I can't hear anything,' she said after a moment. 'Wind from outside, that's all.'

Butler pulled Artemis from the rack wreckage. 'Let's keep going, Artemis. We need to get to my weapons before it occurs to Juliet's passenger.'

Holly opened the door a crack and peeped through. The cellar door opened to a corridor and halfway down was a bunch of pirates armed with automatic weapons. They stood absolutely still, probably in an attempt to stop their bones from rattling.

Butler crept up behind her. 'How are we doing?' he asked.

Holly held her breath as she closed the door. 'Not great,' she said.

They squatted behind a rack of 1990s Californian reds and spoke in urgent whispers.

'What do we have?' asked Artemis.

Butler held up his fists. 'I've got these. That's it.'

Holly searched the pockets of her jumpsuit. 'Some plasti-cuffs. A couple of flares. Not much of an inventory.'

Artemis touched the tip of each finger against the pad of his thumb, one of his focusing exercises. 'We have something else,' he said. 'We have the house.'

CHAPTER 10: SİBLİnG RİVALRY

FOWL MAnOR

 GOBDAW and Bellico followed the hounds up Fowl Manor's grand stairs and along the hallway to Artemis's laboratory. Once through the door, the dogs leaped upon Artemis's white coat, which was hanging from a peg, using their teeth and claws to slash and chew the material.

'They smell the human,' said Gobdaw, disappointed not to have an opportunity to use the baby Glock that fitted so neatly in Myles's little hand.

They had raided Butler's arms room, which was hidden behind a false wall in his quarters. Only four people knew the location of and passcode to the keypad – five now, if Bellico could be counted as a separate person from Juliet. Gobdaw helped himself to the small gun and several blades while Bellico chose a machine pistol and a carbon-graphite recurve bow with a quiver of aluminium arrows. The pirates took more or less everything else, dancing happy jigs as they clattered downstairs to lie in wait.

'We should keep looking,' said Gobdaw.

Bellico did not agree, as she had Juliet's knowledge of the manor. 'No. Artemis's office adjoins this room so they will come here. We have warriors in the basement and the safe room. Let the hounds and the pirates herd them towards us.'

Gobdaw had enough leader's experience to know a good plan when he heard it. 'Very well. We wait here, but if I don't get to fire this gun before sunrise, I shall be most disappointed.'

'Don't worry. You will need every bullet for the big human.'

Bellico grabbed the hounds by their collars and yanked them from the coat. 'You two should be ashamed,' she said. 'Do not lose yourselves inside those beasts.'

One hound butted the second, as though the mistake had been his alone.

'Go now,' said Bellico, kicking their rumps. 'And find us some Mud People.'

Gobdaw and Bellico squatted behind the worktop, one nocking an arrow and the other disengaging the safety on his stolen handgun.

'The house is a virtual fortress,' explained Artemis. 'Once the siege function has been engaged on the security panel, then it would take an army to penetrate the defences, all of which were designed and installed before Opal jumped from her timeline, so there is no chance any of the components will have exploded.'

'And where is this panel?' asked Holly.

Artemis tapped his watch. 'Usually I can access it remotely on my watch or phone, but the Fowl network is down. I upgraded the router recently and perhaps a Koboi component crept in, so we will have to use the panel in my office.'

Butler knew it was his function to play devil's advocate. 'Won't that just lock us in here with a bunch of pirates?'

Artemis smiled. 'Or lock them in here with us.'

Salton Finnacre was bemoaning the loss of his own body to his mate J'Heez.

'Remember those arm muscles I had?' he said wistfully. 'They woz like tree trunks. Now look at me.' He jiggled his left arm to demonstrate how the flaps of flesh hung loosely from his bones. 'I can barely hold this fire stick.'

'It ain't a fire stick,' said J'Heez. 'They're called *guns*. That's a simple enough word to remember, ain't it?'

Salton looked at the automatic handgun in his bony fingers. 'I suppose. Just point and pull, is it?'

'That's what Bellico said.'

'Did you hear that, Berserkers?' Salton asked the half-dozen pirates squashed into the stairwell behind him. 'Just point and shoot. And don't worry about hitting the person in front of you because we are already dead.'

They stood in the red-bricked corridor, praying for some

humans to wander past. After all this time it would be a shame if they didn't get to kill anyone.

Three metres below, in the wine cellar, Butler hefted two bottles of Macallan 1926 Fine and Rare whiskey.

'Your father will not be pleased,' he said to Artemis. 'This is thirty thousand Euro per missile.'

Artemis wrapped his fingers round the door handle. 'I feel certain he will understand given the circumstances.'

Butler chuckled briefly. 'Oh, we're telling your father about the circumstances this time? That will be a first.'

'Well, perhaps not *all* the circumstances,' said Artemis and opened the door wide.

Butler stepped into the gap and lobbed the bottles at the ceiling over the pirates' heads. Both smashed, showering the Berserkers with high-alcohol liquid. Holly stepped under Butler's legs and shot a single flare into their midst. In less than a second the entire bunch of pirates was engulfed in the *whoosh* of blue and orange flames that painted the ceiling black. It didn't seem to bother the pirates too much, except for the one with the peg legs who was soon left without a leg to stand on. The rest lived on as skeletons, bringing their guns around to bear on the cellar door.

'The house will save us?' said Holly nervously. 'That's what you said.'

'Three,' said Artemis. 'Two . . . one.'

Right on cue the manor's fire-safe system registered the rise in temperature and instructed eight of its two hundred nozzles to submerge the flames in sub-zero extinguisher foam. The pirates were driven to their knees by the force of the spray and they yanked their triggers blindly, sending ricochets zinging off the walls and down the stairs. The bullets played out their kinetic energy on the steel banisters and fell to the ground smoking. In the corridor, the pirates' bone temperature dropped over a hundred degrees in less than ten seconds, making them as brittle as pressed leaves.

'Here we go,' said Butler and he charged up the stairs, crashing through the disorientated pirates like a vengeful bowling ball. The unfortunate Berserkers shattered under the lightest impact, disintegrating into a million bone crystals that fluttered in the air like snowflakes. Holly and Artemis followed the bodyguard, racing down the corridor, their feet crunching on bone shards, not stopping to collect weapons, most of which had exploded in the fire, rendering them useless.

As usual, Artemis was sandwiched between Butler and Holly as they fled.

'Keep moving,' Holly called from behind. 'There will be more of them, count on it.'

There were more pirates in the panic room, feeling very pleased with themselves.

'This is the smartest thing we ever done,' said Pronk O'Chtayle, acting commander. 'They comes in here to hide from us, but we is already here.' He gathered his bony crew around him. 'Let's go over it again. What does we do when we hears them?'

'We hides,' said the pirates.

'And what does we do when they comes in?'

'We pops up real sudden,' said the pirates gleefully.

Pronk pointed a bony finger. 'What does you do, specifically?'

A small pirate who seemed to be wearing the remains of a barrel stood by the wall. 'I bangs on this here button, dropping the steel door so's we're all trapped in here.'

'Good,' said Pronk. 'Good.'

The sounds of staccato gunfire bounced off the vaulted ceilings and echoed along the corridor to the panic room.

'They're coming, comrades,' said Pronk. 'Remember to kill 'em several times just to be sure. Stop slicing when yer arms fall off.'

They squatted in the gloom, light from the outside glinting on their blades.

If Bellico had probed a little deeper into Juliet's memories, she would have realized that the panic room could be accessed or sealed from the outside, remotely or with a voice-activation program. But, even if she had known, it would not have made any sense for the humans to lock themselves out of their own haven. That would be pure insanity.

Butler barely paused on his way past the panic-room door to talk into the small speaker set into the steel frame. 'Butler D.,' he said clearly. 'Authorization prime. Lock.'

A heavy door dropped down, sealing the panic room completely and locking the giddy bunch of Berserker pirates inside. Artemis had barely a second to glance under the door.

Is that a pirate wearing a barrel? he thought. *Nothing would surprise me today.*

On reaching the laboratory / office work suite, Butler held up his fist. Artemis was not familiar with military hand signals and crashed into the bodyguard's broad back. Fortunately the teen did not have the heft behind him to budge the bodyguard, for if Butler had taken so much as a stumbled step forward he would have surely been skewered by one of his sister's arrows.

'I see,' whispered Artemis. 'The raised fist means stop.'

Butler placed a finger to his lips.

'And that would mean you wish me to be quiet. Oh, I understand.'

Artemis's words were enough to elicit a reaction from inside the lab. The reaction taking the form of an aluminium arrow that penetrated the partition wall, thunking through the plasterboard, sending flakes fluttering.

Butler and Holly did not discuss a strategy as they were both experienced soldiers and knew the best time to attack was directly after shots had been fired, or in this case arrows.

'Left,' said Butler, and that was all he needed to say. Translated for the layman, he was saying that he would take any hostiles on the left of the room, leaving the right side for Holly.

They darted low inside, splitting into two targets as they

crossed the floor. Butler had the advantage of being extremely familiar with the lab's layout and he knew that the only logical hiding place would be behind the long stainless-steel workbench where Artemis played around with the unknown and built his experimental models.

I have always wondered how secure this thing is, he thought, before charging it like a rugby player entering a scrum where the cost of losing the match was death. He heard an arrow whistle past his ear a second before his shoulder rammed the stainless steel, lifting the bench from its supply cables in a flurry of sparks and a hiss of gas.

Gobdaw clambered on top of the bench, and he had both a short sword and fire stick raised to strike when the Bunsen burner gas said hello to the electric cable. Sparks and a brief explosion resulted, flipping the Berserker backwards into the velvet curtains.

Bellico assessed the situation quickly and bolted towards the office.

Butler saw her go. 'I'm after Juliet,' he barked at Holly. 'You subdue Myles.'

Perhaps the boy is unconscious, thought Holly, but this hope faded as she saw Myles Fowl disentangle himself from the velvet curtains. The look in his eyes told her that there was still a Berserker in that body and that he was not in the mood for surrender. He was armed only with a short blade now, but Holly knew that the Berserkers would fight to the last drop of blood, even if the blood was not strictly speaking their own.

156

'Don't hurt him,' said Artemis. 'He's only four years old.'

Gobdaw grinned, showing a mouthful of baby teeth, which Myles cleaned religiously with a toothbrush modelled on Einstein's head, the bristles being Einstein's trademark spiky hair. 'That's right, traitor. Gobdaw is only four years old, so don't hurt me.'

Holly wished that Artemis would stay out of it. This Gobdaw might look innocent, but he had far more battle experience than she would ever wish to have and, judging by the way he was twirling the blade on his palm, he hadn't lost any of his knife skills.

If this guy was in his own body, he would take me apart, she realized.

Holly's problem was that her heart was not in this fight. Quite apart from the fact that she was battling Artemis's little brother, this was Gobdaw, for heaven's sake. Gobdaw the legend. Gobdaw who had led the charge at Taillte. Gobdaw who had carried a wounded comrade across an icy lake at Bellannon. Gobdaw who'd been cornered by two wolves in a cave after the Cooley raid and come out of that cave wearing a new fur coat.

The two soldiers circled each other.

'Is it true about the wolves?' Holly asked in Gnommish.

Gobdaw missed a step, surprised. 'The wolves at Cooley? How do you know this tale?'

'Are you kidding?' said Holly. 'Everyone knows that. At school, it was part of the pageant, every year. To be honest, I am sick of that story. Two wolves, right?'

'There were two,' said Gobdaw. 'One was sickly though.'

Gobdaw began his strike in mid-sentence, as Holly had known he would. His blade hand darted forward, aiming for his opponent's midriff, but he didn't have quite the reach he used to possess and Holly rapped him hard in the nerve cluster in his deltoid, deadening the arm. That arm was about as much use now as a lead pipe hanging from his shoulder.

'D'Arvit,' swore Gobdaw. 'You are a tricky one. Females were ever treacherous.'

'Keep talking,' said Holly. 'I am liking you less and less, which should make my job a lot easier.'

Gobdaw took three running steps and jumped on to a Regency hall chair, grabbing one of two crossed reproduction pikes from the wall.

'Be careful, Myles!' shouted Artemis, from force of habit. 'That's very sharp.'

'Sharp, is it, Mud Boy? That's the way I like my spears.' The warrior's face twisted as though on the point of sneezing, then Myles broke through for a second.

'It's not a spear, idiot. It's a pike. You call yourself a warrior.'

Then the features twisted again and Gobdaw was back. 'Shaddup, boy. I'm in charge of this body.'

This brief breakthrough gave Artemis hope. His brother was in there somewhere and he hadn't lost a lick of his acid tongue.

Gobdaw tucked the pike under the crook of his good arm and charged. The pike seemed as big as a jousting lance in his hand. He fanned the tip from side to side in a flashing arc, slicing Holly's elbow before she could sidestep the attack.

The wound was not serious, but it was painful and Holly did not have the magic for a quick heal.

'By Danu's Beard,' said Gobdaw. 'First blood to the Berserkers.'

The two soldiers faced each other a second time, but now Holly was backed into the corner with less room to manoeuvre and Gobdaw's deadened arm was coming back to life. The Berserker grabbed the pike with both hands, increasing the speed and steadiness of his sweep. He inched closer, giving Holly no space to make a move.

'I take no pleasure in this,' he said. 'But then I don't feel much sorrow either. You chose your worm, elf.'

Chose your worm was a reference to the fairy game of chewing root worms. A group of kids would dig up five worms and each would choose one to pop in their mouth. Statistically at least one of the worms would be in its dying cycle and have begun to rot from the inside, so one of the kids would be in for a putrid mouthful. But it didn't matter, because the rules of the game dictated that you had to swallow the lot regardless. A human equivalent of this saying would be: *You made your bed so now you have to lie in it.*

This looks bad, thought Holly. *I don't see any way of taking out Gobdaw without hurting Myles.*

Suddenly Artemis waved his arms and shouted, 'Myles! The tip of that pike is steel. Where does steel sit on the periodic table?'

Gobdaw's features twisted and Myles emerged. 'Artemis, steel isn't on the table. It is not an element as you well know. It is composed of two elements: carbon and iron.'

Towards the end of the last sentence Gobdaw took control once more, just in time to feel his arms being yanked behind his back and to hear the sounds of the plasti-cuffs ratcheting over his wrists.

'You tricked me,' he said, not sure exactly how he'd been hoodwinked.

'Sorry, Gobdaw,' said Holly, lifting him by the collar. 'The human doesn't play fair.'

'When did humans ever play fair?' muttered Gobdaw, who at that moment would have gladly vacated young Myles Fowl's head if another host had been available. But then he realized how clever Artemis had been.

That is not a bad strategy, he thought. *Perhaps I can show the butterfly its own wings and turn that human's trick against him.*

Suddenly Myles's eyes rolled back in his head and he hung slack in Holly's arms.

'I think Gobdaw has gone,' said Holly. 'Artemis, it looks like you have your brother back.'

Butler pursued Bellico into the office where she was two steps away from sabotaging the siege box. Her fist was drawn back for the strike when Butler hooked his own arm through the crook of her elbow and they spun like dancers away from the security terminal and on to the rug. Bellico's arm slipped free and she pirouetted to the wall.

'You're finished,' said Butler. 'Why don't you release my sister?'

'Both of us will die first, human!' said Bellico, circling warily.

Butler stood his ground. 'If you have access to my sister's memories, have a flick through them. You can never defeat me. She never has and you never will.'

Bellico froze for a moment, accessing the database of Juliet's mind. It was true, Butler had easily defeated his sister a thousand times. His talents were far superior to hers . . . but wait. There was a vision of the big human on his back, with pain on his brow. He was speaking:

You really nailed me with that move, Jules. It came out of nowhere. How is your big old brother supposed to defend himself against that?

Bellico's eyes flashed. *Which move was the big human speaking of?*

She dug a little deeper and found a fifty-four-step kata that Juliet Butler had developed herself, loosely based on the teachings of Kanō Jigorō, the founder of judo.

I have found the human's weak spot.

Bellico allowed the memory to fully surface and send instructions to the body. Juliet's limbs began to seamlessly perform the kata.

Butler frowned and dropped into a boxer's defensive stance. 'Hey, what are you doing?'

Bellico did not answer. There was anxiety in the Mud Man's voice and that was enough to assure Bellico that she had chosen the correct course of action. She swept around

the office like a dancer, her speed increasing with each revolution.

'Stand still!' said Butler, struggling to keep her in his
eyeline. 'You can't win!'

Bellico could win, she was certain of it. This old man was
no match for the young powerful body she inhabited. Faster
and faster she spun, her feet barely touching the ground, air
whistling through the jade ring in her long ponytail.

'I'll give you one more chance, Juliet, or whoever the hell
you are. Then I will have to hurt you.'

He was bluffing. A scared obvious bluff.

I will win, thought Bellico, feeling invulnerable now.

On the fifty-second step, Bellico launched herself high
into the air backwards, then braced her hind leg against the
wall, switching direction and increasing her altitude. She
descended on Butler in a blur of speed, her heel aimed like
an arrowhead at the nerve cluster in his neck.

Once the human is disabled, I will destroy the siege box, thought
Bellico, already celebrating her victory.

Butler slapped her heel with his left palm and jabbed
the fingers of his right hand into Bellico's gut, just hard
enough to wind her, and there is not a warrior on the
planet who can fight when they cannot breathe. Bellico
dropped like a sack of stones to the rug and lay whooping
in the foetal position.

'How?' she gasped. 'How?'

Butler lifted her by the collar. 'That day was Juliet's birthday. I let her win.'

He marched her towards the security panel and had typed in the lockdown sequence when he heard a snare-drum roll of claws clicking on the floor behind him. He recognized the pattern instantly.

The hound is attacking me.

But he was wrong. The hound hurled itself at Bellico, propelling them both underneath the descending steel shutter and through the office window, leaving Butler with a patch of material in his hand. He stared blankly at the fallen shutter, thinking.

I did not even see her land. I don't know if my sister is alive or dead.

He hurried to Artemis's desk and activated the security cameras, just in time to see Juliet pat the dog and limp out of sight – back towards Opal, he supposed.

'Alive for now,' muttered the bodyguard.

And, where there was life, there was hope. For a few more hours at least.

CHAPTER II: **DEATH BY BUNNY**

NOBODY, human or fairy, had been declared dead more times than Mulch Diggums, and it was a record he was inordinately proud of. In Mulch's eyes, being declared dead by the LEP was just a less embarrassing way for them to admit that he had escaped for the umpteenth time. In the Sozzled Parrot fugitives' bar, LEP death certificates were printed up and tacked to the Wall of Heroes.

Mulch had fond memories of the very first time he had faked his own death to throw police officers off his trail.

My gods, could that really be over two hundred years ago now? Time flies faster than wind through a bum-flap, as Grandmother used to say, bless her.

He'd been on a job with his cousin Nord, on Haven's moneyed mountain, when the homeowner had come home unexpectedly from the convention in Atlantis where he was supposed to be living it up on taxpayers' gold for two more days.

I hate it when they come home early, thought Mulch. *Why do people do that when there's a very good chance they will find burglars in their sitting rooms?*

Anyway, the homeowner happened to be ex-law enforcement and the registered owner of a buzz baton, which he had used on the dwarf cousins with great gusto. Nord managed to escape into their tunnel, but Mulch had been forced to clutch his heart, faking a cardiac, and then crash through a window, playing dead all the way down to the river below.

Corpsing was the hard part, remembered Mulch. *There is nothing more unnatural than keeping your arms slack when they want to be pin-wheeling.*

LEP had interviewed the ex-law-enforcement homeowner who had emphatically claimed that: *Yeah, I killed him. It was an accident of course; I only meant to maim that dwarf then kick him senseless, but you can put that sucker down as dead. Nobody can corpse for three storeys.*

And so Mulch Diggums was declared deceased for the first time. There would be twelve more official occasions where people mistakenly thought Mulch had flown the final coop, and he was, unbeknownst to himself, tunnelling towards an unofficial one at this very moment.

His instructions were simple enough. Dig a parallel tunnel to the one he had recently collapsed, sneak into the crashed *Cupid*, and then steal any weapons that were in the locker. Dig, sneak and steal. Three of Mulch's four favourite verbs.

I do not know why I am doing this, Mulch thought as he tunnelled. *I should be heading down to the crust to find myself a nice crevice. They say that Opal's death wave will only kill humans, but why take such irresponsible chances with the great gift of life?*

Mulch knew that this reasoning was a crock of troll patties, but he found he could dig better if he was annoyed, even if he was the object of his own annoyance. And so the dwarf fumed silently as he churned through the earth towards the shuttle wreck.

Six metres up and thirty metres to the south, Opal Koboi was sinking her hands into the deep algebraic enchantments of the second Berserker lock. Symbols wrapped themselves like glow-worms round her fingers and surrendered their power one by one as she discovered their secrets. Some could be beaten into submission by the sheer force of her black magic, but others had to be coaxed with sly hexes or magical tickles.

I am close, she thought. *I can feel the Earth's strength.*

The wave of death would be in the form of geothermal energy, she presumed, and would be drawn from the entire planet's resources and not just the shallow hydrothermal reservoirs. This would put quite a dent in the world's reserves and could theoretically plunge the Earth into another ice age.

We'll survive, she thought callously. *I have some nice heated boots in storage.*

The work was challenging but manageable and it gave Opal some satisfaction to know that she was the only fairy alive who had done enough research on the intricacies of ancient magicks to open the second lock. The first had been simple – that had required little more than a blast of black magic – but the second needed an encyclopaedic knowledge of spellcraft.

That techno-fool Foaly would never have managed this. Not in a million years.

Opal was not aware of it, but so self-satisfied was she at that moment that she rolled her shoulders and made a purring noise.

Everything is going so well.

This plan had been outlandish, even by her standards, but unlikely or not all the elements were falling into place. Her initial thought had been to sacrifice her younger self and use the ill-gotten power to escape from the Deeps. It then occurred to her that this power would have to be jettisoned almost immediately to prevent it eating her alive, so why not put it to good use?

Opportunity had presented itself to Opal when her younger self had made telepathic contact.

One morning Opal had been deep in a cleansing coma and – *ping!* – suddenly there was a voice in her head calling her sister and asking for help. It had occurred to her briefly that she could in fact be insane, but, little by little, the information filtered through. *A younger Opal had followed Artemis Fowl from the past.*

I have no memory of this, Opal realized. *Therefore my younger self must have been captured and sent back with these events wiped from her mind.*

Unless . . .

Unless the timeline *had* split. Then anything was possible.

Opal was surprised to find her younger self a little whiney, even boring. Had she really been so self-absorbed?

It's all me, me, me, thought Opal. *I injured my leg in the explosion. My magic is fading. I need to get back to my own time.*

None of this was in the least helpful to Opal stuck in her prison.

What you need to do is get me out of here, she broadcast to her younger self. *Then we can see to your injuries and send you home.*

But how to accomplish this? That darned centaur Foaly had incarcerated her in the most technologically advanced cell in the world.

The answer was simple: *I have to force them to release me because the alternative would be simply too horrible to even contemplate.*

Opal wrestled with the problem for several minutes before she accepted that the younger Opal would have to be sacrificed and, once that piece of the puzzle clunked into place, she quickly built the rest of the plan around it.

Pip and Kip were two sleeper gnomes who worked in the civil service. The Council had sent them to do an audit on one of her factory's accounts a few years ago and Opal had hypnotized them using forbidden runes and dark magic. All it took was a phone call from young Opal to activate their loyalty, even at the cost of one or both of their lives. She broadcast instructions to young Opal, telling her exactly how to set up the fake kidnapping and how to use the traces of dark magic still left in her system to find the legendary Berserker Gate. The gate was the way back to the past – or at least that was the story Opal sent out.

Younger Opal could not know but the instructions for Pip and Kip were very specific for a reason. Hidden inside the words was a simple code, which Opal had implanted along with their loyalty bonds. If young Opal had thought to write down all the letters that corresponded to prime numbers, she would have found a far more sinister message than the one she thought she was delivering: *Kill the hostage when time runs out.*

You had to keep it simple for civil servants.

Everything had worked out exactly as she had foreseen, except for the arrival of Fowl and Short. But, in a way, that too was a stroke of good fortune. Now she could kill them up close and personal.

Every cloud has a silver lining.

Suddenly Opal felt her stomach churn as a wave of nausea assailed her. The pixie's first thought was that the black magic was struggling with her own antibodies, but then she realized that the source was external.

Something offends my enhanced magical senses, she thought. *Something over there.*

The wrecked shuttle stood beyond the circle of warriors that stood guard over their queen.

Below the shuttle. Something is coated in a substance that sickens me.

It was that cursed dwarf, sticking his bum-flap in where it didn't belong and not for the first time.

Opal scowled. How many times must she bear humiliation from a flatulent dwarf? It was intolerable.

Sent to retrieve weapons from the ship, no doubt.

Opal raised her gaze fifteen degrees to the shuttle. Crushed though the *Cupid* was, her sixth sense could see a corona of power winding round the fuselage like a fat snake. This particular wavelength would not help to open the second lock, but it could certainly provide enough juice for an extremely visible demonstration of her power.

Opal withdrew a hand from the sluggishly heaving rock and formed the fingers into a claw, arranging the molecules to attract any energy inside the *Cupid*. The power left the vehicle in a glowing morass, shrinking the *Cupid* to a wizened wreck and hovering in the air over the awed Berserkers.

'See what your queen can accomplish!' she cried, eyes bright. Her tiny fingers twirled, manipulating the energy into a sharp wedge which she sent crashing through the earth to where the dwarf laboured. There was a solid thump and a spume of dirt and rocks jetted skywards, leaving a scorched crater in their wake.

Opal returned her attention to the second lock. 'Can you see the dwarf?' she asked Oro, who stood peering into the hole.

'I see one foot and some blood. The foot is jittering about, so he's still alive. I'll go and bring him up.'

'No,' said Opal. 'You do not leave Mummy's sight. Send the earth creatures to kill him.'

If the fairy bonds did not have Oro's free will in such a tight bind, he would have taken Opal to task for repeatedly disrespecting her elders, but, as it was, even the thought of reprimanding his queen cost him a severe stomach cramp.

When the pain passed, he raised two fingers to his lips to whistle for his diggers. He found out that it was not an easy thing to whistle with strange fingers, and all that emerged from his mouth was a watery slobbering noise.

'Don't know that signal, chief,' said Yezhwi Khan, who had once been a pretty handy axe gnome. 'Is that tea break?'

'No!' shouted Oro. 'I need my diggers. Gather round.'

A dozen rabbits hopped quickly to bunch at his feet. Their little whiskers quivered with anticipation of finally seeing some action.

'Get the dwarf,' Oro ordered. 'I would say bring him back alive, but you do not really have the skills for parlay.'

The rabbits thumped their hind legs in agreement.

'So the order is simple,' said Oro, with a touch of regret. 'Kill him.'

The rabbits piled en masse into the hole, eagerly scrabbling towards the injured dwarf.

Death by bunny, thought Oro. *Not a nice way to go.*

Oro did not wish to look. Dwarfs were part of the fairy world and in other circumstances they could have been allies. From behind him he heard the crunch of bone and the rattled whoosh of earth collapsing. Oro shuddered. He would face a troll any day before a bunch of carnivorous rabbits.

On the dais, Opal felt a load lift from her heart as another enemy suffered.

Soon it will be your turn to suffer, Foaly, she thought. *But death would be too easy for you. Perhaps you are already suffering. Perhaps your lovely wife has already opened the gift my little gnomes sent to her.*

Opal sang a little ditty as she worked on the second lock.

> *'Hey, hey, hey,*
> *This is the day,*
> *Things are gonna go my way.'*

Opal was not consciously aware of it, but this was a popular song from the Pip and Kip show.

CHAPTER 12: **THE DORK POSSE**

 THINGS were as grim as they had ever been in Haven City. Even the groups of empath elves who could clearly perceive residual images from bygone millennia, and who liked to lecture school fairies on how life was a bucket of sweet chillies compared to how it used to be in the prospecting days, had to admit that this was the darkest day in Haven's history.

The citizens of Haven were weathering their darkest night, made darker still by the absence of mains power, which meant the only lights were the emergency lamps powered by the old geothermal generators. Dwarf spit had suddenly become a very valuable commodity and many of Mulch's relatives could be seen roving the refugee camp that had sprung up around the statue of Frond, selling jars of luminous spit for an ingot or two.

The LEP were coping the best they could, working in most

cases with limited equipment. The main problem was coordination. The net of cameras and wireless hubs, suspended on gossamer wire from the cavern ceiling, had been upgraded three years previously with lenses from Koboi Labs. The entire network had caught fire and rained down on the citizens of Haven, branding many of them with a lattice of scars. This meant that the LEP were operating without intelligence, and relying on old radios for audio communication. Some of the younger police officers had never been in the field without full support from their precious helmets and were feeling a little exposed without constant updates of information from Police Plaza.

Fifty per cent of the force was currently committed to fighting a huge fire at Koboi Labs, which had been taken over by the Krom automobile company. The explosion and subsequent fire had collapsed a large section of the underground cavern and a pressure leak was barely being contained by plasti-gel cannons. The LEP had bulldozed through the rubble and bolstered the roof with pneumatic columns, but the fire was still liquefying the metal struts, and several types of toxic gas were jetting from cylinders around the compound.

Another ten per cent of the officers were rounding up escaped prisoners from Howler's Peak, which had, until its containment field flickered out, housed most of the criminal goblin kingpins behind Haven's organized crime syndicates as well as their enforcers and racketeers. These goblins were now scurrying around the backstreets of goblin town with their subcutaneous sleeper tags not responding to the frantic signals being repeatedly sent from headquarters. A few more recently tagged goblins were unfortunate enough to have second-generation tags, which exploded inside their scalps, blowing holes in their skulls small enough to plug with a penny but large enough to be fatal to the cold-blooded creatures.

More of the officers were up to their eyeballs in the miscellaneous rescues, crowd control and pursuit of opportunistic felons that went with a catastrophe of this magnitude.

And the rest of the LEP fairies had been put out of action by the explosion of the free mobile phones they had recently won in a competition, which they couldn't remember entering, sent no doubt by Opal's minions. In this manner, the evil pixie had managed to take out most of the Council, effectively crippling the People's government in this time of emergency.

Foaly and his brainiacs were left in Police Plaza, trying to somehow revive a network that had literally been fried. Commander Kelp had barely paused on his way out the door to issue instructions to the centaur.

'Just get the tech working,' he said, strapping on a fourth holster. 'Quick as you can.'

'You don't understand!' Foaly objected.

Trouble cut him off with a chop of his hand through the air. 'I never understand. That's why we pay you and your dork posse.'

Foaly objected again. 'They are not dorks!'

Trouble found space for yet another holster. 'Really? That guy brings a beanie toy to work every day. And your nephew, Mayne, speaks fluent Unicorn.'

'They're not *all* dorks,' said Foaly, correcting himself.

'Just get this city working again,' said Trouble. 'Lives depend on it.'

Foaly blocked the commander's way. 'You do understand that the old network is vaporized? Are you giving me free rein, to coin an offensive phrase, to do whatever I need to do?'

Trouble brushed him aside. 'Do whatever you need to do.'

Foaly almost grinned.

Whatever I need to do.

Foaly knew that the secret of a successful product launch was often in the name. A catchy name is more likely to pique the investors' curiosity and help the new invention to take off, whereas some plodding series of letters and numbers will put everyone to sleep and ensure the product crashes and burns.

The lab name for Foaly's latest pet project was Aerial Radiation-Coded Light-Sensitive Surveillance Pterygota 2.0, which the centaur knew had far too many syllables for potential investors. Rich people liked to feel *cool*, and embarrassing themselves by mispronouncing that mouthful was never going to help them to achieve that, so Foaly nicknamed the little guys ARClights.

The ARClights were the latest in a series of experimental bio-mech organisms that Foaly was convinced were the future of technology. The centaur had met considerable resistance from the Council on ethical grounds because he was marrying technology to living beings, even though he argued that most of the LEP officers now had little chips implanted in their cerebellums to help them control their helmets. The Council's counter-argument was that the officers could choose whether or not to have the implants, whereas Foaly's little experiments were grown that way.

And so Foaly had not been given the go-ahead for public trials. Which is not to say that he hadn't conducted any. He just hadn't released his precious ARClights in public, not in the fairy public at any rate. On the Fowl Estate, now that was another matter.

The entire ARClight project was contained in a single battered field-kit case hidden in plain view on top of a locker in the lab. Foaly reared up on his hind legs to snag the case and plonked it down on his workstation.

His nephew, Mayne, clopped up behind him to see what was going on. '*Dung navarr, Oncle?*' he said.

'No unicorn speak today, Mayne,' said Foaly, settling into his modified office harness. 'I don't have time.'

Mayne folded his arms. 'The unicorns are our cousins, Uncle. We should respect their tongue.'

Foaly moved closer to the case so the scanner could identify him and pop the locks. 'I do respect the unicorns, Mayne.

But real unicorns cannot talk. That gibberish you're spouting came from a mini-series.'

'Written by an *empath*,' said Mayne pointedly.

Foaly opened the case. 'Listen, nephew, if you want to strap a horn to your forehead and go to conventions on the weekends, that's completely fine. But today I need you in *this* universe. Understood?'

'Understood,' said Mayne grumpily. His mood lifted when he saw what was in the case. 'Are those Critters?'

'No,' said Foaly. 'Critters are micro-organisms. These are ARClights. The next generation.'

Mayne remembered something. 'You were refused permission for trials with those, weren't you?'

It irritated Foaly immensely that a centaur of his genius was being forced to justify himself to an assistant for the sake of relations with his sister.

'I got permission just now, from Commander Kelp. It's all on video.'

'Wow,' said Mayne. 'In that case, let's see those little fellows in action.'

Maybe he's not so bad, thought Foaly, keying in the activation code on an old-fashioned manual keyboard in the case.

Once the code was punched in, the case synched with the lab's wall screen, splitting it into a dozen blank boxes. This was nothing particularly special and would have absolutely no one clapping their hands and saying *Ooooh*. What *would* have people applauding and gushing was the swarm of miniature genetically modified dragonflies waking up inside the case. The insects shook their sleepy heads and set their wings buzzing, then lifted off in perfect synchronized formation to hover at Foaly's eye level.

'Oooh,' said Mayne, clapping his hands.

'Just wait,' said Foaly, activating the little dragonflies' sensors. 'Prepare to be amazed.'

The cloud of dragonflies jittered as though suddenly charged and their tiny eyes glowed green. Eleven of the twelve on-screen boxes displayed composite 3D views of Foaly, stitched together from the viewpoint of each insect. Not only did the insects read the visible spectrum but also infra-red, UV and thermal. A constantly updating stream of data scrolled down the side of the screens, displaying reams of information on Foaly's heart rate, blood pressure, pulse and gas emissions.

'These little beauties can go anywhere and see everything. They can glean information from every microbe. And all anyone can see is a swarm of dragonflies. My little ARClights could fly through the X-ray in an airport and no one could tell they are stuffed with bio-tech. They go where I send them and spy on who I tell them to.'

Mayne pointed at a corner of the screen. 'That section is blank.'

Foaly harrumphed. 'I did a trial in Fowl Manor. And Artemis somehow detected the virtually undetectable. I imagine my beauties are lying in pieces under an electron microscope in his laboratory.'

'I didn't read that in any report.'

'No. I forgot to mention it. That trial wasn't exactly an unqualified success, but this one will be.'

Foaly's fingers were clicking blurs on the keyboard. 'Once I program in the mission parameters, then my ARClights will have citywide surveillance restored in minutes.' Foaly instructed a single bug to land on his index finger. 'You, my little fellow, are special, because you will be going to my home, just to make sure my beloved Caballine is all right.'

Mayne leaned in, peering at the little bug. 'You can do that?'

Foaly wiggled his finger and the bug flew off, winding sideways through a vent.

'I can do whatever I like. They are even coded to my voice. Watch.' Foaly leaned back in his chair and cleared his throat. 'ARClight activation code alpha alpha one. I am Foaly. Foaly is my name. Immediate deployment to downtown Haven. Scenario three. All sections. Citywide disaster. Fly, my pretties, fly.'

The ARClights moved like a shoal of silver fish through water, gliding through the air in perfect synchronized flight, then forming into a tight cylinder and shooting through the vent. Their wings skittered against the chute wall, sending back data from every centimetre covered.

The theatricality appealed to Mayne's graphic-novel-loving sensibility. 'Fly, my pretties, fly. Cool. Did you make that up yourself?'

Foaly began analysing the data that was already flooding in from his ARClights.

'Absolutely,' he said. 'Every word a Foaly original.'

The ARClights could be steered manually or, if that function was off-line, they would fly to preordained irradiated spots on the cavern roof. The tiny bio-tech insects performed perfectly, and within minutes Foaly had a functioning network suspended above Haven that could be manipulated with a word or gesture.

'Now, Mayne,' he said to his nephew. 'I want you to take over here and feed information to Commander Kelp over the –' he shuddered – 'radio. I am going to take a minute to check on your Aunty Caballine.'

'*Mak dak jiball, Oncle,*' said Mayne, saluting. Something else actual unicorns could not do.

Humans have a saying that *beauty is in the eye of the beholder*, which basically means if you *think* it's beautiful, then it *is* beautiful. The elfin version of this saying was composed by the great poet B.O. Selecta who said that: *Even the plainest of the plain shall deign to reign*, which critics have always thought was a bit rhymey. The dwarf version of the maxim is: *If it don't stink, marry it*, which is slightly less romantic, but the gist is the same.

Foaly had no need of these sayings, for in his mind beauty was personified by his wife, Caballine. If anyone had ever asked him for a definition of beauty, he would simply have directed their gaze to his wrist and then activated the hologram crystal built into his wrist computer, projecting a revolving CG rendering of his wife into mid-air.

᚛ᚒᚔᚑᚔᚠᚏᚔᚄᚓᚔᚑᚄᚑᚋᚑᚃᚑᚏᚔᚏᚔᚑ᚜

Foaly was so in love with his wife that he sighed whenever Caballine crossed his mind, which was several times an hour. As far as the centaur was concerned, he had found his soulmate.

Love had tugged Foaly's fetlock relatively late in life. When all the other centaurs had been gambolling around the simpasture, pawing the dirt, texting the fillies and sending their chosen ones candied carrots, Foaly had been up to his armpits in laboratory equipment, trying to get his radical inventions out of his head and into the real world. By the time he realized that love might be passing him by, it had already disappeared over the horizon. So the centaur convinced himself that he didn't need companionship and was content to live for his job and work friends.

Then, when Holly Short was missing in another dimension, he met Caballine in Police Plaza. At least that was what he told everyone. *Met* might be a slightly misleading verb to use as it implies that the situation was pleasant, or at least non-violent. What actually happened was that one of Foaly's face-recognition software programs malfunctioned in a bank camera and identified Caballine as a goblin bank robber. She was immediately pounced on by the security-guard jumbo pixies and *ridden* to Police Plaza. The ultimate ignominy for a centaur.

By the time the entire mess was traced back to software error, Caballine had been confined to a gel cell for over three hours. She had missed her mother's birthday high tea and was extremely anxious to throttle the person responsible for the mix-up. Foaly was told by Commander Kelp in no uncertain terms to get down to the holding cells and take responsibility for his foul-up.

Foaly trudged down there, ready to spout one of a dozen standard excuses, all of which evaporated when he came face to face with Caballine in the hospitality suite. Foaly didn't meet many centaurs and he certainly would never bump into one as beautiful as Caballine, with her chestnut eyes, strong wide nose and glossy hair down to her waist.

'Just my luck,' he blurted, without thinking. 'That's just typical of my luck.'

Caballine had herself all psyched up to tear metaphorical strips off the hide of whatever imbecile had been responsible for her incarceration, and perhaps actual strips too, but Foaly's reaction gave her pause and she decided to give him one chance to dig himself out of the hole he was in.

'What is just typical of your luck?' she said, regarding him frankly, letting him know that his answer better be a good one.

Foaly knew the pressure was on and so thought carefully before answering.

'It's just typical of my luck,' he said eventually, 'that I finally meet someone as beautiful as you, and all you want to do is kill me.'

This was a pretty good line and, judging by the misery in Foaly's eyes, there was also more than a grain of truth in it.

Caballine decided to take pity on the dejected centaur before her and dial down her antagonism a few notches, but it was too early to let Foaly off the hook completely.

'And why wouldn't I want to kill you? You think I look like a criminal.'

'I don't think that. I would never think that.'

'Really? Because the algorithm that identified me as a goblin bank robber is based on your thought patterns.'

This lady is smart, Foaly realized. *Smart and gorgeous.*

'True,' he said. 'But I imagine there were secondary factors involved.'

'Such as?'

Foaly decided to go for broke. He felt an attraction towards this centaur that was short-circuiting his brain. The closest he could come to describing the sensation was a sustained low-level electrical shock, like the ones he inflicted on volunteers in his sleep-deprivation experiments.

'Such as my machine is incredibly stupid because you are the opposite of a goblin bank robber.'

Caballine was amused but not won over just yet.

'Which is?'

'Which is a non-goblin deposit-account holder making a deposit.'

'Which is what I am, dummy.'

Foaly flinched. 'What?'

'Dummy. Your machine is a dummy.'

'Yes. Absolutely. I will have it disassembled immediately and reassembled as a toaster.'

Caballine bit her lip and could conceivably have been holding back a smile.

'That's a start. But you still have a long way to go before we're quits.'

'I understand. If you have any capital crimes in your past, I could wipe them from your record. In fact, if you'd like to disappear altogether, I could arrange that.' Foaly rethought this last sentence. 'That sounded like I was going to have you killed, which I totally am not. The last thing I would ever do is have you killed. Quite the opposite.'

Caballine took her handbag from the back of a chair and slung it across her fringed blouse. 'You are quite fond of opposites, Mister Foaly. What is the opposite of having me killed?'

Foaly met her gaze for the first time. 'Keeping you happy and alive forever.'

Caballine moved to leave and Foaly thought, *Stupid donkey. You blew it*.

But she stopped at the door and threw Foaly a lifeline.

'I do have a parking ticket that I did pay, but your machines seem to have it in for me and they swear I didn't. You could have a look at that.'

'No problem,' said Foaly. 'Consider it done and that machine compacted.'

'I'm going to tell all my friends about this,' said Caballine, already leaving the room, 'when I see them at the Hoovre Gallery launch this weekend. Do you like art, Mister Foaly?'

Foaly stood there for a full minute after she was gone,

staring at the spot where Caballine's head had been when she'd last spoken. Later on, he had to rewind the suite's surveillance footage to make sure Caballine had kind of, sort of, asked him on a date.

And now they were married and Foaly considered himself the luckiest dummy in the world and, even though the city was mired in a crisis the likes of which had never before been visited on the subterranean metropolis, he had no hesitation in taking a moment to check on his gorgeous wife who would probably be at this moment at home worrying about him.

Caballine, he thought. *I will be with you soon.*

Since their wedding ritual Foaly and his wife had shared a mental bond like the one often experienced by twins.

I know she is alive, he thought.

But that was all he knew. She could be hurt, trapped, distressed or in danger. Foaly did not know. And he had to know.

The ARClight Foaly had dispatched to check on Caballine had been built especially for that purpose and knew exactly where to go. Foaly had months ago painted a corner of the kitchen ceiling with a laser that would attract the bug from hundreds of kilometres away if need be.

Foaly shunted the other ARClight feeds to the main situations room where Mayne could monitor them and then concentrated on Caballine's bug.

Fly, my pretty. Fly.

The modified dragonfly zipped through Police Plaza's vent system and out over the city, darting through the chaos that permeated the streets and buildings. Fires flared in the piazza and on the freeway. The billboards that lined every street were reduced to carbonized frames and floodwater filled the sunken open-air amphitheatre as far as Row H.

Mayne can handle that for five minutes, thought Foaly. *I am coming, Caballine.*

The ARClight buzzed beyond the central plaza to the southern suburb, which had more of a rural feel. Genetically modified trees grew in small copses and there were even controlled amounts of woodland creatures that were carefully monitored and released above ground when they multiplied to nuisance levels. The dwellings here were modest, less modern in their architecture, and outside the evacuation zone. Foaly and Caballine lived in a small split-level with adobe walls and curved windows. The colour scheme was autumnal throughout and the decor had always been a little *back to nature* for Foaly's taste though he would never dream of mentioning it.

Foaly pulled his v-board towards him and expertly controlled the little bug with numerical co-ordinates though it would have been easier to use a joystick or even voice control. It was ironic that someone who was responsible for so many technological breakthroughs still preferred to use an ancient virtual keyboard that he had made from a window frame when he was in university.

⊕▯◊⟲•⟲♨•◉ ⚿◈▯ ◉ ⟩♒♒⚥•◉•♊⚿

The top half of the door was ajar and so Foaly had his ARClight dip inside the lobby, which was decorated with woven wall hangings depicting great moments in centaurian history such as the discovery of fire by King Thurgood and the accidental discovery of penicillin by the stable hand, Shammy Sod, whose name had entered the popular vernacular to mean an extremely lucky person, for example: *He's won the lottery for the second time, the shammy sod.*

The dragonfly whirred along the corridor to find Caballine sitting on her yoga blanket staring at the mobile phone in her hand. She looked shaken but unhurt and was scrolling through the menus on her screen looking for a network.

You will have no luck there, my love, thought Foaly, then sent a text to her phone directly from the ARClight.

There's a little dragonfly watching over you, said the text. Caballine read it and raised her face, searching for the bug. Foaly set the eyes flashing green to help her. Foaly's wife raised her hand and the bug swooped down to land on her finger.

'My clever husband,' she said, smiling. 'What is happening to our city?'

Foaly sent another message, and made a mental note to add a voice box to the next version of the ARClights.

You are safe at home. We have had some major explosions, but all is under control.

Caballine nodded. 'Will you be home soon?' she asked the bug.

Not soon. It could be a long night.

'Don't worry, honey. I know they need you. Is Holly OK?'

I don't know. We've lost contact, but if anyone can look after herself it's Holly Short.

Caballine lifted her finger and the dragonfly hovered before her face. 'You need to look after yourself too, Mister Technical Consultant.'

I will, texted Foaly.

Caballine took a beribboned box from the low table. 'While I'm waiting for you, I will open this lovely gift that someone sent to me, you romantic centaur.'

Back in the lab, Foaly felt a stab of jealousy. A gift? Who would have sent a present? His jealousy was quickly trumped by anxiety. After all, this was the day of Opal Koboi's great revenge and there was no one the pixie hated more than him.

Don't open it, he sent quickly. *I did not send it and bad things are happening.*

But Caballine did not need to open the box for it was both time- and DNA-coded, and, as soon as she touched it, the omni-sensor on the side scanned her finger and set the opening mechanism whirring. The lid pinged away from the box, spinning away to slap the wall, and inside was . . . nothing. Literally nothing. A black absence that seemed to repel ambient light.

Caballine peered into the box. 'What is this?' she asked. 'One of your gizmos?' Which was as much as Foaly heard because the blackness or whatever it was shorted out the ARClight, leaving Foaly ignorant as to his wife's fate.

'No!' he blurted. 'No. No.'

Something was happening. Something sinister. Opal had decided to target Caballine specifically to torture him. He was sure of it. The pixie's accomplice, whoever it was, had mailed his wife this seemingly innocuous box, but it was far from harmless; Foaly would bet his two hundred plus patents on it.

What has she done?

The centaur agonized over the question for about five seconds until Mayne stuck his head into the room.

'We have something from the ARClights. I think I should push it across to your screens.'

Foaly stamped a hoof. 'Not now, stupid pony. Caballine is in danger.'

'You need to see this,' said Mayne, standing his ground.

Something in his nephew's tone, a bite of steel that hinted at the centaur this boy would become, made Foaly look up. 'Very well. Shunt it across.'

The screens immediately came to life with overhead shots of Haven from dozens of angles. Each shot was black and white but for clusters of red dots.

'The dots are the escaped goblin sleeper/seekers,' explained Mayne. 'The ARClights can detect their radiation signatures, but not activate them.'

'But this is good news,' said Foaly irritably. 'Send the co-ordinates to the agents on the ground.'

'They were moving randomly, but seconds ago they all changed direction, at exactly the same time.'

Foaly knew then what Opal had done, how her weapon had got past the courier's security scans. She had used a sonix bomb.

'And they're headed for my house,' he said.

Mayne swallowed. 'Exactly. Just as fast as they can run. The first group will arrive in less than five minutes.'

At this point, Mayne was talking to thin air as Foaly had already galloped out through the side door.

CHAPTER 13: LUCKY DIP

 MYLES Fowl sat behind Artemis's desk in the mini office chair that his big brother had given to him as a birthday present. Artemis claimed it was custom built, but actually the chair came from Elf Aralto, the famous design store that specialized in beautiful yet practical furniture for elves.

Myles was ratcheted up high sipping his favourite beverage: acai juice from a Martini glass. Two ice cubes, no straw.

'This is my favourite drink,' he said, dabbing the corner of his mouth with a napkin monogrammed with the Fowl motto *Aurum potestas est*. 'I know that because I am me again and not a fairy warrior.'

Artemis sat facing him in a similar but larger chair. 'So you keep saying, Myles. Should I call you Myles?'

'Yes, of course,' said Myles. 'Because that is who I am. Don't you believe me?'

'Of course I do, little man. I know my own brother's face when I see it.'

Myles toyed with the stem of his Martini glass. 'I need to talk with you alone, Arty. Can't Butler wait outside for a few moments? It's family talk.'

'Butler is family. You know that, brother.'

Myles pouted. 'I know but this is embarrassing.'

'Butler has seen it all before. We have no secrets from him.'

'Couldn't he just step outside for a minute?'

Butler stood silently behind Artemis, arms folded in an aggressive manner, which is not difficult to do with forearms the size of baked hams and sleeves that creak like old chairs.

'No, Myles. Butler stays.'

'Very well, Arty. You know best.'

Artemis leaned back in his chair. 'What happened to the Berserker inside you, Myles?'

The four-year-old shrugged. 'He went away. He was driving my head, then he left.'

'What was his name?'

Myles rolled his eyeballs upwards, checking out his own brain. 'Em . . . Mister Gobdaw, I believe.'

Artemis nodded like someone with a great deal of knowledge on the subject of this Gobdaw person would. 'Ah yes. Gobdaw. I have heard all about Gobdaw from our fairy friends.'

'I think he was called Gobdaw the Legendary Warrior.'

Artemis chuckled. 'I am sure he would like you to think that.'

'Because it's true,' said Myles, with a slight tension around his mouth.

'That's not what we heard, is it, Butler?'

Butler did not answer or gesture in any way, but somehow gave the impression of a negative response.

'No,' continued Artemis. 'What we heard from our fairy sources was that this Gobdaw person is a bit of a joke, to be frank.'

Myles's fingers squeaked on the neck of his glass. 'Joke? Who says that?'

'Everybody,' said Artemis, opening his laptop and checking the screen. 'It's in all the fairy history books. Here it is, look. Gobdaw the Gullible they call him, which is nice because of the alliteration. There's another article that refers to your Berserker friend as Gobdaw the Stinkworm, which I believe is a term used to describe a person who gets blamed for everything. We humans would call that a fall guy, or a scapegoat.'

Myles's cheeks were rosy-red now. 'Stinkworm? Stinkworm, you say? Why would I . . . why would Gobdaw be called a stinkworm?'

'It's sad really, pathetic, but apparently this Gobdaw character was the one who convinced his leader to let the entire Berserker unit get themselves buried around a gate.'

'A *magical* gate,' said Myles. 'That protected the fairy elements.'

'That is what they were told, but in truth the gate was nothing more than a pile of stones. A diversion leading

194

nowhere. The Berserkers spent ten thousand years guarding rocks.'

Myles kneaded his eyes. 'No. That's not . . . no. I saw it, in Gobdaw's memories. The gate is real.'

Artemis laughed softly. 'Gobdaw the Gullible. It's a little cruel. There's a rhyme, you know.'

'A rhyme?' rasped Myles, and rasping is unusual in four-year-olds.

'Oh yes, a schoolyard rhyme. Would you care to hear it?'

Myles seemed to be wrestling with his own face. 'No. Yes, tell me.'

'Very well. Here goes.' Artemis cleared his throat theatrically.

> '*Gobdaw, Gobdaw,*
> *Buried in the ground*
> *Watching over sticks and stones*
> *Never to be found.*'

Artemis hid a smile behind his hand. 'Children can be so cruel.'

Myles snapped in two ways. Firstly, his patience snapped, revealing him to be in fact Gobdaw, and, secondly, his fingers snapped the Martini glass's stem, leaving him with a deadly weapon clasped in his tiny fingers.

'Death to the humans!' he squealed in Gnommish, vaulting on to the desk and racing across towards Artemis.

In combat, Gobdaw liked to visualize his strikes just

before executing them. He found that it helped him to focus. So, in his mind, he leaped gracefully from the lip of the desk, landed on Artemis's chest and plunged his glass stiletto into Artemis's neck. This would have the double effect of killing the Mud Boy and also showering Gobdaw himself in arterial blood, which would help to make him look a little more fearsome.

What actually happened was a little different. Butler reached out and plucked Gobdaw from the air in mid-leap, flicked the glass stem from his grasp and then wrapped him firmly in the prison of his meaty arms.

Artemis leaned forward in his chair. 'There is a second verse,' he said. 'But perhaps now is not the time.'

Gobdaw struggled furiously, but he had been utterly neutralized. In desperation, he tried the fairy *mesmer*.

'*You will order Butler to release me,*' he intoned.

Artemis was amused. 'I doubt it,' he said. 'You have barely enough magic to keep Myles in check.'

'Just kill me then and be done with it,' said Gobdaw without the slightest quiver in his voice.

'I cannot kill my own brother so I need to get you out of his body without harming him.'

Gobdaw sneered. 'That's not possible, human. To get me you must slay the boy.'

'You are misinformed,' said Artemis. 'There is a way to exorcise your feisty soul without damaging Myles.'

'I would like to see you try it,' said Gobdaw with perhaps a glimmer of doubt in his eyes.

'Your wish is my command and so on and so forth,' said Artemis, pressing a button on the desk intercom. 'Bring it in, would you, Holly?'

The office door swung open, and a barrel trundled into the room, seemingly under its own power, until Holly was revealed behind it.

'I don't like this, Artemis,' she said, playing good cop, just as they had planned. 'This is nasty stuff. A person's soul might never get into the afterlife trapped in this gunk.'

'Traitorous elf,' said Gobdaw, kicking his little feet. 'You side with the humans.'

Holly waltzed the barrel trolley into the centre of the office, parking it on the wooden floor and not on one of the precious Afghan rugs that Artemis insisted on describing in great historical detail every time she visited the office.

'I side with the Earth,' she said, meeting Gobdaw's eyes. 'You have been in the ground for ten thousand years, warrior. Things have changed.'

'I have consulted my host's memories,' said Gobdaw sullenly. 'The humans have almost succeeded in destroying the entire planet. Things have not changed so much.'

Artemis rose from his chair and unscrewed the barrel lock. 'Do you also see a spacecraft which shoots bubbles from its exhaust?'

Gobdaw had a quick rifle in Myles's brain. 'Yes. Yes, I do. It's made of gold, is it not?'

'This is one of Myles's dream projects,' said Artemis slowly. 'Merely a dream. The bubble jet. If you delve deeper into my brother's imagination, you will find a robotic pony that does homework and a monkey that has been taught to speak. The boy you inhabit is highly intelligent, Gobdaw, but he is only four. At that age there is a very fine line between reality and imagination.'

Gobdaw's puffed-up chest deflated as he located these items in Myles's brain. 'Why are you telling me this, human?'

'I want you to see that you have been tricked. Opal Koboi is not the saviour she pretends to be. She is a convicted murderer who has escaped from prison. She would undo ten thousand years of peace.'

'Peace!' said Gobdaw, then barked a laugh. 'Peaceful humans? Even buried beneath the ground we felt your violence.' He wriggled in Butler's arms, a mini Artemis with black hair and dark suit. 'Do you call this *peace?*'

'No, and I apologize for your treatment, but I need my brother.' Artemis nodded at Butler who hoisted Gobdaw over the open barrel. The little Berserker laughed.

'For millennia I was in the earth. Do you think Gobdaw fears imprisonment in a barrel?'

'You will not be imprisoned. A quick dunking is all that will be necessary.'

Gobdaw looked down between his dangling feet. The barrel was filled with a viscous off-white liquid with congealed skin on its surface.

Holly turned her back. 'I don't care to watch this. I know what it feels like.'

'What is that?' asked Gobdaw nervously, feeling a cold sickness tipping at his toes from the stuff's aura.

'That is a gift from Opal,' said Artemis. 'A few years ago she stole a demon warlock's power using that very barrel. I stored it in the basement because you never know, correct?'

'What is it?' Gobdaw repeated.

'One of two natural magic inhibitors,' explained Artemis. 'Rendered animal fat. Disgusting stuff, I admit. And I am sorry to dunk my brother in it because he loves those shoes. We dip him down and the rendered fat traps your soul. Myles comes out intact and you are held in limbo for all eternity. Not exactly the reward you expected for your sacrifice.'

Something fizzed in the barrel, sending out tiny electrical bolts. 'What the *bleep* is that?' squeaked Gobdaw, panic causing his voice to shoot up an octave.

'Oh, that is the second natural magic inhibitor. I had my dwarf friend spit into the barrel just to give it that extra zing.'

Gobdaw managed to free one arm and beat it against Butler's bicep, but he might as well have been beating a boulder for all the effect it had.

'I will tell you nothing,' he said, his little pointed chin quivering.

Artemis held Gobdaw's shins so that they would drop cleanly into the vat. 'I know. Myles will tell me everything in a moment. I am sorry to do this to you, Gobdaw. You were a valiant warrior.'

'Not Gobdaw the Gullible then?'

'No,' admitted Artemis. 'That was a fiction to force you into revealing yourself. I had to be certain.'

Holly elbowed Artemis out of the way. 'Berserker, listen to me. I know you are bound to Opal and cannot betray her, but this human is going in the vat one way or another. So vacate his body and move on to the afterlife. There is nothing more you can do here. This is not a fitting end for a mighty Berserker.'

Gobdaw sagged in Butler's arms. 'Ten thousand years. So many lifetimes.'

Holly touched Gobdaw's cheek. 'You have done everything asked of you. To rest now is no betrayal.'

'Perhaps the human is toying with me. This is a bluff.'

Holly shuddered. 'The vat is no bluff. Opal imprisoned me in it once. It was as though my soul grew sick. Save yourself, I beg you.'

Artemis nodded towards Butler. 'Very well, no more delays. Drop him in.'

Butler shifted his grip to Gobdaw's shoulders, lowering him slowly.

'Wait, Artemis!' cried Holly. 'This is a fairy hero.'

'Sorry, Holly, there is no more time.'

Gobdaw's toes hit the gunk, sending vaporous tendrils curling round his legs, and he knew in that instant that this was no bluff. His soul would be imprisoned forever in the rendered fat.

'Forgive me, Oro,' he said, casting his eyes to the heavens.

Gobdaw's spirit peeled away from Myles and hovered in

the air, etched in silver. For several moments it hung, seeming confused and anxious, until a dollop of light blossomed
on its chest and began to swirl like a tiny cyclone. Gobdaw
smiled then and the hurt of the ages dropped from his face.
The spinning light grew larger with each revolution, spread-
ing its ripples to swallow Gobdaw's limbs, torso and finally
face, which at the moment of transition wore an expression
that could only be described as blissful.

For the observers, it was impossible to look upon that
ghostly face and not feel just a little jealous.

Bliss, thought Artemis. *Will I ever attain that state?*

Myles shattered the moment by kicking his feet vigorously,
sending ribbons of fat flying.

'Artemis! Get me out of here!' he ordered. 'These are my
favourite loafers!'

Artemis smiled. His little brother was back in control of
his own mind.

Myles would not speak until he had cleaned his shoes with a
wet wipe.

'That fairy ran through the mud in my shoes,' he
complained, sipping a second glass of acai juice. 'These are
kidskin shoes, Arty.'

'He's quite precocious, *n'est-ce pas?*' Artemis whispered
from the side of his mouth.

'Look who's talking, *plume de ma tante*,' Butler whispered
right back at him.

Artemis picked Myles up and sat him on the edge of the

desk. 'Very well, little man. I need you to tell me everything you remember from your possession. The memories will soon begin to dissipate. That means . . .'

'I know what *dissipate* means, Arty. I'm not three, for heaven's sake.'

Holly knew from long experience that shouting at Myles and Artemis would not hurry them along, but she also knew that she would feel better. And at the moment she felt glum and dirty after her treatment of one of the People's most illustrious warriors. Yelling at Mud Boys might be just the thing to cheer her up a little.

She settled for a prod at medium volume. 'Can you two get a move on? There is no time-stop in operation here. Morning is on the way.'

Myles waved at her. 'Hello, fairy. You sound funny. Have you been sucking helium? Helium is an inert monatomic gas by the way.'

Holly snorted. 'Oh, he's your brother all right. We need whatever information he has in his head, Artemis.'

Artemis nodded. 'Very well, Holly. I am working on it. Myles, what do you remember from Gobdaw's visit?'

'I remember everything,' replied Myles proudly. 'Would you like to hear about Opal's plan to destroy humanity or how she plans to open the second lock?'

Artemis took his brother's hand. 'I need to know everything, Myles. Start at the beginning.'

'I will start at the beginning, before the memories start to *dissipate*.'

Myles told them everything in language that was a decade beyond his years. He did not stray from the point or become confused, and at no point did he seem worried about his future. This was because Artemis had often told his little brother that intelligence will always win out in the end, and there was nobody more intelligent than Artemis.

Unfortunately, following the events of the past six hours, Artemis did not have the same faith in his own maxim that he used to. And, as Myles told his story, Artemis began to believe that even his intelligence would not be enough to forge a happy ending from the mess they were mired in.

Perhaps we can win, he thought. *But there will be no happy ending.*

CHAPTER 14: ΠΙΠE STICKS

 FOALY did not have much of a plan in his mind as he ran. All he knew was that he had to get to Caballine's side no matter how he achieved it. No matter what the cost.

This is what love does, he realized and in that moment he understood why Artemis had kidnapped a fairy to get the money to find his father.

Love makes everything else seem inconsequential.

Even with the world crumbling around his ears, all Foaly could think about was Caballine's plight.

There are goblin criminals converging on our house.

Opal had known that, as an LEP consultant, Foaly would require that all deliveries to his house be scanned as a matter of routine. So she had sent an ornate gift box that would appear empty to the scanners, whereas in fact no box is ever truly empty. This one would be packed with micro-organisms that vibrated at a high frequency, producing an ultrasonic whine that would knock out surveillance and drive goblins absolutely crazy – so much so that they would do anything to stop it.

Goblins were not bright creatures at the best of times. There was only one example of a goblin ever winning a science prize and he turned out to be a genetic experiment who had entered himself in the competition.

This sonix bomb would strip away any higher brain functions and turn the goblins into marauding fire-breathing lizards. Foaly knew all of this because he had pitched a mini-version of the sonix bomb to the LEP as a crime deterrent, but the Council refused grant aid because his device gave the wearer nosebleeds.

Police Plaza was eighty per cent rubble now with only the top storey left, clinging to the rock ceiling like a flat barnacle. The lower floors had collapsed on to the reserved parking spaces below, forming a rough rubble pyramid that steamed and sparked. Luckily the covered bridge that led to the adjoining parking structure was still relatively intact. Foaly hurried across the bridge, trying not to see the gaps in the floor where a hoof could slip through, trying not to hear the tortured screech of metal struts as they twisted under the weight of their overload.

Don't look down. Visualize reaching the other side.

As Foaly ran, the bridge collapsed in sections behind him until it felt like the plinking keys of a piano falling into the abyss. The automatic door on the other side was stuck on a kink in the rail and juddered back and forth, leaving barely enough room for Foaly to squeeze through and collapse panting on the fourth-storey floor.

This is so melodramatic, he thought. *Is this how things are for Holly every day?*

Encouraged by the crash of masonry and the stink of burning cars, Foaly hurried across the car park to his van, which was parked in a prime spot near the walkway. The van was an ancient crock that could easily be mistaken for a derelict vehicle instead of the chosen conveyance of the fairy responsible for most of the city's technological advancements. If a person did happen to know who the van belonged to, then that person might suppose Foaly had disguised the exterior to discourage potential car-jackers. But, no, the van was simply a heap of rust mites and should have been replaced decades ago. In the same way that many decorators never painted their own houses, Foaly, an expert in automobile advancements, did not care what he himself drove. This was a daily disadvantage as the centaur-mobile emitted noise output several decibels above regulation and regularly set off sonic alarms all over the city. Today, though, the van's antiquity was a definite advantage as it was one of the few vehicles that could run independently of Haven's automated magnetic rail system and was actually fully functional.

Foaly beeped open the front-loading doors and backed up to the cab, waiting for the extendable harness to buzz out and cradle his equine torso. The harness cinched round him, beeping all the while, then lifted the centaur backwards into the cab. Once the beetle-wing doors had folded down, the van's sensors detected Foaly's proximity and started its own engines. It took a few seconds to mount up and get going in this vehicle, but it would take a lot longer to try and climb into the automobile with six limbs and a tail, which some equinologists considered a seventh limb or at least an appendage.

Foaly pulled a steering wheel out of its slot on the dash and put his hoof to the metal, screaming out of his parking spot.

'Home!' Foaly shouted into the nav-system bot suspended on a gel string before his face. He had, in a moment of vanity, shaped the bot in his own image.

'The usual route, handsome?' said the system bot, winking fondly at Foaly.

'Negative,' replied Foaly. 'Ignore usual speed and safety parameters. Just get us there as quickly as possible. All normal behavioural restraints are lifted on my authority.'

If the bot had had any hands, it would have rubbed them. 'I have been waiting a long time to hear that,' it said and took over control of the vehicle.

Something was happening to the beautifully inlaid little box in Caballine's hand. It seemed as though a tiny thundercloud was roiling inside there. The thing vibrated like a beehive, but there was absolutely no sound. There was, however, *something*, a feeling that set her teeth on edge and made her eyes water, as though invisible nails were being dragged down a mental blackboard.

Crazy, I know, but that's how it feels.

She flung the box away from her, but not before the tiny thundercloud flowed from the container and coated her hand. The box rolled beneath the coffee table – a petrified giant flat toadstool that Holly had once called *so stereotypical it makes me want to scream* – and it lay there emitting whatever it was that had set Caballine's nerves on edge.

'What is it, darling?' she turned to ask the little ARClight, but it lay dead on the floor, a tiny wisp of smoke curling from its head.

The box did that, she guessed. Whatever this thing was, it hadn't come from Foaly, because it felt somehow *wrong*. And now the *wrongness* was on her hand. Caballine was not in any way a skittish centaur, but she felt a premonition of danger that almost buckled her legs.

Something bad is about to happen. Even worse than all the bad things that have happened today.

Many fairies would fall to pieces under the weight of such ominous circumstances, but if the universe expected such a reaction from Caballine Wanderford Paddox Foaly, then the universe was about to be surprised, for one of the characteristics that had drawn Foaly to his bride-to-be was her fighting spirit. And she did not sustain this spirit with the power of positive thinking alone. Caballine had achieved the level of blue sash in the ancient centaurian martial art of Nine Sticks, which included the head and tail as weapons. She often worked out in the LEP gymnasium with Holly Short, and had indeed once accidentally kicked Holly through a rice-paper wall when the image of an old boyfriend had suddenly popped into her head.

Caballine trotted to a locked tall cupboard in the bedroom and instructed it to open. Inside was her blue sash, which she quickly draped across her chest. The sash would be of no practical use if attackers were on the way. What would help was the long whippy bamboo pole next to it, which whistled as it cut the air and could, in the right hands, skin the hide from a troll's back.

The texture of the pole against her palm soothed Caballine and she felt a little foolish standing there in full Nine Sticks regalia.

Nothing bad is going to happen. I'm just overreacting.

Then the front door exploded.

Foaly's navigation system drove like a maniac, cackling with a glee that Foaly could not remember programming into it. And, even though Foaly was consumed with nightmarish visions of Caballine in the clutches of fire-breathing goblins, he could not help but take notice of the devastation that streaked by the window: clouds of thick smoke and flares of orange and blue flame blurred by the van's manic speed. LEP officers picked through rubble and wreckage, looking for survivors, and smoke pillars rose from a dozen familiar landmarks.

'Take it easy,' he said, slapping the nav-bot. 'I won't be much use to Caballine if I arrive dead.'

'Chill, old dude,' said the tiny bot-head. 'It's not like you're going to be much use anyway. Caballine knows Nine Sticks. What are you going to do? Throw a keyboard?'

Old dude? thought Foaly, wishing now that he had never given the bot an experimental personality chip, wishing even more that the chip did not have his own personality. But the bot was right. What was he going to do? It would be tragic indeed if Caballine were killed trying to save him. Suddenly Foaly felt like an aquaphobic lifeguard. Was he bringing anything of use to this situation?

The nav-bot seemed to read his mind, which was impossible, but Foaly resolved to patent it just in case he had accidentally invented a telepathic robot.

'Play to your strengths, dude,' it said.

Of course, thought Foaly. *My strengths. What are my strengths? And where are they?*

They were, of course, in the back of the van, where he stored a thousand half-finished and quasi-legal experiments and replacement parts. When Foaly thought about it, he realized that there were things in his truck capable of blowing a hole in the time-stream if they ever bumped together, so he had decided long ago not to think about it as the alternative was to clean out his van.

'Keep driving,' he instructed the nav-bot, wriggling out of his harness and backing across the small bridge that linked the cab to the rear carriage. 'I need to look in the back.'

'Mind your head, dude,' said the bot gleefully, a second

before hurtling over a humpbacked bridge outside a pixie dental-care facility built in the shape of a giant molar.

That personality chip must be corrupted, thought Foaly. *I would never be so reckless, and I would absolutely never call anyone 'dude'.*

When the front door exploded, Caballine's reaction was fury. Firstly, because the house's front door was antique rosewood and had been responsibly sourced from Brazil, and, secondly, because the door had been open and only a moron would feel the need to blow up something that was already ajar. Now the door would have to be reconstituted and would never be the same again, even if they could find all the splinters.

Caballine stormed into the lobby to find a crazed goblin slithering into the house on all fours, smoke leaking from its flat nostrils, its lizard-like head waving from side to side as though there were a hornet in its skull.

'How dare you!' said Caballine, dealing the lizard-like creature a smart blow to the side of its head that literally knocked the goblin out of its skin, which it had been on the point of shedding.

Well, that was upsetting, she thought, believing the assault to be over, when a second goblin appeared in the blackened doorway, head weaving in the same disconcerting manner as the first. Two more began pawing at the window and something began scrabbling inside the waste disposal.

Don't tell me. Another goblin.

Caballine turned her back on the goblin in the doorway and dealt him a double-barrelled kick with her hind legs that knocked a puff of smoke from his open mouth and sent him flying backwards over the boundary wall as though yanked by a bungee cord. She simultaneously punctured holes in the window with two lightning jabs of her bamboo, dislodging the goblins from her window sill, which had just been painted. Through the cracked pane she saw dozens of goblins converging on the property and felt something close to real panic.

I hope Foaly doesn't come home, she thought, bending her knees in a fighter's stance. *I don't think I can rescue us both.*

Foaly rummaged around the van, looking for something, *anything*, that could save his beloved.

Even if I could call for help, he thought, *everybody is up to their necks in one disaster or other. It's up to me.*

The van was a jumble of clutter, the shelves piled high with robot casings, specimen jars, incubators, power sources and bionic body parts.

But no weapons. Not one single gun.

He found a jar of bio-hybrid eyes, which glared at him, and a specimen jar full of some kind of liquid that he could not remember collecting.

'Any luck?' asked the nav-bot from a gel speaker adhered to a wall panel.

'Not yet,' said Foaly. 'How long till we get there?'

'Two minutes,' replied the bot.

'Can't you shave a minute off that time?'

'I could, if I run over a few pedestrians.'

Foaly considered it. 'No. Better not. Wasn't there a plasma cannon back here somewhere?'

'No. You donated that to the orphanage.'

Foaly did not waste time wondering why he would have donated a plasma cannon to an orphanage, but instead kept digging through the junk in the van.

If I had an hour, I could assemble something, but two minutes?

Fibre optics. Inside-outers. Voodoo mannequins. Cameras. *Nothing useful.*

At the very back of the van Foaly found an old obsolete lithium-ion magic battery that he should have drained years ago. He patted the large cylinder fondly.

We set off the famous time-stop at Fowl Manor with a series of you guys.

Foaly froze. A time-stop!

He could set off a time-stop, and everyone inside would be stuck there until the battery ran out. But time-stops required complicated calculations and precise vectors. You couldn't set off a time-stop in the suburbs.

Normally, no. But these were not normal circumstances.

It would need to be concentrated. Almost pure magic, with a diameter no wider than the property itself.

'I see you looking at that magic battery,' said the nav-bot. 'You're not thinking of setting off a time-stop, are you, dude? You need a few dozen permits before you can do that.'

Foaly synched the battery's timer with the nav computer, something Holly couldn't have done in a million years.

'No,' he said. 'I'm not setting it off. You are.'

Caballine's hide was scorched and there were bite marks on her hind legs, but she would not allow herself to give up. More than a dozen goblins surrounded her now, gnashing the air, their eyeballs rolling wildly, being driven crazy by something. There were more on the roof, chewing their way through, and every window and door was a mass of wriggling bodies.

I never got to say goodbye, thought Caballine, determined to take down as many of these lizards as possible before they buried her under sheer numbers.

Goodbye, Foaly, I love you, she thought, hoping the sentiment would somehow reach him. Then her husband crashed his van through the side of the house.

The nav-bot understood his instructions immediately.

'It's an insane plan,' said the artificial intelligence. 'But it's what I would do.'

'Good,' said Foaly, settling himself into the passenger-seat harness. 'Because you'll be doing it.'

'I love you, dude,' said the little bot, a gelatinous tear rolling down its cheek.

'Calm down, program,' said Foaly. 'I'll see you in a minute.'

*

Caballine didn't really understand what happened next until her mind had time to flick through the images. Her husband's work van jack-knifed into the house, swatting half a dozen goblins. The driver's door was open with its harness extended and Caballine did not have time to register this before she was scooped up, backwards, and dumped face-down into the hindquarter's cradle.

'Hi, honey,' said Foaly, an attempt at jauntiness that was belied by the nervous sweat on his brow.

The van's conduit section was torn asunder as the rear section braked and the front careened on through the opposite wall.

'My house!' said Caballine into the padded seating, as masonry thunked against the doors and sparks fizzled on the windscreen.

Foaly had intended to manually steer the front section to a gradual halt a safe distance from the house, but battered vehicles are unpredictable and this one insisted on flipping on to its side and skidding into the yard, dipping its wheel into the family recycling pit, which contained several of Foaly's ancestors.

The goblins were flummoxed for a moment, then their poor tortured senses picked up the hated sonic signature on Caballine's hand and their heads turned towards the van's front section. There were so many goblins on the house now that it resembled one giant green-scaled creature. Each goblin inflated its chest to hurl a fireball.

'Nice rescue. Shame it wasn't a total success,' said Caballine. 'But I appreciate the gesture.'

Foaly helped her up. 'Wait for it,' he said.

Before a single fireball could be launched, a bolt of blue magic burst through the rear section of the van, shot six metres straight up, then mushroomed into a hemisphere of gelatinous ectoplasm that dropped neatly over the Foaly residence.

'I take it back,' said Caballine. 'That was a spectacular rescue.'

Foaly had just sealed Caballine's hand inside a hazmat glove and assured the assembled neighbours that the emergency was past, when the time-stop fizzled out, revealing a large group of docile goblins.

'Foaly!' shouted Caballine. 'The blue force field is dead.'

'Don't worry,' said Foaly. 'Your hand was driving them crazy, but I smothered the signal. We're safe now.'

Caballine shielded her husband with her own body as the goblins wandered dazed from the ruins of her house. 'They're still criminals, Foaly.'

'They've done their time,' said Foaly. 'That was a concentrated time-stop. Almost a hundred per cent pure. Five seconds for us was five years for them.'

'So they're rehabilitated?' asked Caballine.

Foaly picked his way around the small fires and piles of rubble that were all that was left of his family home.

'As rehabilitated as they'll ever be,' he said, guiding confused goblins towards the remaining posts of his front gate. 'Go home,' he told them. 'Go to your families.'

There wasn't much left of the van's rear section, just the bones of a chassis and some mangled tread. Foaly poked his head inside the door frame and a voice said: 'Dude, I've missed you. It's been a long time. How did we do?'

Foaly smiled and patted a coms box. 'We did good,' he said, and then added, 'Dude.'

CHAPTER 15: **CRICKET ALERT**

 MYLES had grown suddenly exhausted after his ordeal with Gobdaw and was tucked into bed with his laminated copy of the periodic table clutched to his chest.

'Possession can take a lot out of a person,' said Holly. 'Believe me, I know. He'll be fine in the morning.'

The three sat around Artemis's desk, like a war council, which in a very real way they were.

Butler took inventory. 'We have two fighters and no weapons.'

Artemis felt he should object. 'I can fight if need be,' he said, not even convincing himself.

'We have to presume the worst about Mulch,' continued Butler, ignoring Artemis's limp objection. 'Though he does have a way of spectacularly cheating death.'

'What's our objective, specifically?' asked Holly.

This question was directed at Artemis, the planner. 'The Berserker Gate. We need to shut it down.'

'What are we going to do? Write a harsh letter?'

'Normal weapons won't penetrate Opal's magic; in fact, she would absorb the energy. But if we had a super-laser it might be enough to overload the gate. It would be like putting out a fire with an explosion.'

Holly patted her pockets. 'Well, what do you know? I seem to have left my super-laser in another pocket.'

'Even you can't build a super-laser in an hour,' said Butler, wondering why Artemis was even bringing this up.

For some reason, Artemis looked suddenly guilty. 'I might know where there is one.'

'And where would that be, Artemis?'

'In the barn, attached to my solar glider Mark Two.'

Now Butler understood Artemis's embarrassment. 'In the barn where we set up the gym? Where you are supposed to be practising your self-defence routines?'

'Yes. That barn.'

In spite of the situation, Butler felt disappointed. 'You promised me, Artemis. You said that you needed privacy.'

'It's so boring, Butler. I tried, really, but I don't know how you do it. Forty-five minutes punching a leather bag.'

'So you worked on your solar plane instead of keeping your promise to me?'

'The cells were so efficient that there was juice left over, so in my spare time I designed a lightweight super-laser and built it from scratch.'

'Of course. Who doesn't need a super-laser in the nose of their family plane?'

'Please, girls,' said Holly. 'Let's put the BFF fight on hold for later, OK? Artemis, how powerful is this laser?'

'Oh, about as powerful as a solar flare,' said Artemis. 'At its most concentrated it should have enough force to put a hole in the gate, without injuring anyone on the grounds.'

'I really wish you had mentioned this before.'

'The laser is untested,' said Artemis. 'I would never unleash this kind of power unless there was absolutely no alternative. And, from what Myles told us, we have no other card to play.'

'And Juliet doesn't know about this?' asked Holly.

'No, I kept it to myself.'

'Good. Then we might have a chance.'

Butler kitted them all in camouflage gear from his locker and even forced Artemis to endure the application of waxy stripes of black and olive make-up on his face.

'Is this really necessary?' asked Artemis, scowling.

'Completely,' said Butler, energetically applying the stick. 'Of course, if you would stay here and allow me to go, then you and Myles could relax in your favourite loafers.'

Artemis put up with the dig, correctly assuming Butler was still a little miffed about the super-laser deception.

'I must come along, Butler. This is a super-laser, not a point-and-shoot toy. There is an entire activation system involved and there is no time to teach you the sequence.'

Butler slung a heavy flak jacket over Artemis's thin

shoulders. 'OK. If you must go, then it's my job to keep you safe. So, let's make a deal. If you do not voice all those withering comments as to the weight or uselessness of this jacket, which are no doubt swirling in that big brain of yours, then I will not mention the super-laser episode again. Agreed?'

This jacket is really cutting into my shoulders, thought Artemis. *And it's so heavy that I could not outrun a slug.*

But he said, 'Agreed.'

Once Artemis's security system assured them that their perimeter was clear, the group sneaked in single file from the office, out of the kitchen, across the yard, and slipped into the alley between the stables.

There were no sentries, which Butler found strange. 'I don't see anything. Opal must know by now that we escaped her pirates.'

'She can't afford to commit more troops,' whispered Holly. 'The gate is her priority and she needs to have as many Berserkers watching her back as possible. We are secondary at this point.'

'That will be her undoing,' gasped Artemis, already suffering under the weight of the flak jacket. 'Artemis Fowl will never be *secondary*.'

'I thought you were Artemis Fowl the Second?' said Holly.

'That is different. And *I thought* we were on a mission.'

'True,' said Holly, then turned to Butler. 'This is your backyard, old friend.'

'That it is,' said Butler. 'I'll take point.'

They crossed the estate with cautious speed, wary of every living thing that crossed their path. Perhaps the Berserkers inhabited the very worms in the earth or the oversized crickets that flourished on the Fowl grounds and sawed their wings in the moonlight, sounding like an orchestra of tiny carpenters.

'Don't step on the crickets,' said Artemis. 'Mother is fond of their song.'

The crickets, which had been nicknamed Jiminies by Dublin entomologists, were seen all year round only on the Fowl Estate and they could grow to the size of mice. Artemis now guessed this was an effect of the magical radiation seeping through the earth. What he could not have guessed was that the magic had infected the crickets' nervous systems with a degree of sympathy for the Berserkers. This did not manifest itself in bunches of crickets sitting in circles around miniature campfires telling stories of valiant elfin warriors, but in an aggression towards whatever threatened the Berserkers. Or simply put: if Opal didn't like you, then the crickets didn't care for you much either.

Butler dropped his foot slowly towards a cluster of crickets, expecting them to move out of his path. They did not.

I should crush these little guys, he thought. *I do not have time to play nice with insects.*

'Artemis,' he called over his shoulder. 'These Jiminies are giving me attitude.'

Artemis dropped to his knees fascinated. 'Look, they display no natural prudence whatsoever. It's almost as if these crickets don't like us. I should really conduct a study in the laboratory.'

The biggest bug in the cluster opened its lantern jaws wide, jumped high and bit Artemis on the knee. Even though the bug's teeth did not penetrate the thick combat trousers, Artemis fell backwards in shock and would have landed flat on his backside had Butler not scooped him up and set off running with his principal tucked under his arm.

'Let's leave that lab study for later.'

Artemis was inclined to agree.

The crickets followed, pistoning their powerful hind legs to fling themselves into the air. They jumped as one, a bustling green wave that mirrored Butler's path exactly. More and more crickets joined the posse, pouring from dips in the landscape and holes in the earth. The wave crackled as it moved, so tightly were the crickets packed.

At least these ones can't fly, thought Butler. *Or there would be no escape.*

Artemis found purchase and ran on his own two feet, wiggling out from Butler's grip. The big cricket was still clamped to his knee, worrying the combat material. Artemis slapped at it with his palm and it felt like hitting a toy car. The cricket was still there and now his hand was sore.

It was difficult even for Artemis to think in these circum-stances, or rather it was difficult to pluck a sensible thought from the jumble zinging off his cranial curves.

Crickets. Murderous crickets. Flak jacket heavy. Too much noise. Too much. Insane crickets. Perhaps I am delusional again.

'Four!' he said aloud, just to be sure. 'Four.'

Butler guessed what Artemis was doing. 'It's happening all right. Don't worry, you're not imagining it.'

Artemis almost wished that he was.

'This is serious!' he shouted over the sound of his own heart beating in his ears.

'We need to get to the lake,' said Holly. 'Crickets don't swim so well.'

The barn was built on a hilltop overlooking a lake known as the Red Pool because of the way it glowed at sunset when viewed from the manor's drawing-room bay window. The effect was spectacular as though the flames of Hades lurked below fresh water. By day a playground for ducks but by night the gateway to hell. The idea that a body of water could have a secret identity had always amused Artemis and it was one of the few subjects on which he allowed his imagination free rein. Now the lake simply seemed like a safe haven.

I'll probably be dragged straight down by the weight of this flak jacket.

Holly crowded him from behind, elbowing him repeatedly in his hip.

'Hurry!' she said. 'Get that glassy look off your face. Remember there are killer crickets after us.'

Artemis picked up his feet, trying to run fast like he had seen Beckett do so often, on a whim it seemed, as though running for half a day took no particular effort.

They raced across a series of allotments, which had been sectioned off with makeshift fences of shrub and posts. Butler barged through whatever blocked their way. His boots kicked new potatoes from their beds, clearing a path for Artemis and Holly. The crickets were not impeded by barriers, simply buzz-sawing through or flowing around with no discernible loss of pace. Their noise was dense and ominous, a cacophony of mutters. Scheming insects.

The lead crickets nipped at Holly's boots, latching on to her ankles, grinding their pugnacious jaws. Holly's instinct told her to stop and dislodge the insects, but her soldier's sense told her to run on and bear the pinching. To stop now would surely be a fatal mistake. She felt them piling up around her ankles, felt their carapaces crack and ooze beneath her boots. It was like running on ping-pong balls.

'How far?' she called. 'How far?' Butler answered her by raising two fingers.

What was that? Two seconds? Twenty seconds? Two hundred metres?

They ran through the allotments and down the ploughed hill towards the water's edge. The moon was reflected in the surface like the white of a god's eye and on the far side was the gentle ski-slope rise of Artemis's runway. The crickets were on them now, waist-high for Holly. They were swarming from every corner of the estate.

We never had a cricket problem, thought Artemis. *Where have they all come from?*

They felt the bites on their legs like tiny burns and running became next to impossible with a writhing skin of crickets coating each limb. Holly went down first, then Artemis, both believing that this must surely be the worst possible way to die. Artemis had stopped struggling when a hand reached down through the electric buzzing and hauled him free of the morass.

In the moonlight he saw a cricket clamped on to his nose and reached up to crush it with his fingers. The body crunched in his fist and for the first time Artemis felt the adrenalin rush of combat. He felt like squashing all of these crickets.

Of course it was Butler who had rescued him, and as he dangled from the bodyguard's grip, he saw Holly hanging from the other hand.

'Deep breath,' said Butler and tossed them both into the lake.

Five minutes later Artemis arrived gasping at the other side minus one flak jacket, which he felt sure Butler would have something to say about, but it had been either ditch the jacket or drown and there wasn't much point in being bulletproof at the bottom of a lake.

He was relieved to find that he was flanked by Holly and Butler who seemed considerably less out of breath than he himself was.

'We lost the crickets,' said Butler, causing Holly to break down in a splutter of hysterical giggles, which she stifled in her sopping sleeve.

'*We lost the crickets*,' she said. 'Even you can't make that sound tough.'

Butler rubbed water from his close-cropped hair. 'I am Butler,' he said straight-faced. 'Everything I say sounds tough. Now get out of the lake, fairy.'

It seemed to Artemis that his clothes and boots must have absorbed half the lake, judging by their weight as he dragged himself painfully from the water. He often noticed actors on TV ads exiting pools gracefully, surging from the water to land poolside, but Artemis himself had always been forced to climb out at the shallow end or to execute a sort of double flop that left him on his belly beside the pool. His exit from the lake was even less graceful, a combined shimmy-wiggle that would remind onlookers of the movements of a clumsy seal. Eventually Butler put him out of his misery with a helping hand beneath one elbow.

'Up we come, Artemis. Time is wasting.'

Artemis rose gratefully, sheets of night-cold water sliding from his combat trousers.

'Nearly there,' said Butler. 'Two hundred metres.'

Artemis had long since given up being amazed at his bodyguard's ability to compartmentalize his emotions. By rights, the three of them should have been in shock after what they had been through, but Butler had always been able to fold all that trauma into a drawer to be dealt with later when the world was not in imminent danger of ending. Just standing at his shoulder gave Artemis strength.

'What are we waiting for?' Artemis asked and he set off up the hill.

The chitter of the crickets receded behind them until it merged with the wind in the tall pines, and no other animal adversaries were encountered on the brief hunched jog up the runway. They crested the hill to find the barn unguarded.

And why wouldn't it be? After all, what kind of strategist deserts a stronghold to hide out in a highly combustible barn?

Finally a touch of luck, Artemis thought. *Sometimes being devious pays off.*

They got lucky again inside the barn where Butler recovered a Sig Sauer handgun from a coded lockbox bolted to the blind side of a rafter.

'You're not the only one with barn secrets,' he said to Artemis, smiling as he checked the weapon's load and action.

'That's great,' said Holly drily. 'Now we can shoot a dozen grasshoppers.'

'Crickets,' corrected Artemis. 'But let's get this plane in the sky and shoot a big hole in Opal's plans instead.'

The light aircraft's body and wings were coated with solar foil, which powered the engine for lift-off. Once airborne, the plane switched between powered flight and gliding, depending on the directions from the computer. If a pilot were content to take the long way around and ride the thermals, then it was possible to engage the engine for take-off only and some trips could actually create a zero carbon footprint.

'That plane over there,' said Butler. 'Beyond the unused punchbag and the gleaming weights with their unworn handles.'

Artemis groaned. 'Yes, that plane. Now can you forget about the weights and pull out the wheel blocks while I get her started?' he said, giving Butler something to do. 'Let's leave the door closed until we are ready for take-off.'

'Good plan,' said Holly. 'Let me check inside.'

She jogged across the barn, leaving muddy footprints in her wake, and pulled open the plane's rear door.

The plane, which Artemis had named the *Khufu* after the pharaoh for whom a solar barge was built by the ancient Egyptians, was a light sports aircraft that had been radically modified by Artemis in his quest to design a practical green passenger vehicle. The wings were fifty per cent longer than they had been with micro-fine struts webbed above and below. Every surface, including the hubcaps, was coated in solar foil, which would recharge the battery in the air. A power cable ran from the *Khufu*'s tail socket to the south-facing slope of the barn roof so that the craft would have enough charge to take off whenever Artemis needed to make a test flight.

Holly's head emerged from the darkness of the interior. 'All clear,' she said, in a hushed tone in case loud noises would break their streak of luck.

'Good,' said Artemis, hurrying to the door, already running the start-up sequence in his head. 'Butler, would you open the doors as soon as I get the prop going?'

The bodyguard nodded, then kicked the white wedge of wood from under the forward wheel. Two more to go.

Artemis climbed into the plane and knew right away that something was wrong. 'I smell something. Juliet's perfume.'

He knelt between the passenger seats, tugging open a metal hatch to reveal a compartment below. Thick cables thronged the box and there was a rectangular space in the middle where something box-like should have sat.

'The battery?' asked Holly.

'Yes,' said Artemis.

'So we can't take off?'

Artemis dropped the hatch, allowing it to clang shut. Noise hardly mattered any more.

'We can't take off. We can't shoot.'

Butler poked his head into the plane. 'Why are we making noise all of a sudden?' One look at Artemis's face was all the answer he needed.

'So it's a trap. It looks like Juliet was keeping closer tabs on you than we thought.' He pulled the Sig Sauer from his waistband. 'OK, Artemis, you stay in here. It's time for the soldiers to take over.'

Butler's features then stretched in an expression of surprise and pain as a bolt of magic sizzled into the barn from outside, engulfing the bodyguard's head and torso, permanently melting every hair follicle on his head and tossing him into the rear of the plane where he lay motionless.

'It's a trap all right,' said Holly grimly. 'And we walked straight into it.'

CHAPTER 16: A WARNING SHOT

 MULCH Diggums was not dead, but he had discovered the limits of his digestive abilities: that it *was* possible to eat too many rabbits. He lay on his back in the half-collapsed tunnel, his stomach stretched as tight as the skin of a ripe peach.

'Uuuugh,' he moaned, releasing a burst of gas that drove him three metres further along the tunnel. 'That's a little better.'

It took a lot to put Mulch off a food source, but after this latest gorging on unskinned rabbit he didn't think he would be able to look at one for at least a week.

Maybe a nice hare though. With parsnips.

Those rabbits had just kept coming, making that creepy hissing noise, hurling themselves down his gullet like they couldn't wait for their skulls to be chomped. Why couldn't all rabbits be that reckless? It would make hunting a lot easier.

It wasn't the rabbits themselves that made me queasy, Mulch realized. *It was the Berserkers inside them.*

The souls of the Berserker warriors could not have been very comfortable inside his stomach. For one thing, his arms were covered in rune tattoos as dwarfs had a fanatical fear of possession and, for another, dwarf phlegm had been used to ward off spirits since time immemorial. So, as soon as their rabbit hosts died, the warrior spirits transitioned to the after-life with unusual speed. They didn't move calmly towards the light as much as sprint howling into heaven. Ectoplasm flashed and slopped inside Mulch's gut, giving him a bad case of heartburn and painting a sour scorch on the lower bell curve in his tummy.

After maybe ten more minutes of self-pity and gradual deflation, Mulch felt ready to move. He experimentally waggled his hands and feet and when his stomach did not flip violently, he rolled on to all fours.

I should get away from here, he thought. *Far, far away from the surface before Opal releases the power of Danu, if there even is such a thing.*

Mulch knew that if he were anywhere in the vicinity when something terrible happened the LEP would try to blame him for the terrible happening.

Look, there's Mulch Diggums. Let's arrest him and throw away the access chip. Case closed, Your Honour.

OK, maybe it wouldn't happen exactly like that, but Mulch knew that whenever there were accusing fingers to be pointed they always seemed to swivel around to point in his direction and, as his lawyer had once famously said: '*Three or four per cent of the time my client was not a hundred per cent accountable*

for the particular crime he was being accused of, which was to say
that there were a significant number of incidents where Mr Diggums's
involvement in the said incidents was negligible even if he might
have technically been involved in wrongdoing adjacent to the crime
scene on a slightly different date than specified on the LEP warrant.'
This single statement broke three analytical mainframes and
had the pundits tied up in knots for weeks.

Mulch grinned in the dark, his luminous teeth lighting the
tunnel.

Lawyers. Everyone should have one.

'Aw, well,' he said to the worms wriggling on the tunnel
wall. 'Time to go.'

*Farewell, old friends. We gave it our best try, but you can't win
'em all. Cowardice is the key to survival, Holly. You never understood
that.*

Mulch sighed long and hard with a hitching burp at the
end, because he knew he was kidding himself.

I can't run away.

Because there was more at stake here than his own life.
There was life itself. A lot of it, about to be snuffed out by a
crazy pixie.

I am not making any heroic promises, he consoled himself.
*I'm just taking a quick peek at the Berserker Gate to see just how
far up the creek we really are. Maybe Artemis has already saved the
day and I can retire to my tunnels. And perhaps take a few priceless
masterpieces with me for company. Don't I deserve that?*

Mulch's stomach grazed the tunnel floor as he moved, still
swollen and making strange animalistic noises.

I have enough energy for six metres of tunnelling, he realized. *No more, or my stomach walls will split.*

As it turned out, Mulch did not have to swallow a single bite of tunnel clay. When he looked up, he saw a pair of glowing red eyes looking back at him. There were scything tusks poking from the dark beneath the night eyes and a shaggy dreadlocked head arranged around them.

'Gruffff,' said the troll, and all Mulch could do was laugh.

'Really?' he said. 'After the day I've had.'

'Gruffff,' said the troll again and it lumbered forward, with paralysing venom dripping from its tusks.

Mulch went through fear, past panic and around to anger and outrage.

'This is my home, troll!' he shouted, shunting forward. 'This is where I live. You think you can take a dwarf? In a tunnel?'

Gruff did indeed think this and increased his pace, even though the walls constricted his natural gait.

He's a lot bigger than a rabbit, thought Mulch, and then the two collided in a blur of ivory, flesh and blubber, with exactly the sound you would expect to hear when a lean killing machine hits a corpulent gassy dwarf.

In the barn, Artemis and Holly were in a pretty desperate situation. They were down to two bullets in a gun that Holly could barely lift and Artemis couldn't hit a barn door with, in spite of the fact there was one close by.

They hunched in the back of Artemis's solar plane, basically waiting for the Berserkers to launch their attack. Butler lay unconscious across the rear seats with smoke literally coming out of his ears, a symptom that had never been professionally diagnosed as a good thing.

Holly cradled Butler's head, pressing her thumbs gently into his eye sockets, and forced her last watery squib of magic into the bodyguard's cranium.

'He's OK,' she panted. 'But that bolt stopped his heart for a while. If it hadn't been for the Kevlar in his chest —'

Holly didn't finish her sentence, but Artemis knew that his bodyguard had escaped death by a whisker for the umpteenth time and *umpteen* was the absolute limit of the number of extra lives handed out by the universe to any one person.

'His heart will never be the same, Artemis. No more shenanigans. He's going to be out for hours,' said Holly, checking the fuselage's porthole. 'And the Berserkers are getting ready to make their move. What's the plan, Arty?'

'I had a plan,' said Artemis numbly. 'And it didn't work.'

Holly shook his shoulder roughly, and Artemis knew her next step would be to slap him in the face. 'Come on, Mud Boy. Snap out of it. Plenty of time for self-doubt later.'

Artemis nodded. This was his function. He was the planner.

'Very well. Fire a warning shot. They cannot know how many bullets we have left and it might give them pause, buy me a moment to think.'

Holly's rolled eyes spoke clearly and what they said was: *A warning shot? I could have thought of that myself, genius.*

But this was no time to knock Artemis's shrinking confidence, so she hefted Butler's Sig Sauer and opened the window a slit, resting the barrel on the frame.

This gun is so big and unwieldy, she thought. *I can hardly be blamed if I accidentally hit something.*

In siege situations, it was standard practice to send in a scout. *Send in* being a nicer way of saying *sacrifice*. And the Berserkers decided to do just that, ordering one of the Fowl hunting dogs to literally sniff around. The large grey hound flitted through the moonlight streaming in through the barn door, planning to lose itself in the shadows.

Not so fast, thought Holly, and fired a single shot from the Sig, which hit the dog like a hammer blow high in its shoulder, sending it tumbling back outside to its comrades.

Oops, she thought. *I was aiming for the leg.*

When the plane finished vibrating and the gunshot echo faded from Artemis's cranium, he asked, 'Warning shot, correct?'

Holly felt a little guilty about the dog, but she could thrash that out in therapy if any of them survived. 'Oh, they're warned all right. You have your minute to think.'

The dog had exited the barn a lot faster than it went in. Bellico and her magical coterie were more than a little jealous when they saw a soul drift from the canine corpse, smile briefly then disappear in a blue flash, on its way to the next world.

'We don't need to enter,' said Salton the pirate, sliding

the barn door closed. 'All we need to do is stop them coming out.'

Bellico disagreed. 'Our orders are to kill them. We can't do that from here, can we? And mayhap there's something in there my host, Juliet, doesn't know about. Another tunnel or a hot-air balloon. We go in.'

Opal had been very specific when Bellico had presented her with the information about the *Khufu*.

'My host protects the Fowl children,' Bellico had said. 'The boy Myles is very inquisitive and followed Artemis to his hill-top workshop. So Juliet followed the boy. There is a sky craft in there, powered by the sun. Perhaps a weapon of some sort.'

Opal had paused in her spell-casting. 'Artemis has no choice but to go for the weapon. Take a team and remove the craft's battery, then wait for them to enter the workshop.' Opal clasped Bellico's forearm and squeezed until her nails bit into the flesh. A slug of power crawled from Opal's heart, along her arm and into Bellico. Bellico felt instantly nauseous and knew that the magic was poison.

'This is black magic and will eat into your soul,' said Opal matter-of-factly. 'You should release it as soon as possible. There's enough there for one bolt. Make it count.'

Bellico held her own hand before her face, watching the magic coil round her fingers.

One bolt, she thought. *Enough to take down the big one.*

Holly hovered anxiously around Artemis. He was in his think-ing trance and hated to be interrupted, but there was bustling under the barn door and shadows criss-crossing in the moon-light and her soldier sense told her that their refuge was about to be breached.

'Artemis,' she said urgently. 'Artemis, do you have anything?'

Artemis opened his eyes and brushed back a hank of black hair from his forehead.

'Nothing. There is no rational plan that will save even one of us, if Opal succeeds in opening the second lock.'

Holly returned to the window. 'Well then, first in gets another warning shot.'

Bellico ordered the archers to line up outside the barn's sliding door.

'When the door opens, fire whatever you're carrying into the machine. Then we rush it. The elf will have time for two shots, no more. And if any of us happen to be killed, well then that's our good fortune.'

The Chinese warriors could not speak, sealed as their mummified remains were inside enchanted clay sepulchres, but they nodded stiffly and drew their massive bows.

'Pirates,' called Bellico. 'Stand behind the archers.'

'We are not pirates,' said Salton Finnacre sulkily, scratching his femur. 'We are *inhabiting* pirates. Isn't that right, me hearties?'

'Arrr, Cap'n,' said the other pirates.

'I admit it,' said Finnacre sheepishly. 'That sounded fairly pirate-like. But it bleeds through. Two more days in this body and I could sail a brig single-handed.'

'I understand,' said Bellico. 'We will be with our ancestors soon. Our duty will be done.'

'Woof,' said the remaining hound with feeling, barely resisting his host's urge to sniff other people's personal areas.

Bellico wrapped Juliet's fingers round the door handle, testing it for weight.

'One more glorious charge, my warriors, and the humans are forever vanquished. Our descendants can forever live in peace.'

The moment buzzed with impending violence. Holly could sense the Berserkers psyching themselves up.

It's down to me, she realized. *I have to save us.*

'OK, Artemis,' she said brusquely. 'We climb to the rafters. Perhaps it will take the Berserkers time to find us. Time that you can spend planning.'

Artemis peered over her shoulder, through the porthole. 'Too late,' he said.

The barn door trundled across on oiled castors and six implacable Chinese clay warriors stood silhouetted in the moonlit rectangle.

'Archers,' said Holly. 'Lie flat.'

Artemis seemed dazed by the utter collapse of his plans. He had acted *predictably*. When had he become so predictable?

Holly saw that her words were not penetrating Artemis's skull and she realized that Artemis had two major weaknesses. One, he was physically hamstrung not only by his hamstrings but by a lack of coordination that would embarrass a four-year-old, and, two, he was so confident in the superiority of his own intellect that he rarely developed a plan B. If plan A proved to be a dud, there was no fallback.

Like now.

Holly hurled herself at Artemis, latching on to his torso and knocking him flat in the narrow aisle. A second later she heard the command from outside.

'Fire!'

It was Juliet's voice. Ordering the murder of her own brother.

As battle veterans know all too well, the urge to look at the instrument of your own death is almost overpowering. And Holly felt that pull now, to sit up and watch the arrows as they arced towards their targets. But she resisted it, forcing herself down, squashing herself and Artemis into the walkway so the corrugated steel pressed into their cheeks.

Metre-long arrows punched through the fuselage, rocking the plane on its gear and embedding themselves deep in the seating upholstery. One was so close to Holly that it actually passed through her epaulette, pinning her to the seat.

'D'Arvit,' said Holly, yanking herself free.

'Fire!' came the command from outside and instantly a series of whistles filled the air.

It sounds like birds, thought Holly.

But it wasn't birds. It was a second volley. Each arrow battered the aircraft, destroying solar panels; one even passed clean through two portholes. The craft was driven sideways, tilting on to the starboard wing.

And yet again the command came. 'Fire.' But she heard no whistling noise this time. Instead there was a sharp crackling. Holly surrendered to her curiosity, clambering up the slanted floor to the porthole and peeping out. Juliet was lighting the terracotta soldiers' arrows.

Oh, thought Holly. *That kind of fire.*

Bellico squinted into the barn's interior and was pleased to see the plane keeled over. Her host's memory assured her that this craft had indeed flown through the sky using the energy of the sun to power its engine, but Bellico found this difficult to believe. Perhaps the human's dreams and recollections were becoming intertwined, so that to Bellico daydreams and figments would seem real.

The sooner I am out of this body, the better, she thought.

She wound a torch from a hank of hay and lit the tip with a lighter taken from the human girl's pocket.

This fire machine is real enough, she thought. *And not too far removed in its mechanics from a simple flint box.*

A straw torch would not burn for long, but long enough to light her warriors' arrows. She walked along the rank, briefly touching the arrowheads, which had been soaked in fuel from a punctured jerrycan.

Suddenly the hound raised its sleek head and barked at the moon. Bellico was about to ask the dog what was the matter, but then she felt it too.

I am afraid, she realized. *Why would I be afraid of anything when I long for death?*

Bellico dropped the torch as it was burning her fingers, but in the second before she stamped on its dying embers she thought she saw something familiar storming across the field to the east. An unmistakable lurching shape.

No, she thought. *That is not possible.*

'Is that . . .' she said, pointing. 'Could that be?'

The hound managed to wrap its vocal cords round a single syllable that wasn't too far out of its doggie range. 'Troll!' it howled. '*Trooooolllll.*'

And not just a troll, Bellico realized. A troll and its rider.

Mulch Diggums was clamped to the back of the troll's head with a hank of dreadlocks in each hand. Beneath him the troll's shoulder muscles bunched and released as it loped across the field towards the barn.

Loped is perhaps the wrong word as it implies a certain slow awkwardness, but, while the troll did appear to shamble, it did so at incredible speed. This was one of the many weapons in a troll's considerable arsenal. If the intended prey noticed a troll coming from a long way off, seemingly bumbling along, it thought to itself, *OK, yeah, I see a troll, but he's like a million miles away so I'm just gonna finish off chewing this leaf* – then *BAM* the troll was chewing off the prey's hind leg.

Bellico, however, had often seen the troll-rider brigade in action and she knew exactly how fast a troll could move.

'Archers!' she yelled, drawing her sword. 'New target. Turn! Turn!'

The terracotta army creaked as they moved, red sand sifting from their joints. They were slow, painfully slow.

They are not going to make it, Bellico realized, and then she had a grasping-at-straws moment. *Perhaps that troll and its rider are on our side.*

Sadly for the Berserkers, the troll rider was most definitely not on their side and the troll was just doing what he was told.

Gruff did indeed make a fearsome spectacle as he emerged from night shadows into the pale moon glow bathing the field. Even for a troll he was a massive specimen, over nine feet tall, with his bouncing dreadlocks giving the illusion of another foot or two. His heavy-boned brow was like a battering ram over glittering night eyes. Two vicious tusks curved upwards from a pugnacious jaw, beads of venom twinkling at the pointy ends. A shaggy humanoid frame cabled with muscle and sinew, and hands with the strength to make dust of small rocks and big heads.

Mulch yanked on the troll's dreadlocks, instinctively resurrecting an age-old troll-steering technique. His grandad had often told stories around the spit-fire of the great troll riders who had rampaged across the countryside doing whatever they felt like and nobody could even catch them to argue.

'*The good old days*,' his grandad used to say. '*We dwarfs were kings. Even the demons would turn tail when they seen a mounted dwarf comin' over the hill atop a sweat-steamin' troll.'*

This doesn't feel like a good day, thought Mulch. *This feels like the end of the world.*

Mulch decided on a direct approach rather than pussyfooting around with battle tactics and steered Gruff directly into the throng of Berserkers.

'Don't hold back,' he shouted into the troll's ear.

Bellico's breath caught in her throat.

Scatter! she wanted to shout to her troops. *Take cover!*

But the troll was upon them, smashing terracotta warriors with scything swipes of its massive arms, knocking them over like toy soldiers. The troll kicked the dog into the lower atmosphere and sideswiped Bellico herself into a water barrel. In seconds, several pirates were reduced to a dog's dinner and, even though Salton Finnacre managed to jab a sword into Gruff's thigh, the massive troll lumbered on, seemingly unhindered by the length of steel sticking out of his leg.

Mulch's toes located the nerve clusters between Gruff's ribs, and the dwarf used them to steer the troll into the barn.

I am a troll rider, he realized with a bolt of pride. *I was born to do this, and steal stuff and eat loads.*

Mulch resolved to find a way of combining these three pursuits if he made it through the night.

Inside the barn the plane lay balanced on a wheel and wing tip with arrows piercing its body. Holly's face was pressed to the glass, her mouth a disbelieving O.

I don't know why she's surprised, thought Mulch. *She should be used to me rescuing her by now.*

Mulch heard the clamour of ranks re-forming behind him and he knew that it was only a matter of heartbeats before the archers launched a salvo at the troll.

And as big as my mount is, even he will go down with half a dozen arrows puncturing his vitals.

There was no time to open the glider door and scoop up its three passengers, so Mulch yanked on the dreadlocks, dug in his toes and whispered in the troll's ear, hoping that his message was getting through.

Inside the solar plane Holly used the few moments before all hell would surely break loose to hustle a dazed Artemis into the pilot's seat. She strapped herself in beside him.

'I'm flying?' asked Artemis.

Holly flip-flapped her feet. 'I can't reach the pedals.'

'I see,' said Artemis.

It was a banal yet necessary conversation as Artemis's piloting skills were soon to be called into use.

Gruff shouldered the plane upright then put his weight behind it, heaving the light craft towards the open doorway. The plane hobbled forward on damaged gear, lurching with each rotation.

'I did not foresee any of these events,' said Artemis through clattering teeth, more to himself than his co-pilot. Holly placed both hands on the dash, to brace herself against an impact towards which they were rolling at full speed.

'Wow,' said Holly, watching arrows thunk into the nose and wings. 'You didn't foresee a troll-riding dwarf pushing your plane down the runway. You must be losing your touch, Artemis.'

He tried to connect himself to the moment, but it was too surreal. Watching the Berserker soldiers grow larger through the double frames of windscreen and barn door-way made the entire thing seem like a movie. A very realistic 3D movie with vibro-chairs, but a movie all the same. This feeling of detachment coupled with the old Artemis Fowl slow reflexes almost cost him his life as he sat dreamily watching a Berserker long-arrow arcing towards his head.

Luckily Holly's reactions were stellar and she managed to punch Artemis in the shoulder with enough force to knock him sideways to the limit of his seat belt. The arrow punc-tured the windscreen, making a surprisingly small hole, and thunked into the headrest exactly where Artemis's vacant face would have been.

Suddenly Artemis had no problem *connecting to the moment*.

'I can air-start the plane,' he said, flicking switches on the dash. 'If we get off the ground at all.'

'Doesn't that require coordination?' asked Holly.

'Yes, split-second timing.'

Holly paled. Relying on Artemis's coordination was about as sensible as relying on Mulch's powers of abstinence.

The plane battered its way through the Berserkers, decap-itating a terracotta warrior. Solar panels tinkled and cracked

246

and the landing gear buckled. Gruff kept pushing, ignoring various wounds that now gushed with blood.

Bellico rallied her troops and hurried in pursuit, but none could match the troll's pace except the hound who latched on to Mulch's back, trying to dislodge him. Mulch was insulted that a dog would interfere in what was possibly the most valiant rescue attempt ever, so he locked its head in the crook of one elbow and shouted into the animal's face.

'Give it up, Fido! I am invincible today. Look at me, riding a troll, for heaven's sake. How often do you see that any more? Never! That's how often. Now, you have two seconds to back off, or I am going to have to eat you.'

Two seconds passed. The dog shook its head, refusing to back off, so Mulch ate him.

It was, he would later tell his fellow dwarf fugitive Barnet Riddles, proprietor of Miami's Sozzled Parrot bar, *a terrible waste to spit out half a dog, but it's difficult to look heroic with a mutt's hindquarters hanging out of yer mouth.*

Seconds after the live hound disagreed with Mulch to his face, the dead dog disagreed with his stomach. It may have been the Berserker soul that caused the onset of indigestion, or it may have been something the dog ate before something ate him – either way Mulch's innards were suddenly cramped by a giant fist wearing a chain-mail glove.

'I gotta trim,' he said through gritted teeth.

If Gruff had realized what Mulch Diggums was about to do, he would have run screaming like a two-year-old pixette and buried himself underground till the storm had passed, but the troll did not speak grunted Dwarfish and so followed the last command given, which had been: *Push downhill*.

The solar plane picked up speed as it ran down the clay ramp with the Berserkers in quick pursuit.

'We are not going to make it,' said Artemis, checking the instruments. 'The gear is shot.'

The runway's end curved before them like the end of a gentle ski jump. If the plane went off with insufficient speed, then it would simply plummet into the lake and they would be sitting ducks alongside the actual ducks that were probably inhabited by Berserkers and would peck them to death. Artemis was almost reconciled to the fact that he was going to die in the immediate future, but he really did not want his skull to be fractured by the bill of a possessed mallard. In fact, *death by aggressive aquatic bird* had just rocketed to number one on Artemis's Least Favourite Ways to Die list, smashing the record-breaking dominance of *death by dwarf gas*, which had haunted his dreams for years.

'Not ducks,' he said. 'Please not ducks. I was going to win the Nobel Prize.'

They could hear commotion from underneath the fuselage. Animal grunting and buckling metal. If the plane did not take off soon, it was going to be shaken to pieces. This was not a strong craft, stripped back as it was to increase the power-to-weight ratio necessary for sustainable flight.

Outside the solar plane Mulch's entire body was twisted in a cramped tree root of pain. He knew what was going to happen. His body was about to react to a combination of stress, bad diet and gas build-up by instantaneously jettisoning up to a third of his own bodyweight. Some more disciplined dwarf yogis can invoke this procedure at will and refer to it as the Once a Decade Detox, but for ordinary dwarfs it goes by the name Trimming the Weight. And you do not want to be in the line of fire when the weight is being trimmed.

The plane reached the bottom of the slope with barely enough momentum to clear the ramp.

Water landing, thought Artemis. *Death by ducks.*

Then something happened. A boost of power came from somewhere. It was as if a giant forefinger had flicked the plane forward into the air. The tail rose and Artemis fought the pedals to keep it down.

How is this happening? Artemis wondered, staring befuddled at the controls until Holly punched his shoulder for the second time in as many minutes.

'Air-start!' she yelled.

Artemis sat bolt upright. *Air-start! Of course.*

The solar plane had a small engine to get the craft off the ground and after that the solar panels took over, but without a battery the engine could not even turn over, unless Artemis hit the throttle at the right time, before the plane began to lose momentum. This might buy them enough time to catch a thermal for a couple of hundred metres, enough to clear the lake and outfly the arrows.

Artemis waited until he sensed the plane was at the apex of its rise, then opened the throttle wide.

*

Bellico and her remaining troops ran hell for leather down the runway, hurling any missiles in their arsenal after the plane. It was a bizarre situation to be involved in even for a resurrected spirit occupying a human body.

I am chasing a plane being pushed down a runway by a troll-riding dwarf, she thought. *Unbelievable.*

But nevertheless it was true and she'd best believe it or her quarry would escape.

They cannot go far.

Unless the vehicle flew as it was designed to do.

It won't fly. We have destroyed the battery.

This thing flies without power once it is airborne. My host has seen this with her own eyes.

Her good sense told her that she should stop and allow the plane to crash into the lake. If the passengers did not drown, then her archers could pick off the swimmers. But good sense was of little use on a night such as this when ghost warriors roamed the earth and dwarfs rode once more on the backs of trolls, so Bellico decided she must do what she could to stop this plane leaving the ground.

She increased her pace, outstripping the other Berserkers, using her long human legs to their full advantage, and hurled herself at the troll's midsection, grabbing tufts of grey fur with one hand and the pirate sword with the other.

Gruff howled but kept pushing.

I am attacking a troll, she thought. *I would never do this with my own body.*

Bellico glanced upwards through the tangle of limbs and

saw the whole of the moon, gleaming above. Beneath that she saw a dwarf in considerable discomfort, changing his grip to hold on to the plane's body, flattening himself to the fuselage.

'Go,' the dwarf instructed the troll. 'Back to your cave.'

That is not good, thought Bellico. *Not good at all.*

The plane swept up the lift-off ramp into the air. At the same moment, Gruff obeyed his master and released his grip, sending himself and Bellico skipping across the lake like skimmed stones, which was a lot more painful than it sounds. Gruff had a coat of fur to protect his hide, but Bellico covered most of the distance on a face that would have water burns for several months.

Overhead, Mulch could hold on no longer. He released a jet stream of watery fat, wind and half-digested foodstuff that gave the solar plane a few extra metres of lift, just enough to send it soaring out over the lake.

Bellico surfaced just in time to be clocked on the forehead by what could have been a dog's skull.

I will not think about that, she thought and swam back towards the shore.

Artemis pumped the throttle for a second time and the plane's engine caught. The single-nose propeller chugged, jerked then spun faster and faster until its blades formed a continuous transparent circle.

'What happened?' Artemis wondered aloud. 'What was that noise?'

•⚖︎⬡⬡•⚛︎⬡•⚜︎⬡⬡•⬡⬡⬡⬡⬡•⬡⬡⬡⬡•⬡⬡⬡⬡•⬡⬡⬡⬡

'Wonder later,' said Holly, 'and fly the plane now.'

This was a good idea as they were by no means out of the woods yet. The engine was running, it was true, but there was no power in the solar battery and they could only glide for a limited time at this altitude.

He pulled the stick back, climbing to thirty metres, and, as the wider world spread out below them, the magnitude of the devastation wrought by Opal's plan became obvious.

The roads into Dublin were lit by engine fires fed by fuel tanks and combustible materials. Dublin itself was blacked out but for patches of orange lighting where generators had been patched up or bonfires lit. Artemis saw two large ships that had collided in the harbour and another beached like a whale on the strand. There were too many fires to count in the city itself and smoke rose and gathered like a thundercloud.

Opal plans to inherit this new Earth, Artemis thought. *I will not let her.*

And it was this thought that pulled Artemis's mind back into focus and set him scheming on a plan that could stop Opal Koboi for the final time.

They flew over the lake but it was not graceful flight – in fact, it was more like prolonged falling. Artemis wrestled with controls that seemed to fight back as he struggled to keep their descent as gradual as possible.

They crested a row of pines and flew directly over the Berserker Gate where Opal Koboi laboured in a magical corona. Holly used the flyover as a chance to recon their enemy's forces.

Opal was surrounded by a ring of Berserkers. There were pirates, clay warriors and other assorted beings in the ring. The estate walls beyond were patrolled by more Berserkers. There were mostly animals on the walls – two foxes and even some stags, clopping along the stone, sniffing the air.

No way in, thought Holly. *And the sky is beginning to lighten.*

Opal had given herself till sunrise to open the second lock.

Perhaps she will fail and the sunlight will do our work for us, thought Holly. But it was unlikely that Opal had made a mistake in her calculations. She had spent too long in her cell obsessing over every detail.

We cannot rely on the elements. If Opal's plan is to fail, we must make it fail.

Beside her, Artemis was thinking the same thing, the only difference being that he had already laid the foundations of a plan in his mind. If Artemis had voiced his plan at that moment, Holly would have been surprised. Not by the plan's genius – she would expect no less – but because of its selflessness. Artemis Fowl planned to attack with the one weapon Opal Koboi would never suspect him of possessing: his humanity.

To deploy this stealth torpedo Artemis would have to trust two people to be true to their own personality defects.

Foaly would need to be as paranoid as he had always been.

And Opal Koboi's rampant narcissism would need to have run so wild that she would not be able to destroy humanity without her enemies at hand to witness her glory.

*

Finally Holly could not sit and watch Artemis's clumsy attempts at aviation any longer.

'Give me the stick,' she said. 'Give it full flaps when we hit the ground. They're going to be on us pretty quickly.'

Artemis relinquished control without objection. This was not the time for macho argument. Holly was undeniably ten times the pilot he would ever be and also several times more macho than he was. Artemis had once seen Holly get in a fist fight with another elf who said her hair looked pretty, because she thought he was being sarcastic, as she was sporting a fresh crew cut on that particular day. Holly didn't go on many dates.

Holly nudged the stick with the heel of her hand, lining up the plane with the manor's pebble driveway.

'The driveway is too short,' said Artemis.

Holly knelt on the seat for a better view. 'Don't worry. The landing gear will probably totally collapse on impact anyway.'

Artemis's mouth twisted in what could have been an ironic smile or a grimace of terror. 'Thank goodness for that. I thought we were in real trouble.'

Holly struggled with the stick as though it were resisting arrest. 'Trouble? Landing a crippled aircraft is just a normal Tuesday morning for us, Mud Boy.'

Artemis looked at Holly then and felt a tremendous affection for her. He wished that he could loop the past ten seconds and study it at a less stressful time so he could properly appreciate how fierce and beautiful his best friend was. Holly never seemed so vital than when she was balancing on the fine line between life and death. Her eyes shone and her wit was sharp. Where others would fall apart or withdraw, Holly attacked the situation with a vigour that made her glow.

She is truly magical, thought Artemis. *Perhaps her qualities are more obvious to me now that I have decided to sacrifice myself.* Then he realized something. *I cannot reveal my plans to her. If Holly knew, she would try to stop me.*

It pained Artemis that his last conversation with Holly would be, by necessity, peppered with misdirection and lies.

For the greater good.

Artemis Fowl, the human who had once lied as a matter of course, was surprised to find that in this instance lying *for the greater good* did not make him feel any better about it.

'Here we go,' shouted Holly over the howl caused by the wind shear. 'Shankle your bootbraces.'

Artemis tightened his seat belt. 'Bootbraces shankled,' he called.

And not a millisecond too soon. The ground seemed to rush up to meet them, filling their view, blocking out the sky. Then with a tremendous clatter they were down, being showered by blurred stones. Long-stemmed flowers fell in funereal bouquets across the windscreen and the propeller buckled with an ear-splitting shriek. Artemis felt his harness bite into both shoulders, arresting his leftward lean, which was just as well because his head would have naturally come to rest exactly where a prop blade had thunked through the seat rest.

The small craft lost its wings sliding down the avenue then flipped on its roof, coming to a shuddering halt at the front steps.

'That could have been a lot worse,' said Holly, smacking her harness buckle.

Indeed, thought Artemis, watching blood on the tip of his nose seem to drip upwards.

Suddenly something that looked like a giant angry peach slid down what was left of the windscreen, buckling the anti-shatter glass and coming to a wobbly stop on the bottom step.

Mulch made it, thought Artemis. *Good.*

Mulch literally crawled up the manor steps, desperate for food to replace his jettisoned fat. 'Can you believe that super-models do that every month?' he moaned.

Artemis beeped the door and the dwarf disappeared inside, clattering down the main hallway towards the kitchen.

It was left to Artemis and Holly to lug Butler the length of the steps, which in the bodyguard's limp unconscious state was about as easy as lugging a sack of anvils. They had made it to the third step when an uncommonly bold robin redbreast fluttered down and landed on Butler's face, hooking its tiny claws over the bridge of the bodyguard's nose. This in itself would have been surprising enough, but the note clamped in the bird's beak made the little creature altogether more sinister.

Artemis dropped Butler's arm. 'That was quick,' he said. 'Opal's ego doesn't waste any time.'

〉◊⊕♨•↑ℛ♆〉◊♆ → •⊕♬•†♨•⨯ℛ◊⊖◊⊖ℬℱ

Holly tugged the tiny scroll free. 'You were expecting this?'

'Yes. Don't even bother reading it, Holly. Opal's words are not worth the paper they are written on, and I can tell that's inexpensive paper.'

Of course, Holly did read the note and her cheeks glowed brighter with every word.

'Opal requests the pleasure of our company for the great cleansing. If we turn ourselves in, just me and you, then she will let your brothers live. Also she promises to spare Foaly, when she is declared empress.'

Holly balled the note and flicked it at the robin redbreast's head. 'You go and tell Opal no deal.'

The bird whistled aggressively and flapped its wings in a way that seemed insulting.

'You want to take me on, Berserker?' said Holly to the tiny bird. 'Because I may have just crawled out of a plane crash, but I can still kick your tail feathers.'

The redbreast took off, its birdsong trailing behind it like a derisive chuckle as it flew back to its mistress.

'You better fly, Tweety!' Holly shouted after it, allowing herself an unprofessional outburst, and it did make her feel marginally better. Once the bird had disappeared over the treeline, she returned to her task.

'We must hurry,' she said, hooking her arm under Butler's armpit. 'This is a trick. Opal will have more Berserkers on our tails. We're probably being watched by . . . *worms* . . . right now.'

•¶⚙⊗□◡•⊖•⅛⅄⊙•¶⅊•◡⊗⚘∪☎◡•¶⚙◡

Artemis did not agree. 'No. The gate is paramount now. She will not risk more soldiers hunting for us. But we must hurry all the same. Dawn is hours away and we have time for only one more assault.'

'So we're ignoring that note, right?'

'Of course. Opal is toying with our emotions for her own gratification. Nothing more. She wishes to place herself in a position of power, emotionally.'

The steps were coated with seasonal ice crystals, which twinkled like movie frost in the moonlight. Eventually Artemis and Holly succeeded in rolling Butler over the threshold and on to a rug, which they dragged underneath the stairs, making the hefty bodyguard as comfortable as possible with some of the throw pillows that Angeline Fowl liked to strew casually on every chair.

Holly's back clicked as she straightened. 'OK. Death cheated one more time. What's next, brainiac?'

Holly's words were glib, but her eyes were wider than usual, with desperation in the whites. They were so close to unthinkable disaster that it seemed even Artemis with his knack of pulling last-minute miraculous rabbits out of his hat could not possibly save humanity.

'I need to think,' said Artemis simply, quickstepping up the stairs. 'Have something to eat and maybe take a nap. This will take ninety minutes at least.'

Holly clambered after him, struggling up the human-size steps.

'Wait! Just wait,' she called, overtaking Artemis and looking him in the eye from one step up. 'I know you, Artemis. You like to play your genius card close to your chest until the big reveal. And that's worked out for us so far. But this time you need to let me in. I can help. So tell me the truth, do you have a plan?'

Artemis met his friend's gaze and lied to her face. 'No,' he said. 'No plan.'

CHAPTER 17: **LAST LIGHT**

POLICE PLAZA, HAVEN CITY, THE LOWER ELEMENTS

 THE LEP had several operatives working undercover in human theme parks around the world because humans did not even bat an eyelid at the sight of a dwarf or fairy so long as they were standing beside a rollercoaster or animatronic unicorn. Foaly had once reviewed footage from a ride in Orlando that the conspiracy theorists on the Council were certain was a training base for a secret government group of fairy killers. In this particular ride, the customers were put on a subway train that drove into an underground station. A station that was promptly subjected to every natural disaster known to man or fairy. First an earthquake split the tunnel, then a hurricane whipped up a storm of debris, then a flood pulled vehicles down from above and finally an honest-to-gods lava stream lapped the windows.

When Foaly finally got back to his office, he looked down

on the streets of Haven from the fourth floor of the Police Plaza building and it occurred to him that his beloved city reminded him of that Orlando subway station. Totally trashed almost beyond recognition.

But my city cannot be reassembled by the touch of a button.

Foaly pressed his forehead against the cool glass and watched the emergency services work their magic.

Paramedic warlocks treated the wounded with rapid bursts of magic from their insulated mitts. Firegnomes cut through girders with buzz lasers, clearing paths for ambulances, and structural engineers abseiled from rock hooks, plugging fissures with flexi-foam.

It's funny, thought Foaly. *I always thought that the humans would destroy us.* The centaur placed his fingertips on the glass. *No. We are not destroyed. We will rebuild.*

Any new tech had exploded, but there was plenty of outdated stuff that had not been recycled due to budget cuts. Most of the fire department vehicles were operational and none of the back-up generators had been refitted in the past five years. Commander Kelp was overseeing a clean-up operation on a scale never before seen in Haven. Atlantis had been hit just as badly, if not worse.

At least the dome was shored up. If that had imploded, the death count would have been huge. Not human huge but pretty big all the same.

All because one psychotic pixie wanted to rule the world.

A lot of families lost someone today. How many fairies are sick with worry right now?

Foaly's thoughts turned to Holly, stranded on the surface, trying to deal with this situation without LEP support.

If she's even alive. If any of them are alive.

Foaly had no way of knowing. All of their long-range communication was out, as most of it was piggybacked on human satellites that had by now been reduced to space garbage.

Foaly tried to comfort himself with the thought that Artemis and Butler were with his friend.

If anyone can thwart Opal, it's Artemis.

And then he thought, *Thwart? I'm using words like 'thwart' now. Opal would love that. It makes her sound like a supervillain.*

Mayne clopped up beside him. '*Mak dak jiball, Oncle.* We've got something on your lab screens.'

Foaly's nephew had no difficulty speaking Unicorn, but the boy had some difficulty getting to the point.

'They're big screens, Mayne. Usually there's something on them.'

Mayne scraped his forehoof. 'I know that, but this is something interesting.'

'Really. Lot of interesting stuff going on today, Mayne. Can you specificate?'

Mayne frowned. '*Specificate* means to identify the species of a creature. Is that what you mean?'

'No. I meant can you be more specific?'

'About what species?'

Foaly scraped a hoof, scoring the tiling. 'Just tell me what's so interesting on the screen. We're all busy here today, Mayne.'

'Have you been drinking sim-coffee?' his nephew

262

wondered. 'Because Aunty Caballine said you get a little jittery after two cups.'

'What's on the screen?' thundered Foaly, in what he thought of as his majestic tone, but was actually a little shrill.

Mayne reared back a few paces, then gathered himself, wondering why people always reacted to him in this way.

'You remember those ARClights you sent to Fowl Manor?'

'Of course I remember. They're all dead. I send them, Artemis finds them. It's a little game we play.'

Mayne jerked a thumb over his shoulder, towards the screen, where the blank square used to be. 'Well, one of those suckers just came back to life. That's what I've been trying to tell you.'

Foaly aimed a kick at Mayne, but the youngster had already trotted out of range.

FOWL MANOR

Artemis locked his office door behind him and gave the perimeter cams and sensors a cursory glance to make sure they were safe for the moment. It was as he expected. The only activity on the estate was over a kilometre away where the Martello tower used to be and where the Berserker Gate now poked from Opal's impact crater. As a precaution, he set the alarm to the SIEGE setting, which featured deterrents not available on standard house systems, such as electrified windowpanes and flash bombs in the locks. Then again, Fowl

Manor hadn't been a standard house since Artemis decided to keep his kidnapped fairy in the basement.

Once he was satisfied they were locked down, Artemis opened a coded drawer in his desk and pulled out a small lead box. He tapped the lid with a nail and was satisfied to hear a skittering inside.

Still alive then.

Artemis slid the box open and inside, latched on to a three-volt battery, was a tiny bio-cam dragonfly. One of Foaly's little toys, which were usually shorted out in Artemis's regular bug sweeps, but he had decided to keep this one and feed it, in case he ever needed a private line through to Foaly. He had hoped to use this camera to announce the success of their assault on the Berserker Gate, but now the little bug would convey a more sombre message.

Artemis shook the bug on to his desk where it skittered around for a while, before its face-recognition software identified Artemis as the prime target and decided to focus in on him. The tiny lenses in its eyes buzzed almost inaudibly and a couple of stemmed microphones extended like an ant's antennae.

Leaning in close, Artemis began to speak softly, so he could not possibly be overheard, even though his own sensors assured him that his was the only warm body of significant mass within six metres.

'Good morning, Foaly. I know there is not so much as an atom of Koboi technology in this little mutation, so in theory it can transmit and I hope you are still alive to receive the transmission. Things are bad up here, my friend, very bad.

Opal has opened the Berserker Gate and is working on the second lock. If she succeeds, then a wave of coded Earth magic will be released to destroy humanity utterly. This, in my opinion, is a bad thing. To stop this disaster from happening I need you to send me a couple of items in one of your drone mining eggs. There is no time for permits and committees, Foaly. These items must be in Fowl Manor in less than two hours or it will be too late. Get what I need, Foaly.'

Artemis leaned in even closer to the tiny living camera and whispered urgently.

'Two things, Foaly. Two things to save the world.'

And he told the little bug what he needed and where exactly he needed them sent.

POLICE PLAZA, HAVEN CITY, THE LOWER ELEMENTS

The colour drained from Foaly's face.

Koboi was working on the second lock.

This was catastrophic – though there were many fairies in Haven who would dance in the streets to celebrate the eradication of humanity, but no rational ones.

Two items.

The first wasn't a problem. It was a *toy*, for heaven's sake.

I think I have one in my desk.

But the second. The second.

That is a problem. A major problem.

There were legal issues and moral issues. If he even

mentioned it to the Council, they would want to form a task force and a subcommittee.

What Artemis asked was technically possible. He did have a prototype mining egg in the testing area. All he had to do was program the co-ordinates into the navigation system and the egg would speed towards the surface. Built to transport miners from cave-ins, the egg could withstand huge pressures and fly at the speed of sound three times around the world. So Artemis's time limit shouldn't be a problem.

Foaly chewed a knuckle. Should he do what Artemis asked? Did he want to? The centaur could ask himself questions until time had run out, but there was really only one question that mattered.

Do I trust Artemis?

Foaly heard breathing behind him and realized that Mayne was in the room.

'Who else has been in here?' he asked the technician.

Mayne snorted. 'In here? You think the alpha fairies are going to hang around dork central when there's a big old crisis going down? No one has been in here and no one has seen this video. Except me.'

Foaly paced the length of his office. 'OK. Mayne, my young friend, how would you like a full-time job?'

Mayne squinted suspiciously. 'What would I have to do?'

Foaly grabbed item number one from his desk drawer and headed for the door.

'Just your usual,' he replied. 'Hang around the lab and be useless.'

Mayne made a copy of Artemis's video just in case he was being implicated in some kind of treason.

'I could do that,' he said.

CHAPTER 18: SOUL SURVIVOR

ARTEMIS was making final preparations in his office, updating his will and trying to master his feelings, tamping down a flat grey sky of sadness that threatened to cloud his resolve. He knew that Doctor Argon would advise him against bottling up his emotions as it would lead to psychological scarring in the long term.

But there will be no long term, Doctor, he thought wryly.

After so many adventures Artemis felt he should have known that things never turned out exactly as planned, but still he felt surprised at the finality of this step he was being forced to take – and also that he was willing to even consider taking it.

The boy who kidnapped Holly Short all those years ago would never have entertained the notion of sacrificing himself.

But he was no longer that boy. His parents were restored to him and he had brothers.

And dear friends.

Something else Artemis had never anticipated.

Artemis watched his hand shake as he signed his last will and testament. How valid many of his bequests were in this new age, he was not sure. The banking system was almost definitely irretrievably damaged, as were the world's stock exchanges. So there went the stocks, bonds and shares.

All that time spent accumulating wealth, Artemis thought. *What a waste.*

Then: *Come now. You are simply being maudlin. You love gold almost as much as Mulch Diggums loves chicken. And, given the chance, you would probably do the same again.*

It was true. Artemis didn't believe in death-bed conversions. They were far too opportunistic. A man must be what he is and take whatever judgements are forthcoming on the chin.

If there is a Saint Peter, I will not argue with him at the Pearly Gates, he promised his subconscious, though Artemis knew that if his theory was correct he could be stuck on this plane as a spirit just as the Berserkers were.

I can be a supernatural bodyguard to Myles and Beckett.

This notion gave Artemis comfort and made him smile. He realized that he was not at all afraid, as if what he was about to attempt was a simulation in a role-playing game rather than an actual course of action. This changed when Artemis sealed the will in an envelope and propped it against the desk lamp. He stared at the document, feeling the finality in the moment.

No going back now.

And then the fear dropped on him like a tonne weight, pinning him to the office chair. He felt a block of lead solidify in his stomach and suddenly his limbs seemed grafted on and out of his control. Artemis took several deep breaths just to stop himself throwing up, and gradually his calm returned.

I had always imagined that there would be time for goodbyes. A moment for meaningful words with those I love.

There was no time. No time for anything but action.

The fear had passed and Artemis was still set on his course.

I can do it, he realized. *I can think with my heart.*

Artemis pushed his oxblood chair back on its castors, clapped his knees once and stood to face his ordeal.

Holly burst into the office with murder in her eyes.

'I saw what came out of the wine cellar, Artemis.'

'Ah,' said Artemis. 'The egg arrived.'

'Yes, it arrived. And I had a look inside.'

Artemis sighed. 'Holly. I am sorry you saw. Mulch was supposed to hide it.'

'Mulch is my friend too, and I told him you would try to pull something. He was digging himself a last-minute escape tunnel when the egg came in on autopilot. Mulch figures this is the something you are trying to pull.'

'Holly, it's not what you think.'

'I know what you're planning. I figured it out.'

'It seems radical, I know,' said Artemis. 'But it's the only way. I have to do this.'

'*You* have to do it!' said Holly, incensed. 'Artemis Fowl makes choices for everyone as usual.'

'Perhaps, but this time I am justified by circumstance.'

Holly actually pulled her gun. 'No. Forget it, Artemis. It's not happening.'

'It has to happen. Perhaps in time, with resources, I could develop an alternate strategy . . .'

'Develop an alternate strategy? This is not a corporate takeover we're talking about, Artemis. It's your life. You intend to go out there to kill yourself. What about Butler?'

Artemis sighed. It pained him to leave Butler unconscious, ignorant of the plan, especially as he knew that his faithful bodyguard would forever consider himself a failure.

Collateral damage. Just as I shall be.

'No. I can't tell him and neither will you . . .'

Holly interrupted with a wave of her gun. 'No orders from you, Mister Civilian. I am the officer in charge. And I am categorically vetoing this tactic.'

Artemis sat in his chair, resting his face in his hands. 'Holly, we have thirty minutes before sunrise then I die anyway. Butler dies and Juliet. My family. Almost everyone I love will be gone. All you're doing is making sure that Opal wins. You would not be saving anyone.'

Holly stood beside him and her touch was light at his shoulder. Artemis realized suddenly that elves had a signature odour.

Grass and citrus. Once I would have filed that information.

'I know you don't like it, Holly my friend, but it's a good plan.'

Holly's fingers travelled to Artemis's neck and he felt a slight tingle.

'I don't like it, Arty,' she said. 'But it is a good plan.'

The tranquillizer pad took a few seconds to work and then Artemis found himself keeling over on to the Afghan rug, his nose parting the fibres in a tree-of-life motif. The drug numbed his mind and he could not fathom exactly what was happening.

'I'm sorry, Artemis,' said Holly, kneeling beside him. 'Opal is one of my people, so this is my sacrifice to make.'

Artemis's left eye rolled in its socket and his hand flapped weakly.

'Don't hate me forever, Arty,' whispered Holly. 'I couldn't bear that.' She took his hand and squeezed it tightly. 'I am the soldier, Artemis, and this is a job for a soldier.'

'You make a good point, Holly,' said Artemis clearly. 'But this is my plan and, with all due respect, I am the only one who can be trusted to execute it.'

Holly was confused. Just a moment ago, Artemis had been on the verge of unconsciousness and now he was lecturing her in his usual supercilious way.

How?

Holly pulled back her hand and saw a small adhesive blister on her palm.

He drugged me! she realized. *That sneaky Mud Boy drugged me.*

Artemis stood and led Holly to the leather sofa, laying her down on the soft cushions.

'I thought Foaly might tattle, so I took an adrenalin shot to counteract your sedative.'

Holly fought the fog clouding her mind. 'How could you . . . How?'

'Logically you have no right to be angry. I simply followed your lead.'

Tears filled Holly's eyes, spilling down her cheeks as the truth called to her from far away, across a misty chasm.

He is really going through with it.

'No,' she managed.

'There is no other way.'

Holly felt the hollowness of dread sour her stomach. 'Please, Arty,' she mumbled. 'Let me . . .' but she said no more as her lips had turned to slack rubber.

Artemis nearly broke – she could see it in his mismatched eyes, one human, one fairy – but then he stepped away from the couch and breathed deeply.

'No. It has to be me, Holly. If the second lock is opened, then I will die, but if my plan succeeds, then all fairy souls inside the magical corona will be drawn to the afterlife. *Fairy* souls. My soul is human, Holly, don't you see? I don't intend to die and there is a chance that I may survive. A small chance, granted. But a chance nonetheless.' Artemis rubbed his eye with a knuckle. 'As a plan, it is far from perfect, but there is no alternative.'

Artemis made Holly comfortable with cushions. 'I want

you to know, my dear friend, that without you I would not be the person I am today.' He leaned in close and whispered. 'I was a broken boy and you fixed me. Thank you.'

Holly was aware that she was crying because her vision was blurred, but she could not feel the tears on her face.

'Opal expects you and me,' she heard Artemis say. 'And that is exactly what she will get.'

It's a trap! Holly wanted to scream. *You are walking into a trap.*

But, even if Artemis could hear her thoughts, Holly knew there was no turning him from his path. Just as she figured that Artemis had left the room, he reappeared in her field of vision, a pensive look on his face.

'I know you can still hear me, Holly,' he said. 'So I would ask one last favour of you. If Opal outwits me and I don't make it out of that crater, I want you to tell Foaly to power up the chrysalis.' He leaned down and kissed Holly's forehead. 'And give him that from me.'

Then the teen genius left, and Holly could not even turn her head to watch him go.

Opal knew that the ranks of her warriors were depleted, but it didn't matter; she had reached the final level of the Berserker Gate's second lock. Satisfaction flushed through her system in a buzz that set sparks jumping from the tips of her ears.

'I need peace,' she called to whatever Berserker was guarding her flank. 'If anyone comes close, kill them.' She hurriedly amended this order to: 'Except the human Fowl, and his pet LEP captain. Do you understand me?'

Oro, in the body of Beckett, understood well enough, but wished the fairy bonds gave him wiggle room to suggest that their leader forget her personal vendetta. However, Bruin Fadda's rules were explicit: total obedience to the fairy who opens the gate.

We should hunt them down, he wanted to say. *If we can capture these last few humans, then there is no need to open the second lock.*

Opal turned and screamed into his face, spittle flying. 'I said, do you understand me?'

'I do,' said Oro. 'Kill anyone, except Fowl and the female.'

Opal tapped his cute button nose. 'Yes, exactly. Mummy is sorry for raising her voice. Mummy is stressed beyond belief. You would not believe the brain cells Mummy is expending on this thing.'

Say 'Mummy' one more time, thought Oro. *And bonds or no bonds . . .*

The most Oro could do against the grip of the fairy bond was scowl slightly and bear the stomach cramps, but his scowling had no effect as Opal had already turned back to her task, a corona of black magic shimmering around her shoulders.

The final tumbler in Bruin Fadda's enchanted lock was the warlock himself. Bruin had interred his own soul in the rock in much the same spiritual fashion as the Berserkers had been preserved in the ground.

As Opal ran her fingers over the rock's surface, the druid's face appeared in the stone, roughly etched but recognizable as elfin.

'Who wakes me from my slumbers?' he asked in a voice of rock and age. 'Who calls me back from the brink of eternity?'

Oh, please, thought Opal. *Who calls me back from the brink of eternity? Is this the kind of troll dung I am going to have to put up with just to wipe out humanity?*

'It is I, Opal Koboi,' she said, playing along. 'From the house of Koboi. High Queen of the fairy families.'

'Greetings, Opal Koboi,' said Bruin. 'It is good to see the face of another fairy. So we are not yet extinct.'

'Not yet, mighty warlock, but, even as we speak, the humans approach the gate. Haven is threatened. We must open the second lock.'

The rock ground like a millstone as Bruin frowned. 'The second lock? That is indeed a momentous request. You would bear the guilt for this action?'

Opal used the penitent face she had developed for parole hearings. 'I would bear it, for the People.'

'You are indeed brave, Queen Opal. The pixies were ever noble in spite of their stature.'

Opal was prepared to let the *stature* remark pass because she liked the sound of *Queen Opal*. Also, time was wasting. In less than an hour the sun would rise and the full moon would pass, and the chances of maintaining this little army for another day even with the humans chasing their own tails were pretty slim.

◊•🦀•⚡◊♒⊕▱◊•⚡∪☎⊕⊕•◊•▱🪃⚭•

'Thank you, mighty Bruin. Now, the time has come for your answer.'

The warlock's frown deepened. 'I must consult. Are my Berserkers by your side?'

This was unforeseen. 'Yes. Captain Oro is at my shoulder. He is in total agreement with me.'

'I would confer with him,' said the stone face.

This Bruin character was really pushing Opal's buttons. A second ago it was all Queen Opal, and now he wanted to consult the help?

'Mighty Bruin, I don't really think there is any need to consult with your soldiers. Time grows short.'

'I would confer with him!' thundered Bruin, and the scored grooves of his face glowed with a power that shook Opal to her core.

Not a problem, she thought. *Oro is bonded to me. My will is his will.*

Oro stepped forward. 'Bruin, comrade. I had thought you gone to the next life.'

The stone face smiled and he seemed to have sunlight instead of teeth. 'Soon, Oro Shaydova. I liked your old face better than this young one, though I can see your soul beneath.'

'A soul that aches to be released, Bruin. The light calls to us all. Some of my warriors have lost their wits, or close to it. We were never meant to be this long in the ground.'

'That time of deliverance is at hand, my friend. Our work is almost done. So tell me, are the People yet under threat?'

'We are. Queen Opal speaks the truth.'

Bruin's eyes narrowed. 'But you are bonded, I see.'

'Yes, Bruin. I am in thrall to the queen.'

Bruin's eyes flashed white in the stone. 'I release you from your bonds so that we may speak freely.'

Not good, thought Opal.

Oro's shoulders slumped and it seemed as though every one of his years was written on Beckett's face.

'The humans have weapons now,' said Oro and it was strange to see the words coming from a mouth full of milk teeth. 'They seem miraculous to me. In this young one's memory I have seen that, without us to hunt readily, they kill each other by their thousands. They destroy the Earth and have annihilated several thousand species.'

The stone face grew troubled. 'Have they not changed?'

'They are more efficient than we remember, that is all.'

'Should I open the second lock?'

Oro rubbed his eyes. 'This I cannot answer for you. It is true that Queen Opal has sabotaged their efforts, but already they mass against us. The gate has been assaulted twice, with two of our own among the attackers. An elf and a dwarf, both cunning adversaries.'

The stone face sighed and white light flowed from its mouth. 'Always have there been traitors.'

'We cannot hold on much longer,' admitted Oro. 'Some of my warriors have already been called to Danu's side. The world is in chaos and, if the humans attack the gate tomorrow, there will be none to defend it. With their new weapons, perhaps they will find a way to dismantle the second lock.'

Opal was quietly delighted and if she could have clapped her tiny hands without seeming unqueenly she would have done. Oro was convincing this craggy idiot better than she ever could.

'The People wither and die without sunlight,' she added, po-faced. 'Soon we will disappear altogether. Suffering is our daily ritual. We must ascend.'

Oro could only agree with this. 'Yes. We must ascend.'

Bruin ruminated for a long moment and his stony features grated as he thought.

'Very well,' he said finally. 'I shall open the lock, but yours is the final choice, Queen Opal. When the end is in sight, then you must choose. Your soul shall bear the consequences as mine already does.'

Yes, yes, yes, thought Opal, barely concealing her delighted eagerness.

'I am prepared for this responsibility,' she said sombrely. And, though she could not see it, Oro rolled his eyes behind her, all too aware that Opal did not have the People's interests at heart. But her motivations were of little importance as the end result, the *extinction of humanity*, would be the same.

Bruin's features were suddenly submerged in a pool of bubbling magma that bled into the rock to reveal two sunken handprints. Opal's original key and a fresh one glowing a deep blood-red.

'Choose selflessly,' said Bruin's voice from deep within

the stone. 'Prudence will close the gate entirely, releasing the souls and destroying the path forever. Desperation will summon the power of Danu and wipe the humans from the face of our land. Fairies shall walk the Earth again.'

Handprint B it is, thought Opal happily. *I have always found desperation a wonderful motivator.*

Now that the climax had actually arrived, Opal paused for a thrilling moment to savour it.

'This time it is impossible for me to lose,' she said to Oro. 'Mummy's gonna press the big button.'

Oro would have pressed the button himself just to stop Opal referring to herself as *Mummy* but alas only the fairy who opened the gate could activate the second lock.

Opal wiggled her fingers. 'Here we go. Mummy's ready.'

Then a voice called from the lip of the crater. 'The human is surrendering himself. And he's brought the elf.'

Until that second, Opal had not realized that this moment was not quite perfect. But now it would be.

'Bring them to me,' she commanded. 'I want them to see it coming.'

Artemis Fowl dragged a hooded figure along the ground, heels digging grooves in the earth. When they arrived at the crater that had been blasted by Opal's arrival, one of the pirates nudged Artemis and he went tumbling down the incline, his face slapping the dirt with each revolution. The second figure skidded beside him and it seemed almost co-ordinated when they rolled to the foot of the Berserker Gate. They made a bedraggled beaten pair. The second figure landed face up. It was Holly Short. Obviously the elf had not come willingly.

'Oh, my,' said Opal, giggling behind her fist. 'Poor dears. How pathetic.' Opal felt proud of herself that she still had some sympathy in her for others.

I actually feel bad for these people, she realized. *Good for me.*

Then Opal remembered how Artemis Fowl and Holly Short had been responsible for her years in maximum-security confinement, and what she had been forced to do to secure her own release, and her *feeling bad for those people* evaporated like morning dew.

'Help them up,' Oro ordered Juliet who was squatting to one side, eating a bloody rabbit.

'No!' said Opal shrilly. 'Search the Mud Boy for weapons, then let them crawl to my feet. Let the boy beg for mankind. I want this one with blood on his knees and tears of despair on his face.'

The fairy spirits sensed that the end was near and that soon their souls would finally be released from duty and granted peace, so they gathered at the base of the Berserker Gate in their borrowed bodies, forming the sealed magic circle. They watched as Artemis hefted Holly painfully up the stairs, his back bent with the effort.

I wish I could see his face, thought Opal. *See what this is costing him.*

Holly's frame was limp as she bumped along the steps and

one leg dangled off the tower's edge. She seemed small and frail and her breathing was ragged. Opal allowed herself to imagine what Fowl had been forced to inflict on the elf in order to subdue her.

I turned them on themselves, she thought. *The ultimate victory. And they did it for nothing, the fools.*

Artemis reached the plateau and dropped Holly like a butcher's sack. He turned to Opal, hatred written large on his normally impassive features.

'Here we are, *Your Majesty*,' he said, spitting the title. 'I am surrendering myself, as ordered, and I have forced Holly to do the same.'

'And I am so glad to see you, Artemis. So very glad. This makes everything simply perfect.'

Artemis leaned elbows on knees, panting for breath, blood dripping from his nose. 'Holly said that you would never keep your word, but I tried to assure her that there was a chance at least and so long as there was a chance we had no choice. She disagreed and so I was forced to sedate my dearest friend.' Artemis made eye contact with the pixie. 'Is there a chance, Opal?'

Opal laughed shrilly. 'A chance? Oh gods, no. There was never a chance. I love you, Artemis. You are too funny.' She wiggled her fingers and sparks danced.

The colour drained from Artemis's face and his hands shook from effort and anger. 'Don't you care about the lives you take?'

'I don't want to kill *everybody*. But either humans or fairies have to go, so that I can lead the others. I decided on your group because I already have quite a lot of support below ground. There's a secret website and you'd be amazed at some of the registered names.'

The remaining Berserkers gazed up from the crater, swaying slightly, muttering prayers to the goddess Danu. Two pirates suddenly dropped, clattering to the ground in a rattle of bones.

'My children are failing,' said Opal. 'Time for Mummy to send them to heaven. Bellico, move the pesky boy genius back a little. It's not likely that Artemis Fowl will actually launch a physical attack, but he does have a knack for destroying my beautiful plans.'

Juliet tossed Artemis backwards into the dirt. No emotion showed on her face; she was simply unable to take any other course of action.

'Should I kill the Mud Boy?' she asked dispassionately.

'Absolutely not,' said Opal. 'I want him to see. I want him to feel the ultimate despair.'

Artemis rolled to his knees. 'Humans are no threat to you, Opal. Most of us don't even know fairies exist.'

'Oh, they do now. Our shuttle ports are all wide open without their shields. I have revealed our existence to the Mud People so now there is no choice but to eliminate them. It's simple logic.'

Juliet placed a foot on Artemis's back, flattening him to the earth. 'He is dangerous, my queen. And, if the elf traitor wakes, she could harm you.'

Opal pointed at the terracotta warriors. 'You restrain the elf and have those moving statues hold the boy. Mummy wishes to do a little grandstanding. It's clichéd, I know, but after this I'll probably have to be regal and selfless in public.'

Juliet lifted Holly by the scruff of the neck, easily hefting her aloft. Two Chinese warriors pinioned Artemis between them, holding him powerless in their grips of baked clay, with only his hands and feet mobile.

He can do nothing, thought Opal, satisfied.

'Bring them here,' she commanded. 'I want them both to see me cleanse the planet.'

Artemis struggled ineffectually, but Holly's head lolled in its hood, which was a little annoying for Opal as she would have preferred to see the elf wide awake and terrified.

Opal positioned herself by the raised dais, tapping her fingers on the stone like a concert pianist. She worked on the Berserker Gate as she spoke, dipping her hands into the rock, which became molten where she touched.

'Humans had magic once,' she said. Perhaps she should gag Artemis's smart mouth in case he contaminated her buoyant mood with some of his snide observations. Though by the vacant look on this Mud Boy's face, the *snide* had been beaten out of him.

'That's right. Humans wielded magic almost as well as demons. That's why Bruin Fadda put so many hexes on this lock. His reasoning being that if any human grew powerful enough to decipher the enchantments, then Bruin had no choice but to unleash the power of Danu, for the good of the

People.' Opal smiled fondly at the Berserker Gate. 'It looks simple now, like a child's toy,' she said. 'Just two handprints on a rock table. But the computations I had to work out. Foaly could never have managed it, I can tell you. That ridiculous centaur has no idea what it took to solve this puzzle: enchanted runes in several dimensions, quantum physics, magic maths. I doubt there are four people in the world who could have brought that old fool Bruin back to life. And I had to do it all mentally. Without screens or paper. Some of it telepathically through my younger self. You know I didn't even lose my memories when she died and I thought I would. Strange, isn't it?'

Artemis did not reply. He had retreated into bruised sulky silence.

'So here's how it works,' said Opal brightly, as though explaining a maths problem to her kindergarten group. 'If I choose the first handprint, then I close the gate forever and all fairy souls inside the circle are released – except mine of course as I am protected by black magic. But if I choose the scary red hand, then the power of Danu is unleashed but on humans only. It's a pity we won't see too much from here, but at least I can watch you die and imagine the magic's effect on everyone else.'

Artemis wrenched one arm free of the clay warrior's grip, tearing his sleeve and a layer of flesh. Before anyone could react, he placed his own hand in the Berserker Gate's first lock.

Of course nothing happened apart from Opal barking with

laughter. 'You don't understand, stupid boy. Only I can choose. Not you, not that pathetic centaur Foaly, not your little elf friend. Only Opal Koboi. That is the whole point. She who opens the lock controls the gate. It is coded right down to my very DNA.' Opal's tiny face grew purple with self-importance and her pointed chin shook. 'I am the messiah. And I will shed blood so that the People may worship me. I will build my temple around this silly gate that leads nowhere and they can parade school tours past to learn about me.'

Artemis had a single strand of defiance left in him. 'I could close it,' he grunted. 'Given a few minutes.'

Opal was nonplussed. 'You could . . . You could close it? Weren't you listening? Didn't I make it simple enough? No one can close it but me.'

Artemis seemed unimpressed. 'I could figure it out. One more hour, ten minutes even. Holly is a fairy, she has magic. I could have used her hand and my brain. I know I could. How difficult could it be if you managed it? You're not even as smart as Foaly.'

'Foaly!' screamed Opal. 'Foaly is a buffoon. Fiddling around with his gadgets when there are entire dimensions left unexplored.'

'I apologize, Holly,' said Artemis formally. 'You warned me and I wouldn't listen. You were our only chance and I tricked you.'

Opal was furious. She skirted the Chinese warriors to where Juliet stood holding Holly whose head was dangling.

'You think this ridiculous *thing* could ever have accomplished what I have accomplished?'

'That is Captain Holly Short of the Lower Elements Police,' said Artemis. 'Show some respect. She beat you before.'

'This is not *before*,' said Opal emphatically. 'This is now. The end of days for humanity.' She grabbed Holly's hand and slapped it vaguely in the area of the handprint on the Berserker Gate. 'Oh, look at that. The gate is not closing. Holly Short has no power here.' Opal laughed cruelly. 'Oh, poor pretty Holly. Imagine, if only your hand would activate the gate, then your suffering could end right now.'

'We could do it,' mumbled Artemis, but his eyes were closing and it seemed as though he had lost faith in himself. His free hand tapped a distracted rhythm on the stone. The human's mind had finally snapped.

'Ridiculous,' said Opal, calming herself. 'And here I am, getting flustered by your claims. You vex me, Artemis, and I will be glad when you are dead.'

Two things happened while Opal was ranting at Holly. The first thing was that Opal had a series of thoughts:

Holly's hand seems very small.

Opal realized that she hadn't closely examined the elf since she'd appeared at the crater's rim. Either she'd been lying down, or Artemis had shielded her body with his own.

But her face. I saw the face. It was definitely her.

The second thing to happen was that the small hand in question, which still rested on the Berserker Gate, began to crab spasmodically towards the handprint, feeling its way with fingertips.

Opal pulled back Holly's hood to take a better look and saw that the face crackled a little on close inspection.

A mask. A child's projection mask. Like the one used by Pip . . .

'No!' she screamed. 'No, I will not permit it!'

She reached under Holly's chin and wrenched off the mask, and of course it was not Holly underneath.

Opal saw her own cloned face beneath the mask and felt instantly traumatized as though blindsided by a massive blow.

'It is me!' she breathed, then giggled hysterically. 'And only I can close the gate.'

Two seconds of stunned inaction followed from Opal, which allowed Nopal's fingers to arrange themselves perfectly in the handprint. The print turned green and radiated a warm light. The smell of summer emanated from the stone and there was birdsong.

Artemis chuckled, showing his blood-rimmed teeth. 'I would imagine that you're *vexed* now.'

Opal sent a vicious magical pulse directly into the clone's torso, twisting her from Juliet's grip and sending her rolling away from the gate, but all she accomplished with her brutality was to let the ethereal light flood through faster. The emerald rays spiralled upwards in a tight coil, then fanned out to form a hemisphere round the magic circle. The Berserkers sighed and bathed their upturned faces in the meadow-green glow.

'It is finally finished, Opal,' said Artemis. 'Your plan has failed. You are finished.'

There were people in the light, smiling and beckoning. There were scenes from times gone by. Fairies farming in this very valley.

Opal did not give up so easily and recovered herself. 'No. I still have power. Perhaps I lose these Berserker fools, but my magic will protect me. There are other fairies to be duped and the next time you will not stop me.'

Opal slapped Oro hard to distract him from the light. 'Make certain that clone is dead,' she ordered. 'The magic may not take the soulless creature. Finish her off if need be. Do it now!'

Oro frowned. 'But she is one of us.'

'What do I care?'

'But it is over, majesty. We are leaving.'

'Do as I say, thrall. It can be your last act before you ascend. Then I am done with you.'

'She is innocent. A helpless pixie.'

Opal was enraged by the argument. 'Innocent? What do I care about that? I have killed a thousand innocent fairies and I will kill ten times that if I deem it necessary. Do as I command.'

Oro drew the dagger, which seemed as big as a sword in his hand. 'No, Opal. Bruin released me from my bonds. You shall kill no more fairies.'

And with a soldier's efficiency he pierced Opal's heart with a single thrust. The tiny pixie dropped, still speaking.

She talked until her brain died, mouthing foul vitriol, still refusing to believe that it was over for her. She died staring into Artemis's face, hating him.

Artemis wanted to hate right back, but all he could feel was sadness for the waste of life.

Something that may have been a spirit, or a dark twisted shadow, flickered behind Opal for a moment like a fleeing thief, then dissolved in the magical light.

All this time. All this strife and nobody wins. What a tragedy.

The light glowed brighter and shards detached themselves from the corona to become liquid, congealing around the Berserkers inside the circle. Some left their bodies easily as though slipping from an old coat; others were yanked out limb by limb, jerking into the sky. Oro dropped his dagger, disgusted by what had been necessary, then vacated Beckett's body in a flash of green fire.

At last, he may have said, though Artemis could not be sure. On either side of him, the clay warriors disintegrated as the Berserker spirits vacated them and Artemis dropped to the ground, coming face to face with Nopal.

The clone lay with her eyes uncharacteristically bright and what might have been a smile on her face. She seemed to focus on Artemis for a moment, then the light died in her eyes and she was gone. She was peaceful at the end and, unlike the other fairies, no soul detached itself from her body.

You were never meant to be, realized Artemis, and then his thoughts turned to his own safety.

I need to escape the magic as quickly as possible.

The odds were in his favour, he knew, but that was no guarantee. He had survived against all odds so many times over the past few years that he knew that sometimes percentages counted for nothing.

It occurred to Artemis that, as a human, he should simply be able to hurl himself through the walls of this magical hemisphere and survive.

With all the genius in my head, I am to be saved by a simple high jump.

He scrambled to his feet and ran towards the edge of the gate tower. It was no more than three metres. Difficult but not impossible from a height.

What I wouldn't give for a set of Foaly's Hummingbird wings now, he thought.

Through the green liquid Artemis saw Holly and Butler cresting the hill, running towards the crater.

Stay back, my friends, he thought. *I am coming.*

And he jumped for his life. Artemis was glad that Butler was there to witness his effort, as it was almost athletic. From this height, Artemis felt as though he were flying.

There was Holly racing down the slope, outrunning Butler for once. Artemis could see by the shape of her mouth that she was shouting his name. His hands reached the skin of the magic bubble and passed through and Artemis felt tremendous relief.

It worked. Everything will be different now. A new world with humans and fairies living together. I could be an ambassador.

Then the spell caught him as neatly as a bug in a jar and Artemis slid down the inside of the magical corona as though it were made of glass.

Holly rushed down the hillside, reaching towards the magical light.

'Stay back!' Artemis shouted, and his voice was slightly out of synch with his lips. 'The spell will kill you.'

Holly did not slow, and Artemis could see that she intended to attempt a rescue.

She does not understand, he thought.

'Butler!' he called. 'Stop her.'

The bodyguard reached out his massive arms and folded Holly in a bear hug. She used every escape manoeuvre in the manual, but there was no slipping such a grip.

'Butler, please. This is not right. It was supposed to be me.'

'Wait,' said Butler. 'Just wait, Holly, Artemis has a plan.' He squinted through the green dome. 'What is your plan, Artemis?'

All Artemis could do was smile and shrug.

Holly stopped struggling. 'The magic shouldn't affect a human, Artemis. Why hasn't it released you yet?'

Artemis felt the magic scanning his person, looking for something. It found that something in his eye socket.

'I have a fairy eye – one of yours, remember?' said Artemis, pointing to the brown iris. 'I thought my human genes could overcome that, but this is perceptive magic. Smart power.'

'I'll get the defibrillator,' said Butler. 'Perhaps there will be a spark left.'

'No,' said Artemis. 'It will be too late.'

Holly's eyes were slits now and a pallor spread across her skin like white paint. She felt sick and broken.

'You knew. Why, Artemis? Why did you do this?'

Artemis did not answer this question. Holly knew him well enough by now to unravel his motives later. He had seconds left and there were more urgent things to be said.

'Butler, you did not fail me. I tricked you. After all, I am a tactical genius and you were unconscious. I want you to remember that, just in case . . .'

'Just in case of what?' Butler shouted through the viscous light.

Again, Artemis did not answer the question. One way or another, Butler would find out.

'Do you remember what I said to you?' said Artemis, touching his own forehead.

'I remember,' said Holly. 'But . . .'

There was no more time for questions. The green mist was sucked backwards into the Berserker Gate as though drawn by a vacuum. For a moment Artemis was left standing, unharmed, and Butler dropped Holly to rush to his charge's side. Then Artemis's fairy eye glowed green and, by the time Butler caught the falling boy in his arms, Artemis Fowl's body was already dead.

Holly dropped to her knees and saw Opal Koboi's twisted body by the lock. The remnants of black magic had eaten through her skin in several places, exposing the ivory gleam of skull.

The sight affected her not one bit at that moment, though the pixie's staring eyes would haunt Holly's dreams for the rest of her life.

CHAPTER 19: **THE ROSES**

 THE world was resilient and so slowly fixed itself. Once the initial thunder strike of devastation had passed, there was a wave of opportunism as a certain type of people, i.e. the majority, tried to take advantage of what had happened.

People who had been sneered at as New Age eco-hippies were now hailed as saviours of humanity as it dawned on people that their traditional methods of hunting and farming could keep families fed through the winter. Faith healers, evangelists and witch doctors shook their fists around campfires and their following blossomed.

A million and one other things happened that would change the way humanity lived on the Earth, but possibly the two most important events following the Great Techno-Crash were the realization that things could be fixed and the detection of fairies.

After the initial months of panic, a Green Lantern fanatic in Sydney got the Internet up and going again, discovering that even though most of the parts in his antenna had exploded he still knew how to fix it. Slowly the modern age began to reassert itself as mobile-phone networks were rigged by amateurs and kids took over the TV stations. Radio made a huge comeback and some of the old velvet-voiced guys from the seventies were wheeled out of retirement to slot actual CDs into disk drives. Water became the new gold, and oil dropped to third on the fuel list after solar and wind.

Across the globe there had been hundreds of sightings of strange creatures who might have been fairies or aliens. One moment these creatures were not there, and the next there was a crackle or a bang and suddenly there were observation posts with little people in them, all over the world. Small flying craft fell from the sky and powerless submarines bobbed to the surface offshore of a hundred major cities.

The trouble was that all of the machinery self-destructed and any of the fairies/aliens taken into custody inexplicably vanished in the following weeks. Humanity knew that it was not alone on the planet, but it didn't know where to find these strange creatures. And, considering mankind had not even managed to explore the planet's oceans, it would be several hundred years before they developed the capacity to probe beneath the Earth's crust.

So the stories were exaggerated until nobody believed them any more and the one video that did survive was not half as convincing as any Saturday morning kids' show.

296

People knew what they had seen and those people would believe it to the day they died, but soon psychiatrists began to assign the fairy sightings to the mass traumatic hallucination scrap heap that was already piled high with dinosaurs, superheroes and Loch Ness monsters.

THE FOWL ESTATE

Ireland became truly an island once more. Communities retreated into themselves and began growing foodstuffs that they would actually eat rather than mechanically suck all the goodness out of, freeze all the additives into and ship off to other continents. Many wealthy landowners voluntarily donated their idle fields to disgruntled hungry people with sharp implements.

Artemis's parents had managed to make their way home from London, where they had been when the world broke down, and, shortly after the funeral ceremony for Artemis, the Fowl Estate was converted into over five hundred separate allotments where people could grow whatever fruit and vegetables the Irish climate permitted.

The ceremony itself was simple and private with only the Fowl and Butler families present. Artemis's body was buried on the high meadow where he had spent so much of his time tinkering on his solar plane. Butler did not attend because he steadfastly refused to believe the evidence presented to him by his own eyes.

Artemis is not gone, he asserted, time after time. *This is not the endgame.*

He would not be persuaded otherwise, no matter how many times Juliet or Angeline Fowl dropped down to his dojo for a talk.

Which was why the bodyguard showed not one whit of surprise when Captain Holly Short appeared at the door of his lodge at dawn one morning.

'Well, it's about time,' he said, grabbing his jacket from the coat stand. 'Artemis leaves instructions and it takes you guys half a year to figure them out.'

Holly hurried after him. 'Artemis's instructions were not exactly simple to follow. And, typically, they were totally illegal.'

In the courtyard, a doorway had been cut into the orange glow of the morning sky and in that doorway stood Foaly, looking decidedly nervous.

'Which do you think seems less suspicious?' asked Butler. 'An alien-looking craft hovering in the yard of a country home? Or a floating doorway with a centaur standing in it?'

Foaly clopped down the gangplank, towing a hover trolley behind him. The shuttle door closed and fizzled out of the visible spectrum.

'Can we get on with this, please?' he wondered. 'Everything we're doing here is against fairy law and possibly immoral. Caballine thinks I'm at Mulch's ceremony. The Council is actually giving Diggums a medal, can you believe that? The little kleptomaniac managed to convince everyone he more or less saved the planet single-handed. He got a book deal. Anyway, I hate lying to my wife. If I stop to think about this for more than ten seconds, I might just change my mind.'

Holly took control of the hover trolley. 'You will not change your mind. We have come too far just to go home without a result.'

'Hey,' said Foaly. 'I was just saying.'

Holly's eyes were hard with a determination that would tolerate no argument. She had been wearing that expression almost every day now for six months ever since she had returned home from the Berserker Gate incident. The first thing she had done was seek out Foaly in Police Plaza.

'I have a message for you from Artemis,' she'd said, once Foaly had released her from a smothering hug.

'Really? What did he say?'

'He said something about a chrysalis. You were to power it up.'

These words had a powerful effect on the centaur. He trotted to the door and locked it behind Holly. Then he ran a bug sweep with a wand he kept on his person. Holly knew then that the word meant something to her friend.

'What chrysalis, Foaly? And why is Artemis so interested in it?'

Foaly took Holly's shoulders and placed her in a lab chair. 'Why *is* Artemis interested? Our friend is dead, Holly. Maybe we should let him go?'

Holly pushed Foaly away and jumped to her feet. 'Let him go? Artemis didn't let me go in Limbo. He didn't let Butler go in London. He didn't let the entire city of Haven go during the goblin revolution. Now tell me, what is this chrysalis?'

So Foaly told her and the bones of Artemis's idea became obvious, but more information was needed.

'Was there anything else?' asked the centaur. 'Did Artemis say or do anything else?'

Holly shook her head miserably. 'No. He got a little sentimental, which is unusual for him, but understandable. He told me to kiss you.'

She stood on tiptoes and kissed Foaly's forehead. 'Just in case, I suppose.'

Foaly was suddenly upset, and almost overwhelmed, but he coughed and swallowed it down for another time.

'He said, "*Kiss Foaly*." Those exact words?'

'No,' said Holly, thinking back. 'He kissed me, and said, "*Give him that from me.*"'

The centaur grinned, then cackled, then dragged her across the lab.

'We need to get your forehead under an electron microscope,' he said.

Holly explained their interpretation of Artemis's plan to Butler as they walked towards the Berserker Gate. Foaly trotted ahead, muttering calculations to himself and keeping an eye out for early-bird humans.

'The chrysalis was what Opal used to grow a clone of herself. It was turned over to Foaly who was supposed to destroy it.'

'But he didn't,' guessed Butler.

'No. And Artemis knew that from hacking into LEP recycling records.'

'So Artemis wanted Foaly to grow a clone? Even an old soldier like me knows that you need DNA for that.'

Holly tapped her forehead. 'That's why he kissed me. There was enough DNA in the saliva for Foaly to grow an army, but it seemed like a natural trace to the airport scanners.'

'A genius to the end,' said Butler. He frowned. 'But aren't clones poor dumb creatures? Nopal could barely stay alive.'

Foaly stopped at the lip of the crater to explain. 'Yes, they are, because they don't have a soul. This is where the magic comes in. When the first Berserker lock was closed, all fairy spirits within the magic circle were released from their bodies, but Artemis may have had enough human in him and enough sheer willpower to remain in this realm, even after his physical body died. His spirit could be a free-floating, ectoplasmic, ethereal organism right now.'

Butler almost stumbled over his own feet. 'Are you saying Artemis is a ghost?' He turned to Holly for a straight answer. 'Is he actually saying that Artemis is a ghost?'

Holly steered the hover trolley down the incline. 'The Berserkers were ghosts for ten thousand years. That's how the spell worked. If they lasted that long, it's possible that Artemis held on for six months.'

'Possible?' said Butler. 'That's all we've got?'

Foaly pointed to a spot near the tower. '*Possible* is being optimistic. I would say *barely conceivable* would be a better bet.'

Holly undid the clips of a refrigerated container on top of

the hover trolley. 'Yes, well, the *barely conceivable* is Artemis Fowl's speciality.'

Butler heaved off the lid and what he saw inside took his breath away, even though he had been expecting it. Artemis's clone lay inside a transparent tent, breath fogging the plastic.

'Artemis,' he said. 'It's him exactly.'

'I had to play with the hothousing,' said Foaly, unhooking the clone from its life-support systems. 'And I didn't have access to my own lab, so he has six toes on his left foot now, but it's close enough for a backstreet job. I never thought I'd say it, but Opal Koboi made good tech.'

'It's . . . He's fifteen now, right?'

Foaly ducked behind a twist of nutrient pipes to hide his face. 'Actually, the timing got away from me a little, so he's a little older. But don't worry, I gave him a total makeover. Skin shrink, bone scrape, marrow injections – I even lubed his brain. Believe me, his own mother wouldn't be able to tell the difference.'

He rubbed his hands and changed the subject. 'Now, to work. Show me where Artemis died.'

'Down there,' said Holly, pointing. 'By the . . .'

She had been about to say *tower*, but her breath caught in her throat at the sight of the incredible roses that grew in thick curved bands emanating from the exact point where Artemis had collapsed.

The Fowl Estate roses were something of a sensation, blooming as they did in a perfect spiral at the foot of the round tower where no roses had been planted. Their unusual

burnished orange petals made them visible from the other
allotments and Juliet had been assigned the task of ensuring
that none of the villagers helped themselves to as much as a
single stem.

Because of recent little-people rumours, the allotment
workers had taken to calling the flowers *fairy roses*, which was
a better name for them than even they suspected.

Butler carried the enclosed clone in his arms and he was
suddenly reminded of a night years ago when he had carried
someone else through a field, watching the tall grass swish
in Artemis's wake.

Except that time I was carrying Holly.

Foaly interrupted his thought. 'Butler, you must place the
body in the roses. At the centre of the spiral. Without life
support we have only minutes before degeneration begins.'

Butler laid the clone gently inside the spiral on a soft patch
where there were no thorns to pierce it.

Holly knelt to open the tent's zip. She pulled the flaps
apart and inside lay Artemis's new body in a hospital gown,
its breath coming in short gasps, sweat sheening its forehead.

Foaly moved quickly around the clone, straightening its
limbs, tilting its head back to clear the airwaves.

'These roses,' he said. 'They are a sign. There's magical
residue here. I would bet this formation is pretty much the
same shape as Bruin Fadda's original rune.'

'You're pinning your hopes on a flower bed sprouting in
the meadow?'

'No, of course not, Butler. Bruin Fadda's magic was

powerful, and someone with Artemis's willpower could easily last a few months.'

Butler held his own skull. 'What if this doesn't work, Holly? What if I let Artemis die?'

Holly turned quickly and saw that Butler was emotionally stretched. He had been hiding behind denial for half a year and would blame himself forever if Artemis didn't come back.

If this does not work, Butler may never recover, she realized.

'It *will* work!' she said. 'Now, less talk and more resurrecting. How long do we have, Foaly?'

'The clone can survive for perhaps fifteen minutes away from the life support.'

Butler knew that the time for objections was past. He would do whatever was necessary to give this plan a chance to succeed.

'Very well, Holly,' he said, standing to attention. 'What should I do?'

Holly squatted a metre from the clone, fingers wrapped round rose stems, oblivious to the thorns piercing her skin. 'It is all done now. Either he appears or we have lost him forever.'

I think we will have lost something of ourselves too, thought Butler.

They waited and nothing out of the ordinary happened. Birds sang, the hedgerow bustled and the sound of a tractor engine drifted to them across the fields. Holly squatted and fretted, dragging flowers out by their roots. While she worried, Butler's gaze rested on the clone's face and he recalled times past spent with his principal.

There never was anyone like Artemis Fowl, he thought. *Though he didn't make my job any easier with all his shenanigans.* Butler smiled. *Artemis always had my back, even though he could barely reach it.*

'Holly,' he said gently. 'He's not coming . . .'

Then the wind changed and suddenly Butler could smell the roses. Holly stumbled forward to her feet.

'Something's happening. I think something is happening.'

The breeze scooped a few rose petals from the flowers and sent them spinning skywards. More and more petals broke free as the wind seemed to curve along the orange spiral, quickly stripping each flower. The petals rose like butterflies, flitting and shimmering, filling the sky, blocking the sun.

'Artemis!' Butler called. 'Come to my voice.'

Has he done it? Is this Artemis Fowl's greatest moment?

The petals swirled with a noise like a chorus of sighs and then suddenly dropped like stones. The clone had not moved.

Holly moved forward slowly, as though learning to use her legs, then dropped to her knees, clasping the clone's hand.

'Artemis,' she said, the word like a prayer. 'Artemis, please.'

Still nothing. Not even breath now.

Butler had no time for his usual impeccable manners

and moved Holly aside. 'Sorry, Captain. This is my area of expertise.'

He knelt over the pale clone and with his palm searched for a heartbeat. There was none.

Butler tilted the clone's head back, pinched its nose and breathed life deep into its lungs.

He felt a weak heartbeat under his hand.

Butler fell backwards. 'Holly. I think . . . I think it worked.'

Holly crawled through the carpet of petals.

'Artemis,' she said urgently. 'Artemis, come back to us.'

Two more breaths passed, then several rapid jerky ones, then Artemis's eyes opened. Both a startling blue. The eyes were initially wide with shock, then fluttered like the wings of a jarred moth.

'Be calm,' said Holly. 'You are safe now.'

Artemis frowned, trying to focus. It was clear that his faculties had not totally returned and he did not yet remember the people leaning over him.

'Stay back,' he said. 'You don't know what you're dealing with.'

Holly took his hand. 'We do know you, Artemis. And you know us. Try to remember.'

Artemis did try, concentrating until some of the clouds lifted.

'Y-you,' he said hesitantly. 'You are my friends?'

Holly wept with sheer relief. 'Yes,' she said. 'We are your friends. Now we need to get you inside, before the locals arrive and see the recently deceased heir being escorted by fairies.'

Butler helped Artemis to his feet, which he was obviously unsteady on.

'Oh, go on then,' said Foaly, offering his broad back. 'Just this once.'

Butler lifted Artemis on to the centaur's back and steadied him with a huge hand.

'You had me worried, Arty,' he said. 'And your parents are devastated. Wait until they see you.'

As they walked across the fields, Holly pointed out areas of shared experience, hoping to jog the teen's memory.

'Tell me,' Artemis said, his voice still weak. 'How do I know you?'

And so Holly began her story: 'It all started in Ho Chi Minh City one summer. It was sweltering by anyone's standards. Needless to say, Artemis Fowl would not have been willing to put up with such discomfort if something extremely important had not been at stake. Important to the plan . . .'

Turn over for a sneak peek at

EOIN COLFER'S
brand-new series

W.A.R.P.

COMING 2013

Chapter 1:

THE KILLING CHAMBER

BEDFORD SQUARE. BLOOMSBURY. LONDON. 1898.

THERE were two smudges in the shadows between the grandfather clock and the velvet drapes. One high and one low. Two pale thumb-prints in a black night made darker still by blackout sheets behind the thick curtains and sackcloth tacked across the skylights.

The lower smudge was the face of a boy, soot blackened and slightly shivering inside the basement chamber. This was young Riley brought this very night on his first killing as a test.

The upper smudge was the face of a man known to his employers as Albert Garrick, though the public had known him by a different name. His stage name was Lombardi, and many years ago he had been the most celebrated illusionist in the West End, until the night he had accidentally lived up to the claims on the Adelphi Theatre playbill by actually sawing his beautiful assistant in half. Garrick discovered on that night that he relished taking a life almost as much as he enjoyed the delighted applause from the stalls, and so the magician made a new career: assassination.

Those who remember the once-famous illusionist would not recognize him now with his flat murderer's eyes, blade scarification on his forehead and the lopsided, sharply healed cheekbones: injuries inflicted during his fledgling attempts at murder for pay.

Garrick gripped Riley's shoulder, long bony fingers pressing through the fabric of the boy's coat, pinching the nerves. He didn't say a word but nodded once, a gesture heavy with reminder and implication.

Think back, said the inclined chin, *to your lesson of this afternoon. Move silently as the Whitechapel fog and slide the blade in until your fingers sink into the wound.*

Garrick had instructed Riley to haul a dog carcass from the Strand to their Holborn rooms and then practise his knife work on the suspended remains so he would be accustomed to the resistance of bone.

Novices have the mistaken impression that a sharp blade will slip in like a hot poker through wax, but it ain't so. Sometimes even a master like myself can come up against bone and muscle, so be ready to lever down and force up. Remember that, boy. Lever down and force up. Use the bone itself as your fulcrum.

Garrick performed the move now with his long stiletto blade, tilting his wide blackened forehead at Riley to make certain the boy took heed.

Riley nodded then took the knife, palming the blade across to the other hand as he had been taught.

Garrick nudged Riley from the shadows towards the large four-poster bed, on which lay the nearly departed.

Nearly departed. This was one of Garrick's witticisms.

I had quite the patter in my theatre days, he often told Riley.

Garrick's Achilles' heel was his ego. He missed the stage and, these days, Riley was his only audience. He needed the boy. Garrick's ego drank from the pools of those eyes as he told his dark stories. And he even treated his apprentice to private magic shows in the Orient Theatre, which he had purchased to store his old illusionist's gear.

Riley had heard so many elaborate tales of Albert Garrick's creative methods of murder that he had started to doubt whether his master's exploits were any more real than Dick Turpin's or Varney the Vampire's from the penny dreadful serials.

Tonight, he doubted no more. This was a real killing, a fat purse paid in advance. Riley knew that he was being tested. Either he snuffed out his first candle or Albert Garrick would leave an extra corpse in this terrible, gloomy chamber and swipe himself a new apprentice from the gutters of London. It would pain him to do it, but Garrick would not see any other option. Riley must learn to do more than fry sausages and polish boots.

Riley swept his feet forward, one at a time, tracing a wide circle with his toes as he had been taught, searching for debris. It slowed the progress, but one crackle of discarded paper could be enough to awaken his intended victim. Riley saw in front of him the blade in his own hand, and he could hardly believe that he was here, about to commit the act that would damn him to hell.

When you have felt the power, you can take your place as my junior in the family enterprise, Garrick would often say. *P'raps we should have cards of business made up, eh, boy? Garrick and Son. Assassins for hire. We may be low but we're not cheap.*

Then Garrick would laugh and it was a dark faraway noise that caused Riley's nerves to throb and his stomach to heave.

Riley could see no way to avoid murdering a human being this night. The room seemed to close in around him, the drapes like curtains of some macabre music hall.

If those curtains open, thought Riley, *there will be an audience of skeletons applauding. I must kill this man or be killed myself.*

These thoughts and more chased their tails round Riley's pounding head till his hand shook and the blade almost slipped from his fingers.

Garrick was instantly at his side like a ghost, touching Riley's elbow with one crooked icicle of a finger.

'From dust thou art . . .' he whispered so softly that the words might have been formed from the gusts of a draught.

'And unto dust thou shall return,' mouthed Riley, completing the Biblical quote. Garrick's favourite.

My own last rites, he'd told Riley one winter's night as they looked out on Leicester Square from their booth in an Italian restaurant. The magician had polished off his second jug of bitter red wine and his gentleman's accent had started to slide off his words like fish from a wet slab.

Every man Jack of us crawled forth from the filth and dust, and unto that bloomin' stuff we shall return, mark you. I just send 'em back quicker like. A few heartbeats early so that we may enjoy life's comforts. That is the way of our situation and if you have no steel in you for it, Riley, then . . .

Garrick never completed his threat, but it was clear that the time had come for Riley to earn his place at the table.

Riley continued onwards, feeling the cracks between each board through the thin soles of his shoes that had been painstakingly shaved down on the lathe in Garrick's workshop. He could now see the mark in the bed. An old man with a thatch of grey hair jutting out from under a puff quilt.

I can't see his face. He was grateful for that much.

Riley approached the bed, feeling Garrick behind him, knowing his time was running out.

Unto dust. Dispatched to dust.

Riley saw the old man's hand resting on the pillow, the index finger a mere nub due to some old injury, and he knew that he could not do it. He was no murderer.

Riley cast his eyes about while keeping his head still. He had been taught to use his surroundings in times of emergency, but his mentor was behind him, observing Riley's every move with his eerie non-blinking intensity. There would be no help from the old man in the bed. What could a grey-hair possibly do against Garrick? What could anyone do?

Four times Riley had run away and four times Garrick had found him.

Death is the only way out for me, Riley had thought. *Mine or Garrick's.*

But Garrick could not be killed, for he was death.

Unto dust.

Riley felt suddenly faint and thought he would sink to the cold floor. Perhaps that would be for the best? Lie senseless and let Garrick do his bloody work, but then the old man would die too and that knowledge would weigh on Riley's soul in the afterlife.

I will fight, decided the boy. He had scant hope of survival, but he had to do something.

Plan after plan flitted through his fevered brain, each one more hopeless than the next. All the time, he moved onwards, feeling the frost of Garrick on his neck like a bad omen. The man on the four-poster grew clearer. He could see an ear now, with holes where a row of rings must have once pierced.

A foreigner perhaps? A sailor?

He saw a ruddy jaw with tallowed runs of flesh tucked underneath and a lanyard that ran to a strange pendant lying on the quilt.

Look for every detail, was one of Garrick's lessons. *Drink it all in with yer eyes and maybe it will save your life.*

No chance of saving my life, not tonight.

Riley took another sweeping step and felt his forward foot grow curiously warm. He glanced down and to his surprise and confusion saw that the toe of his shoe glowed green. In fact a cocoon of light had blossomed round the frame of the sleeping man, its heart an emerald blaze emanating from the strange pendant.

Garrick's words gusted past his ear. 'Hell's bells. Trickery! Dirk him now, boy.'

Riley could not move petrified as he was by the spectral light.

Garrick pushed him further into the strange warm glow, which immediately changed hue, becoming a scarlet hemisphere. An unnatural keening erupted from somewhere in the bed, piercing and horrible, rattling Riley's brain in the gourd of his skull.

The old man in the bed was instantly awake, popping upwards like a wind-up Jack from his box.

'Stupid sensor malfunction,' he muttered, his accent Scottish, his eyes rheumed and blinking. 'I have a pain in my . . .'

The man noticed Riley and the blade shining like an icicle from his fist. He allowed his hand to trail slowly down towards the glowing teardrop pendant resting on his scrawny chest then tapped the centre twice, silencing the dreadful wail. The pendant's heart displayed a glowing series of numbers now, seemingly written in phosphorous. Flickering backwards from twenty.

'Now there, lad,' said the old man. 'Hold on to those horses. We can talk about this. I have funds.'

Riley was transfixed by the pendant. It was magical certainly, but more than that, it was familiar somehow.

Garrick interrupted Riley's thoughts with a sharp prod in the ribs.

'No more delay,' he said briskly. 'Make your bones, boy. Unto dust.'

Riley could not. He would not become like Garrick and damn himself to an eternity in the pit.

'I-I . . .' he stuttered, wishing his mind would supply the words to extricate both himself and this strange old man from these dire straits. The man raised his palms to show they were empty as though fair play was on offer in this dark room.

'I'm not armed,' he said. 'All I have is unlimited currency. I can run you up whatever you need. Easiest thing in the world to print a few thousand pounds. But, if you harm me, men will come to make sure you didn't take my secrets – men with weapons like you have never seen.'

The old man spoke no more as there was a knife suddenly embedded in his chest. Riley saw his own hand on the hilt and for a sickening moment thought that his muscles had betrayed his heart and done the deed, but then he felt the tingle of Garrick's cold fingers releasing his forearm and he knew that his hand had been forced.

'There it is,' said Garrick as the warm blood coated Riley's sleeve. 'Hold on tight and you will feel the life leave him.'

'It wasn't me that did it,' Riley said to the man, the words trickling from his lips. 'It was never me.'

The old man sat stiff as a board, the pendant's chord fraying against the dagger's blade.

'I do not believe this,' he grunted. 'All the people on my tail and you two clowns get me.'

Garrick's words crawled into Riley's ears like slugs. 'This

is not credited to your account, boy. Mine was the hand that found the gap between this pigeon's ribs, but there are circumstances here I'll give you that. So, I may allow you another chance.'

'I do not believe this,' said the old man once more, then his pendant beeped and he was gone. Literally gone. Fizzling into a cloud of orange sparks that were sucked into the pendant's heart.

'Magic,' breathed Garrick, his tone approaching reverence. 'Magic is real.'

The assassin stepped sharply back, protecting himself from whatever the consequences of the vaporization might be, but Riley did not have the presence of mind to follow. Still holding the dagger, all he could do was watch as the cloud spread along his arm dematerializing his very self quicker than a beggar could spit.

'I am going,' he said and it was true, though he could not know where.

He saw his torso turn transparent and his organs were visible for a moment, packed in tight behind translucent ribs, then all the workings were gone too, replaced by sparks.

The gas that Riley had become was sucked into the pendant's heart. He felt himself go in a vortex that reminded him of being tumbled by a wave on Brighton Beach and of a boy watching him from the shore.

Ginger. I remember you.

Then Riley was reduced to a single glowing dot of purest

energy. The dot winked once at Garrick then disappeared. The old man and the boy, both gone.

Garrick reached for the pendant, which had fallen to the sheets thinking, *I have seen this device before, or one like it. Many years ago . . .* But his fingers touched only a smear of soot left behind where the strange talisman had been.

'All my life,' he said. 'All my life.'

He thought the rest but did not say it as he was alone in this room of wonders.

All my life I have searched for real magic, thought Albert Garrick. *And now I know it does exist.*

Garrick was a man of turbulent emotion which he usually kept tucked inside his heart, but now he allowed his happiness to spurt from him in trickles of warm tears, which plopped circles in the blood pool between his feet.

Not simply conjuring. Real magic.

The assassin sank to the ground, his long spindly legs folding so that his knees were level with his ears. Blood soaked through the seat of his expensive breeches, but he cared not one jot, for nothing would ever be the same again. His only fear was that the magic had gone from this place forever. To have been so close and to have missed out by a whisker would indeed be devastation.

I will wait here, Riley, he thought. *The Chinese believe that magic often resides in a place, so waiting is my only card to play. And, when the men come with their fabulous weapons, I will avenge you. Then I will take the magic and bend it to my will and there will be none who can stop me.*

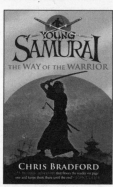

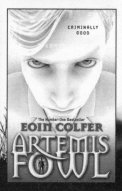
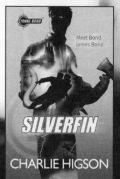

FOALY'S

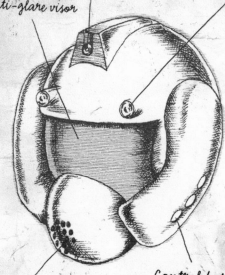

20 mega-pixel camera

200 watt lamps

Anti-glare visor

Detachable
Oxygen / pollution
mask

Control buttons

Counter-beat
wing stabilizers

Super-strength
polymer wings

Exhaust ports

Air intake

GADGETS

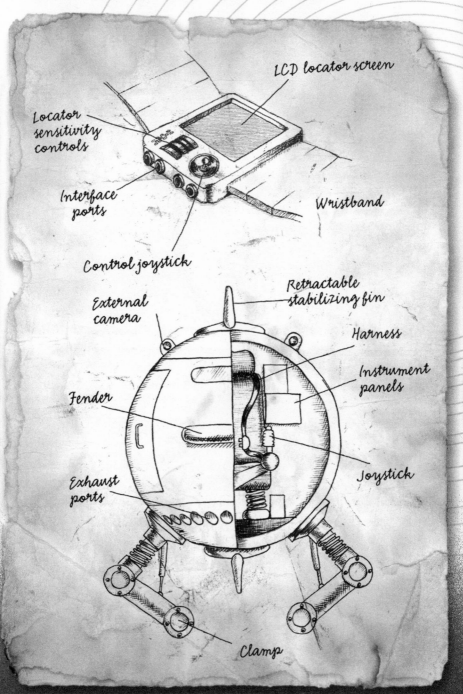

LCD locator screen

Locator sensitivity controls

Interface ports

Control joystick

Wristband

External camera

Retractable stabilizing fin

Harness

Instrument panels

Fender

Exhaust ports

Joystick

Clamp

ARTEMIS FOWL

THE GRAPHIC NOVEL

Of course, it had started with the Internet.
But then it always does.

Alien abductions. UFO sightings. Leylines. Ancient stone circles.

And the People.
It always came back to the People.

Trawling through gigs of data, he had compiled a database from the thousands of references to fairies he'd found from countries all over the world.

Each human civilization had its own term for the People. But there was no doubt that the reports referred to the same hidden race.

Many stories whispered of a special book carried by each fairy.

It was their bible containing the history of their race. It also contained their laws, their rules... and their weaknesses.

RELIVE THE ADVENTURE, THE MAGIC,
THE MIND-BLOWING TECHNOLOGY,
THE BEGINNING.
AS YOU'VE NEVER SEEN IT BEFORE.

ARTEMIS FOWL

THE
GRAPHIC
NOVEL

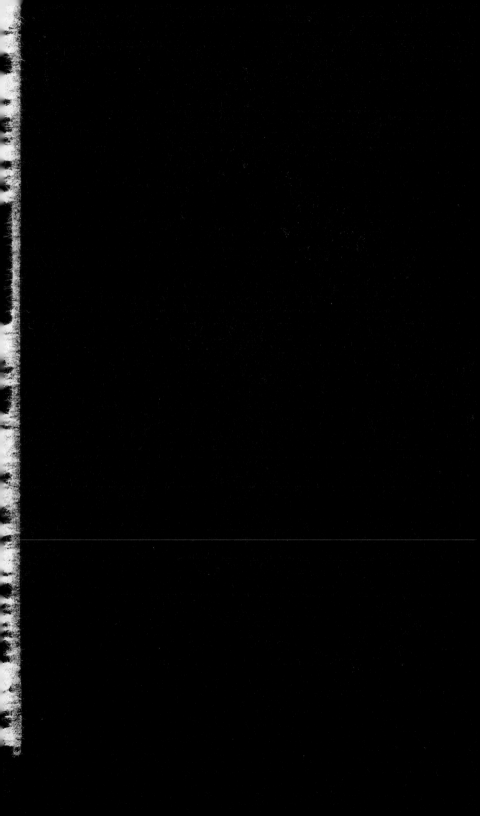